PRAISE FOR *THE SUMMER SON*

"Craig Lancaster really knows how to tell a story. And in this deeply felt, keenly observed, beautifully structured novel, he tells one older than Sophocles, about the tensions between fathers and sons and the secrets that shape—and threaten to destroy—their lives."

— Charles Matthews, former books editor,
San Jose Mercury News

"Lancaster's characters drill into the earth in search of natural gas, and so too do they burrow into their pasts, hunting for the pockets of explosive angst that define who they are today. A compelling dose of realism and a vicious reminder that ancient history is always close enough to kiss us."

— Joshua Mohr, author of
Some Things That Meant the World To Me and *Termite Parade*

"*The Summer Son* is a superb and authentic exploration of family ties and the delicate relationships between fathers and sons, husbands and wives, and the past and present. Lancaster writes from the heart in clear and powerful prose, exposing his characters' flaws and strengths in heartbreaking detail and giving readers exactly what we want from contemporary fiction: characters we believe in from the first page, laugh and cry with throughout, and, finally, deeply understand at the end."

— Kristy Kiernan, award-winning author of
Catching Genius and *Between Friends*

THE SUMMER SON

THE SUMMER SON

A NOVEL BY CRAIG LANCASTER

PUBLISHED BY

amazonencore

Published by AmazonEncore
P.O. Box 400818
Las Vegas, NV 89140

ISBN-13: 9781935597247
ISBN-10: 1935597248

ACKNOWLEDGMENTS

As ever, I owe more thanks than I'll ever be able to account for in this space. My friend Jim Thomsen can always be counted upon to read my work before I inflict it on innocents. His observations and suggestions are appreciated and needed. To my "pre-readers," Crystal Walls, Laura Biafore, Amy Pizarro, Carol Buchanan, R. J. Keller, Kristen Tsetsi, Linda Vandiver, and Jill Munson, thank you for being test subjects. Your feedback was an immense help.

My high school English teacher, Janelle Eklund, has read two drafts of my novels, and I pray that she gets to read many more. And to the faithful readers who asked for a new book, I am indebted to you for the encouragement.

Alex Carr and his editorial team at AmazonEncore produced a beautiful book, and Sarah Tomashek is a marketing whiz of the first order. That *The Summer Son* has made it from my hands to yours is due in large part to AmazonEncore's belief in it, and for that I am eternally grateful.

Finally, all my love to my mother, Leslie; my father, Ron; and my stepfather, Charles. This book is for you.

SAN JOSE, CALIFORNIA | SEPTEMBER 2007

THE FIRST CALL CAME on Tuesday night. I yelled at Cindy from the garage to pick up. On the fourth ring, I dropped the armful of newspapers I was packing into the recycling bin and ran to the extension in the kitchen.

"Hello?"

"Mitch."

My guts coiled.

"Dad?"

"Yeah."

"What's up?" I asked.

"Nothing."

Seven words into the call, we hit the wall again. I counted on hearing from Dad once a year, somewhere around Christmas. I would return the favor of a call in March, on his birthday. We left the rest of the holidays and landmark dates to languish in the inertia of silence. To hear from him outside our usual calendar rattled me. I wasn't sure I wanted to press ahead and find out what prompted the call.

"So," I said, fracturing the uncomfortable silence that had settled over us. "What's been going on?"

"Nothing much. Just sitting here, watching TV."

"Not much happening here, either. You caught me cleaning up in the garage."

"If you're busy, I'll go…"

"No, that's not what I'm saying. I just thought Cindy and the kids were in the house, but I can see now"—I pulled back the kitchen curtains and saw my wife standing at the grill on the patio—"that they're outside."

"What are they doing?"

"Looks like Cindy's grilling up some dinner. Avery and Adia are playing on the swing set."

"You're busy."

"No, Dad, I'm not…"

"I'll call back another time."

He was gone.

We had two more calls, on Thursday and then again Friday, both around the same time. On each call, Dad caught me in the middle of some mundane chore—on Friday, I was plunging the hall toilet—and then used the fact that I wasn't sitting around waiting to hear from him as an excuse to cut things short.

Friday night, as my wife and I lay clinging to our own sides of the bed, ignoring each other in favor of our books, Cindy set hers down and said, "You have to find out what's going on."

"With what?"

"With the national debt. What do you think? With your dad."

I marked my page and put the book away, then grasped the bridge of my nose between my thumb and forefinger.

"How do you propose I do that?"

"Call him first."

"I don't follow."

"The man clearly wants something, and he just as clearly is not going to say what it is. So ask him."

"Just like that? Come on."

"Mitch," she said, turning to make me look at her and see her exasperation. "I don't care how you get him to talk, but you need to find out what's eating at him. The man has some sort of burden. You need to lighten his load, if you can."

"Dad, what do you want?"

It was Saturday, and the direct route that I had decided to take with my father seemed ill considered the moment the words tumbled from my mouth.

"What do you mean, what do I want?"

"I mean, you've called three times this week and haven't had anything to say. Is something going on? Do you need anything?"

In the uncomfortable few seconds of silence that followed, I pictured the frothing on the other end of the line, twelve hundred miles away. Dad didn't do slow burns. His words came with sharp edges and aggression.

"I don't need anything from you. I don't want anything from you."

"OK," I said, backpedaling to a conciliatory tone. "Is there a reason for the calls?"

"I need a reason?"

"Well, hell, Dad. That's the way it's been for thirty years. Why change now?"

"You know what, Mitch? Go screw yourself."

He hung up.

I held tight to the dead receiver in my ear. I closed my eyes and waited for the sting to subside. When it did, I gently set the phone into the cradle. In the living room, Cindy thumbed through a magazine as the twins played on the floor.

"Any other genius ideas?" I asked.

Cindy smirked.

I stomped out.

"You're going to have to go see him."

This was late Sunday afternoon. It was the first thing Cindy had said to me since the previous night, which had been sullied by another quarrel and my wife's proclamation that I had become a disappointment to her. I suggested that she join the club; by this time, I was damned disappointed in myself. For seven months I had been throwing the same weak pitch, blaming her for the trouble we found our marriage in. When I uncovered her little dalliance, I might have had a case, but my moral high ground had eroded. My inability to let go of grudges was rivaled only by my blindness to my inattention to her and the twins. For months now, she had been fighting for our marriage, and I knew I hadn't been meeting her halfway to halfway.

I had been stewing about the most recent fight, about my mounting failures, and about this mystery Dad had dropped on us. In my anger, I wanted to close every door. Cindy, on the other hand, insisted on opening a window and seeing if her ideas—about our marriage, and about Dad—would fly.

"You're kidding, right?" I said. "I can't wrench a conversation out of him on the phone. What do you think he's going to say if I tell him that I'm coming?"

"So you don't announce it. You just go."

"Just like that?"

"Sure."

I shook my head.

"No. That's crazy. He doesn't want me around. He's made that abundantly clear." I had seen my father twice in nearly thirty years, both of the instances pushed along, in part, by Cindy. What made her think I could even get past the door?

"Mitch," she said, and her tone demanded that I face her. "You have to. I want you out of here. I need to think about things, and so do you."

I threw it back at her. "I know why you want me out. This is just a good excuse to do it."

"No, Mitch, I want you out because I want you back. The you I fell in love with—"

"You say that as if I'm the one who strayed."

Cindy sighed.

"Believe what you want to, Mitch. You haven't been here with us—not really—for months now. I don't know what to do about that anymore. For as long as I've known you, you've had almost nothing to say about this man, and when you have said something, it's been how he has kept you on the outside and rejected you—"

"He has. Don't act like he hasn't."

"I know he has. I know something happened a long time ago that still bothers you. But I don't know what it is, and I can't help you with it."

"I don't need help."

"Yeah, Mitch, you do. We need help. You've been reject-ed, and you've rejected us. Are you so blind that you can't see that? You keep your own wife, your own kids, at the end of your arm. You're him all over again, it seems to me."

"That's not fair."

"Maybe it's not. But I know this: we can't live like this. You're a good man, but I've lost you."

"I haven't gone anywhere. Unlike you," I shot back at her.

She shook her head.

"I feared this, Mitch. I did. Before we got married, I asked your mother about this thing between you and your dad. I was scared of it, because you would never talk about him. Do you know what she said?"

I stared at her.

"She said she didn't know, that she could never get you to talk about it either. She said you closed something off inside and that was it. You were done. She told me that you were a good man and that I should marry you, that you were solid and loyal."

"I *am* loyal."

"Yes, you are. But you're not here anymore, not in any way that counts. So you know what? Go see your dad. Set things right. Tell him off. Do whatever. Then come back and set things right with us. We'll be waiting right here for you."

I couldn't help myself. I laughed—a little chuckle at first that blossomed into a full-throated gut-buster. By the time I realized that Cindy was right, that I had to get on an airplane to see my father and that, furthermore, I had to do it not only to uncover whatever the hell his problem was but also to save my marriage, I couldn't catch my breath. She walked out of the room, and I couldn't even find the words to tell her that the joke was on me.

When I reeled myself in, I made a promise to myself. I didn't know if I could fix things with Cindy by walking away from her, but I damned sure could try to make that old man square our accounts. He owed a lot of people, but I was the only one left to collect. I told myself that I didn't care about him, only about what he owed me, whatever that was.

I even tried to believe it.

SAN JOSE | SEPTEMBER 16–17, 2007

I CALLED MY BOSS, John Wallen, on Sunday night to tell him that I would be gone for a few days because...why? Because my father was a hardheaded, prickly, inscrutable bastard? Because my wife and I couldn't last a day without some small spark of a fight threatening to burn down our house? Company policy on leave addressed neither baffling phone calls from manipulative fathers nor marital strife.

The fact was breathtakingly simple. I didn't have a reason that would satisfy John. My sales had been crappy for as long as my marriage had been unraveling, and I lately was spinning through a vicious cycle of bad work, stress, and the subsequent strain with Cindy. All that manifested itself in my increasing slothfulness on the job and extended absences from home. I knew I didn't have much margin of error left, with my boss or with my wife, but by nothing more than dumb luck, I was close on several major sales. If I reeled those in, it would make my year and, I hoped, buy me some grace at work and at home.

Now I was abandoning my post.

"Is he sick?" John asked.

"I don't know."

"Some sort of distress?"

"Maybe."

"Huh."

I had been with John for sixteen years. He'd built our South Bay medical-sales firm into a success story, and for a big chunk of that time, I had been his star salesman. I knew John well enough to know that "huh" meant that he was angry or confused. I hoped it wasn't the former, but when it got right down to it, I really didn't care. If I did, I supposed, I wouldn't be leaving.

"Well, I hope everything's all right," he said.

"I'll be back as soon as I can, John."

He chuckled unhappily. "You'd better."

I booked my ticket for the next day. I got the last seat on both flights, from San Jose to Denver and then from Denver to Billings. I booked the return for Thursday, not having any idea whether I'd be in Montana for days, weeks, or hours. The ticket, bought the day before travel and without a week-end stay, was staggering, nearly thirteen hundred dollars. The toll served only to darken my attitude.

Cindy tried to turn me around.

"Don't fight him, and don't take the bait if he offers it," she said. "Just be."

It was sensible advice that I found hard to imagine taking. I held tight to my biggest grievances with the man, but Cindy could do the math. Twenty-eight years divided by two face-to-face visits equals fucked up. She knew it, and she blamed Dad for it—if for no other reason than I did—and she blamed me for not rising above it. I often threw it back in her face and told her that it was my problem and not hers. I was wrong about that.

The cumulative effect of how far away Dad was from me in distance and degree had consequences in our home. Four years earlier, after years of trying, years of exploring the boundaries of the science of childbirth, we had been blessed with the arrival of Avery and Adia. It delighted me to learn that it really was true, that with children, every day is a discovery. Dad saw none of this. To Avery and Adia, Grandma and Grandpa were Cindy's parents, who were right there in San Jose. My own mother didn't live long enough to meet them. And Dad had seen them once, on a somber visit to Montana just a few months earlier for the funeral of his third wife, Helen. Cindy had insisted that we make that trip, difficult as it was to see him, much as she insisted that I go on this one now.

She thought some good might come from reaching out to him at a difficult time, and she wanted our children to know him.

But Dad was oblivious to the twins, and his grandchildren, in turn, were unimpressed by him. He didn't smile or twinkle or make them laugh. He mostly grunted, if he made any noise at all. More than anything, he hid behind silence and welcomed no one to the other side.

As for Cindy and me, everything we did was for the kids, especially now, when we were coming apart. For all the fights, we never let Avery and Adia see the damage. We had gone so far as to agree that if we ever separated, Cindy, Avery, and Adia would stay in the house and I would go.

We desperately didn't want that. We called in every bit of help we felt comfortable in seeking. Her parents stood ready to sweep in and take the children when the tension smothered us. We auditioned marriage counselors until we finally found the one we both could talk to. We confided in friends. We set aside date nights, and though several eroded into more fights, the point is, we were trying. Cindy was trying, anyway. I kept riding off into the same old ditch, and every bit of progress we made, I ruined by turning accusatory again.

Now I was going away, because I hadn't tried enough or succeeded enough. Because my father had wrenched an opening in our lives big enough for my wife to push me through.

The kids wandered into our bedroom as I closed up my duffel bag.

"Where are you going, Daddy?" Avery asked.

"To see your grandpa."

"You don't need a suitcase for that!" Adia said.

"Not your Grandpa Bobby. Grandpa Jim."

Adia curled up her nose. "I don't like him."

I looked at Cindy, helpless. She rolled her shoulders, as if to say, "Well, can you blame her?" And, of course, I couldn't.

"You'll just have to get to know him better," I said. "Grandpa Jim is a good man."

Look, kids, a fucking lie.

All the way up the 880 to the airport, I kept thinking that if I just said the word, the cab driver would veer off the freeway, turn around, and take me home. I could run up the sidewalk to our house, fling open the front door, and tell Cindy that it had all been a big mistake, that I would be husband of the year from now on. It could be just that easy.

At the exits for Stevens Creek, then the Alameda, and then Coleman, I felt the urge rise in my throat, the words sticking to my wet tongue. Each time, I swallowed hard and choked them back down. The driver pressed on, oblivious to the mental battle spilling into his back seat.

Cindy had left earlier that morning to take the kids in for a checkup—a coincidence that I half-bitterly accused her of having rigged so she wouldn't have to deal with this. I knew, of course, that the kids' appointment had been set weeks earlier, and my wife took my frustrated jibe gently and said, "You'll do fine. You know I'd go if I could. You also know that it will be better if I don't."

I knew. The way I had it figured, disaster or disappointment loomed as the outcome of this trip, whatever the circumstance. But if I were to put Jim Quillen and the battle royale between his son and daughter-in-law in the same room, God save us all.

I stood in line at the ticket counter. I watched people peel off toward their gates, and I wondered what manner of regret they carried. I was being choked by mine, and I worried that my throat wouldn't be wide enough to swallow it again.

As I stood in the terminal, my mind drifted again, inexorably, toward the sun-bleached images that returned to me with enough regularity that they had become part of my existence, an unpleasantness that I long ago assimilated. In the time that it took for my brain's wiring to fire up the memory, I became not a thirty-nine-year-old husband, father of two, and businessman, but instead, an eleven-year-old boy in a strange, small town. As each exquisite detail filled my head, I was as ill equipped now as I was then to set it right. I knew every word I should have said, every action I should have taken, and yet, in the replay in my head, the same things happened, again and again and again, as if on a tape loop.

I shuffled through the security line toward the gate, picking through the words of my past few conversations with my wife and warily looking ahead to what waited at Dad's, and I felt myself go. I knew that I would be exhausted by the time I had gnawed yet again on each bitter scrap, but I welcomed the thoughts, if only as a diversion from the mess I was leaving at home.

It's not as if I should have been surprised. Dad had been on my mind for several days, and this journey through my memories meant going to the twenty-eight-years-earlier version of him, to swallow once more the way in which he broke me down—broke us all down—and left us to pick up the pieces, year after year. It's only in retrospect that I see any of it coming, and by then, it's too late to get out of the way.

As we waited on the tarmac, I pulled out one of the notebooks packed into my carry-on bag. A night earlier, when I had finally confessed to Cindy that I felt sick and scared about what awaited me, she gave me an assignment.

"Tell me what happened," she said.

"To what?"

"To you and your dad. Tell me what happened."

"God, Cindy, it's late."

"Not now. While you're gone. Write it down. Let it out."

I equivocated, but she wouldn't accept no. She stuffed my bag with notebooks and pens.

"Give it a shot," she said.

I uncapped a pen and set the ballpoint onto the paper. I kept it there for a while, arguing with myself about whether to proceed.

"SEATAC, WASHINGTON," I wrote.

I set the pen down and closed my eyes.

I felt the plane lurch backward from the Jetway, but I didn't remember its wheels leaving the ground, nor did I recall the big loop over the South Bay before we turned east. My eyes had been wide open the first time I took this trip, when I lived it, and over the years I found that the endless journeys into my memories went better with them closed tight. I knew what was coming. I'd seen the story before. Parts of it comforted me, particularly the recollections of those moments before I left SeaTac all those years ago. I could see my mother's sweet face, smiling at me as she said good-bye. She tried not to let me see her tears.

In my head, she always returned to me, the vibrant, beautiful mother who inhabits my dreams.

It's my favorite part, but it never lasts.

Grace fades.

Losses linger in your gut, resistant against your best efforts to expel them.

Somewhere between consciousness and sleep, lulled by the jet's engines and the torrent of memory, I returned to that place I've never been able to escape and made another fitful journey through what my eyes took in and my head wouldn't let go.

SEATAC, WASHINGTON | JUNE 14, 1979

"Mitch, hold still." My mother betrayed a hint of frustration with me. She had things to say before I barreled onto the plane for Salt Lake City.

"When you get off the plane, there's supposed to be someone to take you to the next gate. If you don't see someone, just stay there. OK?"

"Yeah."

I knew the drill. Mom had been putting me on planes for six or seven years and putting her trust in the airline personnel to get me to where I was going. I hadn't been lost yet, and I found it embarrassing to be treated like a little kid.

"OK, good," she said. "How often are you going to call?"

"Once a week."

"Right. And tell Jerry it wouldn't kill him to call once in a while, too. I haven't heard from him in weeks."

"OK, Mom."

She knelt down to face me, though she needn't have done so. I was nearly five and a half feet tall—just a wisp shorter than she was.

She smiled. At the corner of her eye, I saw the first tear coming, and I fidgeted. She pulled me into a hug.

"I love you, Mitch."

"I know. Me too."

She let me go, then grasped the bill of my ball cap and gave it a friendly tug. I loved that cap. If I held any regret about leaving for the summer, it would be that my baseball team, the Mariners of Capitol Little League, would finish their final two games without me.

"Tell your dad that I want a phone call tonight, so I know you made it safely."

"OK."

I turned away from her, and the gate attendant gave me a wave of his hand, as if to say, "Come on, let's go."

I skipped down the Jetway.

Eight years earlier, when I was three years old, Mom had split from Dad. She packed my brother Jerry and me into her car and drove us through the night from Billings to Olympia. She had chosen a time when Dad's work took him out of town, but it was an unnecessary precaution. He never came for us, and he never seemed surprised that we had gone. We lived for a little while in my grandparents' basement until Mom could no longer stomach that arrangement. Her parents detested Dad and had always contended that Mom's union with him would end in pain. That their prediction was realized twelve years after it was first made seemed to satisfy them somehow, which never made much sense to me. Who would want to be right about something like that?

Jerry and I spent alternating summers with Dad, one of us always hanging back in Olympia. Mom said that sending one of us away for the summer was so difficult that she couldn't bear to be without both of us at the same time. Separating us ensured that she didn't have to.

After Jerry graduated from Olympia High School in '78, he flat-out told Mom that he wasn't going to college, that he planned to work on Dad's rig. She pleaded with him to reconsider, but it was pointless. Jerry was our father's son in physicality and stubbornness. He didn't linger in Olympia longer than it took for him to turn the tassel on his mortarboard.

One year later, on the summer set aside for my every-other-year visit, I was on my way to join my brother and my father.

In Salt Lake, a gate attendant met my flight, just as Mom said he would, and he whisked me in a cart to a satellite terminal for my puddle-jumper ride to Cedar City. I had scammed a few extra bags of peanuts from the stewardess on the Seattle flight, and they were stuffed into my shirt and pants pockets. I had even accepted the plastic wings that had been offered, after first protesting that I wasn't a little kid.

"Are you from Cedar City?" the shuttle driver asked.

"Nuh uh. That's just where my stepmom is meeting me."

"Where are you headed?"

"Milford."

"You ever been there?"

"Nah."

"Not much to it. How long you staying?"

"All summer."

He whistled and said nothing else.

I rode alone on the flight to Cedar City. Once I was buckled in, the copilot came out. I stuffed peanuts in my mouth while he talked.

"This will be a short flight, Mitch. Since it's just you and us, we'll leave the cockpit door open so you can take a peek and see what we see. Just stay in your seat, OK?"

Up in the cockpit, the pilot turned around and gave me the thumbs-up, which I happily returned.

I waited impatiently, willing the propellers to start. I yearned to see my father and Jerry again, and I was close now. I could feel the coming freedom of hanging out in the field, guzzling soda pop to my heart's content, playing video games in hotel lobbies. The rigid structure I chafed against at home would be thrown off in Milford, I was sure.

Dad was a doodlebugger—that's what guys like him were called, guys who ran truck-mounted drilling rigs and dug exploratory holes for uranium and natural gas. During the energy booms of the sixties, seventies, and early eighties, they roamed the rural West in packs, joined by surveyors and soil scientists. Itinerant workers all, they would blow into a town and take it over for a few weeks.

As a consequence of Dad's work, Jerry and I always headed somewhere new on our separate visits. Jerry spent summers in places like Cuba, New Mexico; and Limon, Colorado; and Rock Springs, Wyoming. I saw Elko, Nevada; and Thermopolis, Wyoming; and Sidney, Montana. Both of us would see Milford. The idea of that thrilled me.

About forty-five minutes into our hour-long flight, I saw the copilot pull out a book that looked like a manual of some sort, and the black grip of fear slipped around me. When I saw the propellers, I tried not to worry, but deep down, I knew that these puddle-jumpers were not safe—or were less safe, anyway, than the jet I had flown from SeaTac. Visions of Jim Croce and those guys from Lynyrd Skynyrd played in my head. They had died in planes just like the one I was on.

My mind reeled.

Doesn't he know how to fly this thing?

Something's wrong, isn't it? Why would he need a book?

Wouldn't they tell me if something is wrong?

I'm just a kid. Maybe they're afraid I'd freak out.

Maybe it's not that bad. They don't look worried.

Of course, I can only see the backs of their heads.

Maybe it's really, really bad. What point would there be in telling me if that were the case?

Aren't they obligated to say something?

Maybe I should ask.

I opened my mouth, but no words came. Instead, I hocked a frothy stew of vomit against the cabin wall and onto the floor. My eyes watering, I looked down and saw peanut chunks sitting atop the carpet.

The sound of my sickness drew the copilot out.

"Mitch, there's a bag there in that front pocket, if you feel sick again. Don't worry about it. We're nearly there."

I slumped in my seat, embarrassed that I had barfed but relieved that we apparently were not going to crash. I rubbed at my eyes, teary from the sheer physical exertion of regurgitation. The acid that didn't make the trip out of my mouth lingered in my throat, burning. The smell of my sick wafted up toward me.

A few minutes later, a stretch that seemed to take forever, we touched down and rolled to the gate. The copilot came back and lifted me over my pool of congealing throw-up.

"You OK, Mitch?"

"Uh-huh."

"Don't sweat it, man. If I had a dollar for every time somebody yakked on this plane, I wouldn't have to work anymore."

Marie waited just inside the door. She didn't disappoint. Dad had an eye for beauties. It was certainly true with Mom, and what he had found in Marie, his second wife, was glamorous in a way that Mom had never been. Marie's jet-black hair, parted in the middle, had been styled into locks that draped her shoulders and framed her porcelain face. Her nails were painted red. She wore big sunglasses, like Elton John's. And she smelled great.

Though Dad had married Marie in '76, because of my every-other-year visiting schedule, this was only the second time I had seen her. Her smile crumbled when she saw the copilot's hand on my shoulder as we entered the terminal.

"Hi, Marie," I said.

"He had a little accident, ma'am," the copilot told her. "He threw up. No big deal, but I wanted to make sure he got to where he was going."

"Are you OK?" she asked me.

"Yeah."

"Looks like you got a little on you," she said, lines creasing her nose as she pointed at my pants. "Let's get that cleaned up."

The copilot pointed me to the men's room, and as I walked away, Marie reached out and touched his arm, thanking him. Jealousy poured over me.

I sat in the passenger seat and nursed a Coca-Cola that Marie bought for me. She said it would calm my stomach. I didn't feel as though I was going to barf again, but that was immaterial. I liked Coke. I also liked riding in Marie's car. It smelled of jasmine, like her.

"How far is it?" I asked.

"About sixty miles. We'll be there in an hour or so."

"Neat."

"How did school go, Mitch?"

"Straight As."

"No kidding?"

"Yep."

"So what happened with that F last year?"

"I hated Mrs. Spinks."

"Why?"

"She played favorites. So I didn't do the work."

"We were worried about you."

"I had Mrs. Allen this year. She's my favorite teacher ever. I won the spelling bee, too."

"Really? That's great, Mitch."

"I lost in the next round, though. I misspelled *duodenum.*"

"What is that?"

"It's something in the body, I think."

"How'd you spell it?"

"D-u-o-d-e-n-i-m."

"That's an easy mistake to make."

"I was also elected student council president."

"Student council president, that's great," she said. "Your dad is going to be really proud."

I preened under her praise, and under the anticipation of his. Maybe he would even tell me so.

"I guess this means you'll want to stay there and not go to that private school."

Mom wanted to get me enrolled at St. Michael's. She said my "brilliance" would be better cultivated there. We weren't devout Catholics, but Mom saw that as a small hurdle. If it improved my chances, we could become devout, she said.

The bigger barrier was money. Mom didn't have much. Her job with the state was sufficient for our needs, but she relied on Dad's child support to make the bigger leaps of putting braces on our teeth (I hadn't needed them, but Jerry had racked up an impressive array of orthodontia), buying school clothes and supplies every year, paying doctors' bills, and the myriad other budget-busting expenses that kids incur. Jerry had left the house a year earlier, and that's where his support payments ended. Mine continued, and Mom had been lobbying Dad to help send me to private school.

"Here's the thing about that, Mitch," Marie said. "We've been talking, and we think you're doing fine in public school. It's a lot of money, more than we have to give. If you're happy, that's great."

Private school was Mom's idea. I liked how Marie talked to me as if I were an adult.

"Yeah, I like it at Garfield."

"Good."

At a highway junction, Marie turned her Buick Skylark left. Milford—and Dad and Jerry, who would be back from the fields soon—waited for us just thirteen miles down the road.

MILFORD, UTAH | JUNE 14, 1979

ON THE FIRST LEG of the trip from Cedar City, I took in plenty of farmland, the deep greens reminding me in some way of what I had left behind in Olympia. Once we made the turn north, the terrain turned more foreboding. This was unrelenting country—desert, almost, with scrub brush, austere buttes, and vast flatlands laid out in a broad valley framed by distant peaks and more sky than I had ever seen. This was the country Dad ventured into, fighting the earth, pushing pipe through the ground, then dropping a charge down the hole to be detonated and picked over by another crew.

As we approached town, the highway crossed the railroad tracks and jogged right, spitting us into downtown. Marie drove past boarded-up storefronts. I took note of the most regal of downtown buildings, the Hotel Milford, with its brick exterior and flat roof. Sitting on the edge of a town block as the hotel did, the front of the hotel curved along with the corner. I wanted to see the inside of that place.

After a few blocks, Marie turned into a trailer park, and I saw up ahead the Holiday Rambler and Dad's pickup. During the warm months, Dad usually pulled a trailer to job sites; it was less expensive than holing up in even a cheap motel. During winter, when just moving the equipment was hard enough, the trailer stayed at his ranch in Montana. As we approached, I looked up and down at Dad's big, sturdy Supercab. My heart sank when I realized that my motorcycle wasn't in the back.

"Looks like they're here," Marie said.

"Yeah."

It seemed interminable, the time it took for Marie to park the car and open the trunk so I could grab my bag and hustle inside to see Dad.

He was sitting on the couch when we came in, his work shirt stripped from his torso and wadded on the floor. Strewn about him were maps of the work areas, and Dad studied them through bifocals. Diesel and dust, the residue from Dad's workday, hung in the air.

"Hi, Dad."

My father looked up and grinned at me.

"How are you, sport? How was your trip?"

"Fine, mostly."

"Mostly?"

"He had a little problem on the flight to Cedar City. Threw up," Marie said, bending over and kissing Dad on the forehead.

"You OK?" he asked.

"Yeah."

I took measure of my summer home. I assumed that Dad and Marie would stay in the back, in the bedroom, and that I would spend the nights on the bed that folded out of the couch. I began to worry about what the sleeping arrangement was going to be, so far as Jerry was concerned. I couldn't imagine that he wanted to share a bed with me any more than I wanted to sleep with him. The Holiday Rambler didn't allow for privacy in the best of circumstances. If I were bedding down with my older brother, there would be none.

"Where's Jerry?" I asked.

"He's off seeing that girl." Dad spat the words out.

"Is he staying here?" Dad, who had returned to studying his maps, didn't answer.

"Oh no," Marie said. "Jerry's not staying here."

"He and the other hand rented a place," Dad said.

Had I not known my father like I did, I might have considered it odd that he would refer to an actual human being as "the hand," or that by extension he would refer to his own son in the same way. But that's what workers were to Dad. They were grist, fodder, a means to an end. He went through them so quickly and ruthlessly sometimes that there wasn't much point in becoming so acquainted that given names were necessary, save for writing out payroll checks.

"Is Jerry—"

"Mitch, look, I'm busy here," Dad said. "There are games in the office. Why don't you go down there and play awhile."

Marie, fussing with her hair in the bathroom, came out without being summoned. She dug into her purse, pulled out change, and poured it into my waiting hands.

About an hour later, Marie came into the office and told me that we would be going to dinner.

"Are you feeling up to it?" she asked.

"Yeah, I'm fine."

"Your dad is real happy to see you," she said. "He's just trying to figure out the work for the next week or so. He's a little run-down. Do you understand?"

"Sure."

Marie offered her hand, and I took it as we walked back to the trailer to meet Dad. Then we all walked down the street to a diner.

Jerry and his girlfriend waited for us in a booth. I very nearly didn't recognize him. In the year that he had been gone, he'd gotten a lot heavier, and from what I saw, the additions were muscle. If you were to look just at Jerry's face, there was no mistaking that he was Dad's son; his countenance had identical chiseled angles, as if it had been carved from stone. Jerry had also grown a robust beard.

"Little brother," he said, jabbing at my ribs as I approached the table. I smiled at him, and at the pretty girl next to him.

"Hey, this is Denise."

"Hi," I said.

"I've heard a lot about you, Mitch."

Dad and Marie slid into the seats opposite Jerry and Denise, who wriggled closer to my brother and patted the seat beside her, beckoning me to sit down.

"So what's the plan, Pop?" Jerry said.

"I've been looking at it. I think we should pull out where we are tomorrow, then cross the highway and start in that new section. We'll be all alone there."

In Dad's business, the biggest money went to the driller who could dig the fastest. Dad got paid a flat rate per foot, so it was in his interest to dig as many holes as he could each day, until the work was gone. Once this place was drilled out, everybody would pull out and chase the next job. I gathered from the conversation that too many rigs had congregated, scrapping it out over too few holes. Dad aimed to expand the field. I also knew that nobody could hang with his endurance. I had seen many a workday extended for one more hole, then one more, then one more, with my father pushing as deep into the clock as possible before the coming of night severed his ambition.

While Dad and Jerry talked shop, Marie and Denise chatted, and the scraps I heard told me I wanted no part of it. Girl talk made no sense to me.

"Jerry, I won the spelling bee at Garfield," I broke in.

My brother nodded at me and said, "That's great," and then he dove right back in with Dad.

Denise leaned over to me and whispered, "That's really cool. I can't spell." That made me smile.

The food came, and the chatter stopped. We tore into our burgers, and for a while, all that could be heard at our table was chewing and soda being sucked through straws.

Between bites, I tried again with Dad.

"Dad?"

"Yeah?"

"Where's my motorcycle?"

"Up at the ranch. We'll get it when we're on break."

"When's that?"

"A couple of weeks."

"Two weeks?"

"Mitch, just eat."

I glanced at Marie, and she gave me a smile and then nodded at my food. I picked up a french fry and chomped it.

When the plates were cleared, Jerry asked if I wanted to go with him and Denise to a convenience store down the street.

"Yeah," I said. "I also need to call Mom and let her know I'm here. She wants to talk to you, too."

"Great," Jerry said. He shook his head.

Dad handed Jerry his calling card. "Five minutes," he said. "No more."

Then Dad turned to me.

"You hurry back," he said. "We get going early, so you're going to need some sleep. You're coming out with us, right?"

"Yeah."

"And you," Dad barked at Jerry. "Ease off on that rutting. I need your strength."

Marie jabbed Dad in the ribs with her elbow. Denise looked like she wished she could burst into flames.

"Yes, Mom."

"No, Mom."

"It was fine."

"Yes, he was at the gate."

"Yes."

"He's right here. I will. OK. I love you too."

I handed the phone to Jerry, who went through a similar ritual. *Are you OK? Do you need anything? Are you eating well? Watch out for your brother. Be careful. I love you.*

His duty done, Jerry hung up the phone.

"Twenty questions," he said.

"Yeah."

"It's good to see you, Mitch. Really. You've grown."

"So have you."

I waited, but he didn't have anything more to offer.

"Do you like it here with Dad?" I asked.

"I knew it wasn't going to be easy working for the old man, and it hasn't been. In a year, he's gone through four other guys."

I had seen enough of Dad's dealing with employees to guess that the partings hadn't been amicable, a fact that Jerry confirmed for me.

"Jesus, Mitch, the last one, up in Rock Springs, that was bad. Dad rode the guy about everything. He couldn't do anything right. Too damn slow. Didn't know the tools. Didn't pay attention. Hell, Dad even told him once that he didn't eat the right way. That last day, he'd finally had enough, I guess. He took a swing at Dad."

I winced. "Really? What happened?"

"You know. Dad beat the shit out of him. Broke his nose. I had to pull him off the guy. I thought he might kill him."

I shuddered, and then I changed the subject.

"Where did you meet her?" I nodded at Denise, who was on the other side of the store, looking at eight-tracks.

Jerry smiled. "Nice, eh?"

That was one way to put it. Denise—her long hair blonde, her tanned legs sprouting out of short cut-off jeans—was perhaps the prettiest girl I had ever seen.

"Yeah."

"Met her right here. She just graduated from high school. Nice girl. A really nice girl." From the deep-voiced way he said it, I could guess what he meant.

Jerry and Denise drove me back to the trailer. In the parking lot, he stopped and said, "Mitch, don't press too hard with Dad, OK? Just be cool about the motorcycle and stuff like that. Things are kind of tough right now."

"What do you mean?"

"I'm not going to get into it now. Just keep your head down, do what you're told, and don't give him a lot of problems. Can you do that?"

"Sure."

"Good. I'll see you in the morning. Early."

I climbed out of the back seat, and Jerry threw the car into reverse and backed out to the street.

I headed for the trailer and wondered what might be waiting for me on the other side of the door.

BILLINGS, MONTANA | SEPTEMBER 17, 2007

I SLEPT ALL THE WAY to Denver, then stared out the window of the smaller jet for the hour-plus ride to Billings. Standing at the baggage carousel in Billings for the second time in four months, I felt as fresh as could be expected. In the face of uncertainty, that gave me heart.

I had called Cindy as the plane taxied to the gate. By rote, we said, "I'm sorry" to each other a lot these days, even if we didn't always know what we were apologizing for. I offered my regrets and sought a last dose of bucking up.

"I'm still wondering if this is the right thing to do."

"It is," she said. "And as a practical matter, it doesn't really make any difference now. You're there."

"That's comforting."

"Mitch, just stay on topic with him. Find out what's wrong, and make your peace. It's long overdue."

"That's easy for you to say. You act as though there's peace to be had."

"Are you arguing with me because you're afraid to argue with him?"

"Maybe."

"Don't argue, then. Just talk to him. Find out what's bugging him. You're the bigger man here. You're smarter, and you're more mature."

"Yeah, yeah. You're right."

"Now that's my big, smart man." The breathy way she said it was playful, something she hadn't been in a long while.

I wished I could go home.

Behind the wheel of the rental car, I plunged into the heart of Billings.

Despite my attitude about being there, I liked the city. My feelings about it came with baggage, a whole lot of it, but I always wondered how things might have been different for me, and for all of us, had Mom never left. Billings had been my home for the first three years of my life, and it's where I spent stretches of some childhood summers. This created an odd duality in which I knew Billings and was a stranger to it.

Until Mom spirited us away to Olympia, we lived in a small ranch-style house on the south side of Interstate 90. When I saw it on the visit a few months earlier, it was much as it seemed in my foggy memories, save for a new coat of paint and a chain-link fence in front where none had been before. Billings, as a whole, was scarcely the same place. Three decades of what some folks refer to as progress had transformed it into a mini-metropolis. But the place where we lived, near the Yellowstone River and in the shadow of Sacrifice Cliff, was the Billings that time forgot.

But I wasn't headed to that old house, nor to the cattle ranch that Dad and Marie bought in the late seventies.

Those were places of a different time and of different people. No longer the self-styled drilling baron, Dad puttered around a double-wide in the middle of town, playing out his days. No longer a wide-eyed, admiring son, I was just a guy in a rented Ford Focus, pushing my way toward an uncertain visit, burdened by fears in the present and thoughts of the past.

There was no sneaking up on the old man. Dad pulled back the curtain in his kitchen, alerted by my car as it spat gravel. He eased down the stairs as I retrieved my duffel bag from the trunk. His gray hair down to a few wisps, his pronounced limp from a long-ago broken hip, his face beaten into leather by the changing seasons on the back of a drilling rig, Dad looked older than his seventy-one years.

"What are you doing here, sport?"

"Figured I'd come out and see how you were doing."

He looked me over. "Why?"

"Do I need a reason?"

He headed back up the stairs toward the front door, and I followed. "You don't need a reason." He paused before opening the door, then said, "Might feel better about this if you offered one, though."

"Well, I guess you're just going to have to live with the truth. You're my dad, and I wanted to see you."

That earned me a Jim Quillen snort—a half-quizzical, half-dismissive acknowledgment that I had been heard if not believed. He opened the door and waved me through.

My desperate, unlikely hope that this might be a simple task was snuffed when I saw and smelled what was inside. Dad's place bore little resemblance to what I had seen months earlier. A home of gingham patterns and throw pillows and country charm had ceded to strewn newspapers and clothes. It looked as though he was simply retrieving the wash and dumping it out into the middle of the floor. I saw dozens of food-stained paper plates set here and there. The place reeked of garbage.

"Holy shit."

"I'd have cleaned up if I'd known you were coming," Dad said. He would have needed a month's notice.

"Where you staying?" Dad asked.

"I was hoping here. Would that be all right?"

Dad didn't say yes or no, in so many words. He simply pointed down the hallway. I followed the direction of his finger while he started plucking up newspapers.

BILLINGS | SEPTEMBER 17, 2007

I GOT THE NEWS that Dad had married a third time in much the same way that I had received the news about his second wife. He called me and said, "You have a new mother." That's where the similarities ended. The first call, in '76, had been to an eight-year-old boy who thrilled at the idea of a whole new member of the family. The second, twenty years later, had been to a twenty-eight-year-old man who barked back, "I have a mother," and reluctantly stayed on the phone to give a perfunctory greeting to Mrs. Quillen number three. Helen had said something like "I'm just so thrilled to have such a talented son." I had shot back, "You're my father's wife. Let's just leave it at that."

In the years that followed, Helen surprised me. If she had been hurt by my coldness, she didn't reveal it. She simply treated me with consistent kindness when I called Dad or he called me. She would hop on the extension and fill the considerable gaps in the conversation. Once, she called me out of the blue and asked why I never came to see Dad. I suggested that she ask him. If she ever did, I didn't hear about it.

When Mom died, one of the most thoughtful and unexpected notes came from Helen.

There is nothing I can or would attempt to say that could make the pain of losing your mother go away. My own parents have been gone for more than thirty years, and not a day goes by that they don't cross my mind.

But please remember this: you're her legacy, her greatest work. And she did a wonderful job with you. You are a good, honest, forthright man, and you're living the life that she gave you a foundation to live. Every day that you wake up is another day that Leila's legacy lives on.

I'm proud to know you, proud to be related to you. And I thank God every day that you're who you are. So, you could say, I also thank God that she was who she was.

A few years later, when Helen began her fight with cancer—an arduous battle that she and Dad bore stoically—I would bring that note out from time to time and reread it as I prayed for her to get better, and then, toward the end, for her to go quietly and without pain. Looking at what had become of their home in her absence, I missed her all over again.

In the kitchen, I was momentarily flummoxed about where to start in taming the filth, and then I figured that a big garbage bag would do for openers. I shoved in paper plates and plastic forks and plastic cups (after I had drained the half-filled ones into the kitchen sink) and anything that carried a hint of garbage. The unopened mail, and there was a lot of it, got stacked on the table until I could go through it with Dad.

"What happened?" I asked. "This place was spotless a few months ago."

"I've been busy."
"Busy doing what?"
"Busy."

I tamed the dining room and kitchen. Next, I ventured to the bathroom. I had already seen the bedroom I would be staying in, and it was mercifully clear of mess. The only bathroom in the place was not. The stench of dried urine knocked me back when I cracked open the door. I peeked in, and my eyes confirmed what my nose suspected. Bath towels that hadn't been washed in who knows how long hung from the shower curtain rod, soap scum ringed the tub, and Dad's errant whizzing had left little yellow puddles between the sink and the tub.

"Do you have rubber gloves?" I yelled to him.
"Just leave it."
"It's no problem."
"Under the kitchen sink."

As I walked back through, I saw that Dad had made a halfhearted attempt at helping, but from what I could see, he had just rearranged the newspapers and other detritus in the living room into more orderly stacks. I found him in his recliner, fiddling with the TV remote.

"What do you want to do with all of this newspaper, Dad? Do you recycle it?"

"Maybe I want to keep it."

I held up a front page of the *Billings Gazette*, dated July 14, 2007.

"You save those sewer-bond stories, eh?" I said.

His anger struck like lightning.

"Don't fucking baby me. Do you hear me? Don't do it."

"Whoa. I'm not babying you. I'm just cracking a little joke."

"It's not funny."

"No, apparently not."

Dad fumed but said nothing else.

I went to the kitchen, dug out the rubber gloves and cleaning solution, and then I trudged down the hallway to finish in the bathroom.

A few minutes later, I heard him coming down the hallway. I sat on my knees with my head pinned between the toilet and the bathroom cabinet as I scrubbed the floor.

"I'm going to lay down for a little while," he said.

"All right, Dad. I'm nearly finished in here."

He stepped down the hall and shut the door. For the next four-plus hours, the house was mine.

By the time Dad emerged, at just past seven, I had made the house habitable again. I had dragged five big, brimming garbage bags to the bin, mopped the floors, washed dishes, collated the mail, and dusted the furniture. The only chore left was to run a vacuum cleaner, something I had left undone while Dad slept.

I sat in his recliner, watched Monday Night Football, and ate a pizza I had found in the freezer. I offered Dad his chair, but he motioned for me to stay put and sat on the couch opposite me.

"Place looks good," he said.

"It'll do. You want something to eat?"

"Not hungry." He turned to the TV. "Who's playing?"

"Washington and Philly."

"Who's up?"

"Washington, 3–0."

The game mattered little. A lifelong Montanan, Dad threw in with the Denver Broncos. Having grown up in Washington, I hitched my allegiance to the Seattle Seahawks. That had made for some good-natured banter between us when I was a kid and they were in the same division, but silence had long since ensured that we had no room in our relationship for a triviality like football.

"So, Dad, what happened with the house?"

"What do you mean?"

"Come on. I just spent four hours cleaning it."

"Nobody asked you to do that."

"It was either me or the HAZMAT crew, Pop."

"I told you. Don't mouth off."

There was much I could say to that—starting with the absurdity of Dad's scolding a grown man as if he were a little boy—but I flushed with shame about my crack. I was doing exactly what Cindy had counseled me not to do. If I teased him, I would go back to California with no more answers than I had when I got here.

"Come on, Dad. Talk to me."

"About what?"

"About the house. About the past week of telephone calls. About anything."

He sighed, then dropped his head and stared at his hands, his fingers interlocking and twisting.

"There just doesn't seem much point to it."

"It..."

"The house. She's gone. What's the point?"

"You're not gone. You live here."

"Yeah."

I waited. I hoped he would say more, that he could give me something more to work with.

"I don't really know what to do with myself. I just sit around here, waiting. For what?"

"Are you feeling depressed?"

"I don't want to talk about all that psycho bullshit. I'm just tired, that's all."

"It's not psycho bullshit. It's real. And somebody can help, if that's your problem."

"I said I'm just tired."

"OK."

We sat in silence. The Eagles kicked a couple of field goals to go ahead, and then, with just a few seconds left in the first half, the Redskins scored on a touchdown pass, and you would have thought we were both fans the way we jumped out of our seats.

When I got up to go into the kitchen for another slice of pizza, Dad followed me.

"I didn't know how much I would miss her," he said. "She was dying for a year, but I can't believe she's gone. I miss her."

I thought he was a real son of a bitch for saying that. I hadn't made the trip so I could feel my heart break for him, yet that's what happened. I wondered if I should feel guilt that his pain had brought us together. And then I discarded the thought. It was his pain or mine.

I wrapped Dad in an awkward hug. He endured it stiffly, his open right hand patting me impatiently on the back until, finally, I let him go.

MILFORD | LATE JUNE 1979

I DIDN'T NEED much time to figure out what Jerry had warned me about that first evening. Dad and Marie were fighting, a lot. They would try to hide it, but how much hiding can one do in a twenty-six-foot-long fifth wheel? I did what I could to stay away from it, pumping quarters into the pinball machines in the trailer park office, tearing around in the city park across the street, and when Jerry would let me, hanging out at his place.

The problem was that Jerry protected his scant hours away from us. That summer reinforced the truth of just how separated my brother and I were, by years and by interests. We had nothing in common, save for a father we tried to please, to varying degrees of success, and a desire to not take on collateral damage when Dad and Marie clashed.

Just as I easily deduced that Dad and Marie were fighting, it was similarly easy to figure out that the source of the quarrels was money, specifically Marie's ability to make it disappear. While she sometimes accompanied us to the field—reading in a lawn chair, under an umbrella, and out of earshot of the loudest grind of the big machinery—Marie often took two- and three-day sojourns to Salt Lake City to visit friends and favored stores. When she came back, she

carried bags of blouses and pantsuits and shoes and jew-
elry. Each unhappy return ratcheted Dad's stress level up a
notch or two. Jerry said he had begun to wonder how many
notches Dad had left. Black dread filled my stomach when
he said that. I knew that when Dad reached the end of his
patience, pain would follow.

The hours in the sagebrush and dust, while arduous,
provided a respite for all of us. The days began early, at
five a.m., when Dad convened a breakfast at the diner. If
Jerry and Dad's other hand, Toby Swint, were more than a
few minutes late, Dad paced around outside the door, mut-
tering under his breath that one more fuck-up—just one
more—and he would by God find somebody who wanted to
do work. When they finally arrived, he greeted their sheep-
ish apologies with a stare and then rushed us through breakfast. Dad ran a tight ship, the tightest of any of the fifteen or
so drillers on the job.

No later than a quarter to six, we hit the road, out the
other side of town. We rode four-wide across the bench seat
of the Supercab; the rear of the cab was generally full of
tools or maps or work clothes. I sat wedged between Jerry
and Dad, who drove, and Toby perched on the outside.
When I fell asleep, and that was nearly every morning, my
heavy head ping-ponged between Dad's right shoulder and
Jerry's left.

The Ely Highway ran between sandy desert buttes and
sage, and although we ventured only twenty-five or thirty
miles from town, the drive seemed endless, coming and
going. It was as if the same scene unfolded in front of us,
mile after mile, and just when I started to think, again, that

we would never reach the end, Dad turned off on some dirt road and headed into the backcountry.

Rather than haul equipment back and forth from Milford, Dad ended each day by parking at the site of next day's first dig. I loved that first sight of the rig each morning. Something about it represented renewal, at least to me. Another day, another chance to lay down eight, ten, a dozen exploratory wells. Another chance to please Dad. Another day to be caught in the crosshairs of his wrath.

Neither Jerry nor Toby found our daily arrivals so invigorating. That's when their work began in earnest. Jerry's first job was to shimmy underneath the truck—an International Harvester Paystar 5000 mounted with a Mayhew rig—and grease it up. First, he would walk the perimeter, giving each wheel well a hard kick. In the late afternoons, after we shut down, rattlesnakes were known to climb into the insides of the wheel wells and stretch out. The last place Jerry wanted to be when he came face-to-face with a surprised rattler was on his back. Better to give the snake plenty of notice and let him crawl away on his own.

Toby did the same under the water truck, a brown Ford with a three-thousand-gallon tank. He also had the task of fetching the explosives Dad would need on the first hole and making sure the shovels and other tools were ready. Once the mast came up, Dad didn't tarry.

The actual digging never failed to enchant me. It was like a crude ballet, with my father playing the role of the maestro. He would drive pipe into the ground segment by segment, controlling the speed and the addition of new pipe with a series of levers, while Jerry did the heavy lifting opposite him. Once a segment was down as far as it could go, Jerry would slap something that looked like a big steel hand around the pipe; then Dad would gun the rig's engine, unhinging the driver from the pipe. Jerry would then take a spring-loaded contraption connected to a cable and jam it into the open end of a new pipe. With levers above his head, Dad manipulated the cable, lifting the pipe and pulling it toward Jerry, who hung off the edge of the rig, ready to catch it. The new pipe was connected to the previous segment, then was pushed down again. Each segment of pipe measured twenty feet, and it took anywhere from eight to twelve of them to finish each well. Pulling them out was the same process in reverse, with Jerry attaching the clutcher to the pipe, which was pulled up and detached, then thrown down a chute— all the while, Dad guiding it with his levers—where it would topple into a transport bay. Toby, the designated number-two hand, handled the shoveling and the other grunt work.

The brittle earth proved a complication in the country we were in. It was the worst kind of drilling, as far as Dad was concerned. He had to tote around a huge steel box with a hole in one end, called a pit. He positioned the open end over the drill site, and into the pit the crew poured water and powdered mud. The mud went down the hole and, propelled by the spinning pipe, clung fast to the earthen walls, fortifying them. Traditional air drilling wouldn't do in such a place; the holes would just collapse onto themselves. The churned-up dirt had to be shoveled out of the pit, a job that fell to Toby and, when Dad allowed it, to me. Dad also would let me shake in the powdered mud, but like everything else, he micromanaged it, often in contradictory ways.

"Not so much, Mitch, not so much."

"More, goddammit, more."

"OK, put that shit away."

"Where's the fucking mud, Mitch?"

I occasionally caught a glimpse of Jerry, who would roll his eyes or scrunch up his nose and silently pretend to be Dad yelling out orders. Dad's bark pushed me to the verge of tears, but Jerry's clowning brought me back around.

Once the hole went to the specified depth, Dad ran a charge down it. The explosives came in big plastic sticks—sometimes white, sometimes red—with threading on each end. The sticks were as thick and half again as long as a rolling pin. The wooden stake that marked each dig included information about how much explosive to run. This involved joining the sticks, wiring them with a blasting cap, and then carefully lowering it all down the hole.

With all the powdered mud he was using, though, getting the explosive down the hole was difficult. He, Jerry, and Toby often took twenty or thirty wooden rods, each ten feet long with metal hooks on the ends, and connected them, using the chain to shove the explosive through the muck and down the hole. It was an imprecise science; one wrong move could separate one rod from another deep in the hole, and Dad could spend an hour or more trying to blindly hook them up again. No bald-faced display of profanity I've seen before or since can compare with the sight of my father kicking empty explosives boxes and blasting out obscenities as the clock wound down on his workday while he tried to figure out how to get his cocksucking rods back.

"Mitch, do you want to learn how to drive?"

Jerry and I stood watching Dad make mercifully easy work of a well.

"Drive what?"

"The Love Boat. I'm thinking the pickup, you goofball."

"Seriously?"

"Sure. I know you're not having too much fun without your mini-bike here. You can start driving the pickup between holes."

We were talking a distance of only a hundred yards or so, but to my eleven-year-old sensibility, it might as well have been a cross-country interstate journey.

"What about him?" I said, nodding toward Dad.

"It'll be our secret. By the time he figures out you're doing it, he'll just be glad you know how. It will make it easier for him to fire Toby."

We both laughed at that.

Sure enough, by the time the hole had been dug, the explosive had been dropped, and Dad had put his report onto the stake, he wasted no time climbing back into the rig and pressing on to the next site. He paid me no mind.

In the pickup, Jerry said, "Now, step on the clutch."

"I know how."

"Oh really?"

"Well, I mean, I've seen you guys do it."

"OK, genius, just take it away." Jerry crossed his arms and waited for me to fail. I did, but only just.

I succeeded in starting the pickup, but I had no appreciation for just how hard the clutch was going to spring back on me as I tried to release it and give the truck some gas.

We lurched and sputtered and came to a stop. Ahead, the rig and the water truck grew smaller.

"You'll get it," Jerry said. "Give it a little more gas."

That worked. The Ford lurched forward in first gear.

"Now, you've got to use your ears. When the engine whines, shift."

I did so, double clutching as I had seen Dad do in the rig.

"No need for that," Jerry said. "Step through the floorboard and hold it until you're in the next gear. You don't want to burn out the clutch."

My other misstep occurred on the stop. I forgot about the clutch and just depressed the brake. The pickup heaved, cutting out and throwing us violently forward. My mouth crashed against the steering wheel.

"Shit, Mitch."

"Sorry."

I drove the rest of the afternoon, with Jerry riding shotgun. By the third attempt, he didn't need to tell me what to do. I had figured out the clutch-release-and-give-it-gas rhythm, and I could arrive at a smooth stop. There was no indication that Dad had a clue what was going on—or he just didn't care, as Jerry predicted.

Jerry and I were laughing and talking as I guided the Ford up to the drill site of the last hole of the day, and I'd grown cocky at my blossoming expertise.

When Jerry said, "Shit," I looked up and saw Dad running at us, waving his arms. I slammed on the brakes—again forgetting the clutch—as Dad reached the driver's-side door.

His face crimson, Dad grabbed the handle and yanked the door open, then pulled me out by the front of my shirt and threw me into the dirt.

"Do you see that motherfucking thing?" he yelled. "Do you see it?"

In front of my face sat a full box of explosives that Toby had set on the ground. I was maybe five feet from running over it.

"Oh fuck," Jerry said. He had come around to where I lay and knew just how lucky we were. Relief was short-lived, though, as Dad's tongue began carving us up.

"What was he doing?" Dad thundered, his face inches from Jerry's, his fists balled up.

"I was teaching him how to drive. It was an accident."

"No, asshole," Dad said. "It wasn't an accident. No thanks to you, though."

I started crying. Dad wheeled back on me.

"Shut up. Don't fucking cry here, Mitch. Don't do it. You're going to be a man, you're going to drive a truck, then you don't get to fucking cry here."

I couldn't stop. The tears came harder, faster, cutting tracks into the dust that had painted my face when he had pushed me down.

Dad loomed over me, grabbing me by the shirt and pulling me to my feet, then spinning me and kicking me square in the ass, which knocked me down again.

"We don't cry here. If you're going to cry, you big fucking baby, you go do it somewhere else."

I loped around to the side of the water truck, out of earshot and out of sight. After a few minutes, while I fretted that Dad might follow me and yell at me some more,

I heard the mast go up and the first segment of pipe go down. The mechanical roar drowned out everything else, and I returned to my whimpering in solitude.

The job went quickly. Dad, Jerry, and Toby finished fourteen holes that day, the best day we had that summer. We marked the occasion by riding to town in silence.

MILFORD | LATE JUNE 1979

I WORRIED THAT DAD'S anger would splash over into the after-hours, but I guess I was fortunate. Larger frustrations awaited.

We dropped Jerry and Toby off at their place on the west side of town, then drove down the hill to the trailer park. Marie's Skylark, which we hadn't seen in a couple of days, was out front. Dad sighed.

"OK," he said.

Marie bounded out and threw her arms around Dad, who tolerated a kiss before shaking her off and heading toward the door. If an army stood between Dad and his bath after a day's work, he would find a way through it. A wife was no match.

I followed closely as he galloped up the steps of the trailer. The dining area and the couch that folded out into my bed were filled with shopping bags from seemingly every department store in Salt Lake City.

"What's this?" he said.

"Just a few things I needed," Marie said.

"What you need and what we can afford are two different things."

"Really? You haven't seen me in two days, and this is what you're going to start in on?"

Dad's shoulders slumped.

"I'm taking a bath. Put the receipts on the table."

It's funny the memories that survive the years, and the ones that don't. I can remember the exact layout of Milford, and if you dropped me on a corner there today, I could find every place that lingers in my head. I remember the gas stations, and I remember the bars. I remember the songs on the jukebox and the radio. If I hear "Sad Eyes" on an oldies station, I'm back in Milford.

Then there are the things I have forgotten. I couldn't tell you the name of the diner or the name of the trailer park. The physical aspects of that little town cling to my memory, immovable even as I pile a lifetime of experience on top of them. The names are just trivialities.

I can also remember that Dad smelled of Aqua Velva when his fight with Marie chased me into the fading light.

Dad emerged from his bath and sat down to his ledger, ready to assess Marie's damage and to cut checks for Jerry and Toby, pay the various notes on his equipment, and settle his fuel charges and the other invoices that trickled in. I sat across from him, watching the black-and-white TV with the sound down so only I could hear it.

Dad recorded each entry, and I saw him rub his face more and more as the unfavorable math piled up. Finally, he turned to Marie, who was reading.

"Five hundred and twenty-two dollars."

"What?"

"Five hundred and twenty-two dollars. That's what we have for the next couple of weeks. For me to keep this crew going, to buy bits, to stock up on supplies, to pay for this spot, and for you to do whatever the hell it is you do. Shit, Marie, it's not enough to cover the fuel."

"So you're saying that because I did a little shopping, we're broke?"

"Because you did a lot of shopping, we're broke."

"What do you want me to say, Jim? What am I supposed to do around here all day?"

"You don't have to come at all. If all you're going to do is break us, I'd prefer you didn't."

"You'd rather I sat up there at that ranch?"

"That's what we bought it for."

"I'm not sitting up there for weeks at a time while I wait for you to come home."

"No, you sit around here, bleeding me dry."

"Fuck you, Jim."

"Fuck me?" he said, standing up and advancing on her.

Marie stood up to meet him.

"Yes. Fuck you." She reared back with a haymaker, which landed harmlessly against Dad's arm. That pissed Marie off more. She shoved past him into the hall and began chucking toiletries. He ducked under a can of shaving cream. It hit the table in front of me and caromed off my forehead.

I bolted. Dad yelled for me, but then a soap dish whizzed by. It crashed into the window at the back of the trailer, and Marie had his full attention again. I heard them screaming at each other as I sprinted down the gravel road, across the street, and up the hill into the park. Atop the hill, where the rows of houses picked up, I stopped and put my hands on my knees and tried to corral my breath. Once I had air again, I zigzagged through the streets until at last I found Jerry's door.

I gave it four raps. I leaned on the doorbell for good measure.

Jerry, looking irritated, threw open the door and saw me standing there, my chest heaving. He stepped aside and waved me in.

By eight o'clock, I could no longer fight a collapse into sleep. My own run-in with Dad had been bad enough; a lingering battle with Marie, I knew, could make things exponentially harder on us all. Dad's urgency about work hit overdrive when he felt stressed, and that impatience would surely get pounded out on the people around him. Half-sick with worry, and having eaten just a few handfuls of potato chips at Jerry's, I fell into a fitful sleep on the floor in front of the television.

Around ten, Jerry shook me awake and told me to answer the phone. I padded into the kitchen, bleary-eyed.

"Hello?"

"Hi, Mitch."

"Marie?"

"Yeah. I'm sorry about tonight. I'm heading back to Montana. It's for the best. I just wanted to call and make sure you were all right."

"Yeah, I guess."

"Good. I wanted to let you know that you shouldn't ask for too much from your dad right now, especially not money. It's a bad time."

"OK."

"I think we need to give him some room."

"OK."

"OK, kiddo. Have fun."

I hung up the phone.

"What'd she say?" Jerry asked.

"That I shouldn't bother Dad about money."

"That's rich. *You* shouldn't bother Dad about money. That takes some gall."

Jerry shook his head. I headed back to my spot on the floor.

BILLINGS | SEPTEMBER 18, 2007

I AWOKE JUST AFTER FIVE A.M., and as hard as I tried to coax a return to sleep, I couldn't get back to it. Finally, after a half hour of futile fighting, I threw back the covers and grumbled a greeting at the day.

In the hallway, I leaned in close to Dad's door and heard his bass-drum snore. The summers that I spent with him, particularly when we would share a motel room or that small trailer, I would have to adjust to his nighttime gasps. Gradually, sleeplessness ceded to assimilation, and his coughing cacophony morphed into white noise.

I couldn't scare up anything reasonable for breakfast, just a hardened heel of bread and some cereal that was a month beyond its best-by date. A peek out the window revealed morning bathed in darkness.

I decided to take a walk.

A few blocks from Dad's place, I stood in the empty parking lot of the Elks Club and watched the sun make its climb. Here, near the nexus of summer and fall, I found it easy to grasp the appeal of Billings and Montana—the cool morning, the early sunlight slowly finding and diffusing the dark.

In San Jose, most of the year brought pleasant reliability, warmth, and clear skies. In Montana, you could never quite be certain what you were going to get. Long ago, I had seen snow in June in this part of the world. That had been quite the sight.

The city found its breath again after its slumber, and behind me on Lewis Avenue I heard a rising flow of traffic. I thought about calling Cindy and telling her that I missed her and the kids, but halfway through dialing, I caught myself. It was five a.m. back home. She wouldn't be pleased to hear my half-baked thoughts about time, place, and weather at such an hour.

I pressed on.

I made a loop through the heart of Billings, into the residential neighborhoods that buffer downtown, across Grand Avenue to Billings Senior High and then Pioneer Park. I ventured west several blocks, huffing through the uphill climb. I passed joggers and moms with strollers, and I greeted each with a hearty "good morning." I was exhilarated at being out there, breathing in the crisp air, and I resolved to make more of an effort at such things once I returned home. In San Jose, as work piled upon family time upon other obligations, I found it too easy to brush off exercise. My expanding gut and strain at climbing Billings's small hills served as penalties for such inactivity.

Up on Grand Avenue, I ducked into Albertsons for a half-dozen doughnuts and a couple of cups of coffee, and I hoped that when I arrived back at the double-wide, Dad might be awake to enjoy breakfast with me.

I found him in his recliner. He wore a blue terrycloth robe well past its prime and watched the local morning show.

"Hey, Pop. Brought you some breakfast."

Dad grunted an acknowledgment and said, "I figured you'd had enough and had gone on home, until I looked and saw that your car was still here."

"Is that what you want? For me to leave?"

"Do what you want. It's a free country."

I shook my head. "Whatever, man. I have breakfast. Have some if you want. Or don't. I really don't give a shit."

He joined me in the dining room and swiped a jelly doughnut and a cup of coffee. I poured sugar and cream—lots of both—into mine.

"Why don't you drink it like a man?"

The anger rose in my throat, and I swallowed it.

"Like this?" I said. I grasped the cup of coffee, then pushed my elbows out and tightened my body. I paced around the room, my torso moving back and forth herky-jerky. In a cartoonish deep voice, I said, "You there. No dairy products in your coffee. Be a man like me. Straight caffeine. Fuck taste."

"A comedian," Dad said, and he waved me off. But I saw a glimmer. He had difficulty hiding his amusement.

I sat on the couch and dialed home on my cell phone.

"You can use my phone," Dad said.

"Unlimited minutes," I said.

He went back to watching his program.

"Hi. ... I got up around five and took a walk. ... Yeah, really, me, a walk. ... He's doing fine. We just had breakfast. … He's watching TV. … How are the kids? … Oh, I'm sure you're enjoying the solitude. … No, no big plans. Just going to hang out around here, unless there's something he wants to do. … I will. … OK. … Bye.

"Avery and Adia are still asleep," I told Dad.

"Uh huh. What's that wife of yours up to?"

"Cindy."

"Yeah."

"Her name's Cindy."

"I know."

"Being a mom, keeping me in line. The usual."

"She still a tree hugger?"

"You mean an environmentalist?"

Dad spit out an "ugh."

"Yeah, she's still involved with that. She's part of a mayor's group that's looking at green policies, in fact."

"Green—I hear that word all the time. I don't even know what that means."

"It means sustainable living and business practices. Reducing greenhouse gases, more recycling, alternative energy, that sort of thing."

"Sounds like a bunch of goddamned hooey to me."

"It's the way of the world now, Dad."

"Tree huggers make me sick. They're why my job went to shit, you know."

I shook my head. "Everything went to pot in '82, '83, right?"

"Around there, yeah."

"Natural gas and oil prices. They hit bottom, huh?"

"Yep."

"People out of work. Housing went all to hell. Right?"

"Yeah, Mitch."

"But it's Cindy's fault that you lost your job. You're a genius, Pop."

His eyes blazed. "Just shut up."

"No, really. An amazing show, Dad."

"You're probably going to raise those two kids to be granola munchers too, aren't you?"

"We're going to raise them to be their own people," I said. "Their names are Avery and Adia, by the way."

"I know their names."

"Yeah, well, you don't know much else. I'm going to tell you something, and I hope it matters to you. When I was packing up to come here, I told the twins where I was going, and Adia said she doesn't like you."

"She doesn't even know me," Dad protested.

"Yeah, well, that's sort of the point."

"That's pretty goddamned judgmental."

"You seem hurt."

"I'm not hurt. But that's not very fair."

"She's just a child, Dad. And you should recognize the logic, seeing as how yours is no more advanced than hers. She calls 'em like she sees 'em. Sound familiar?"

The conversation was done. Dad swatted his paper at me and looked away.

BILLINGS | SEPTEMBER 18, 2007

A FEW HOURS after we retreated to our neutral corners, from which we stared at the TV, Dad asked if I wanted to play a game.

"What do you have in mind?"

"Helen and I used to play *Sorry* a lot."

"The board game?"

"Yeah."

Dad went to his bookcase. The game sat atop his preferred reading, mostly Westerns and a few Grisham titles. As I helped him sort the game pieces and the playing cards, I saw three sheets of plain white paper, each filled with hundreds of slash marks in units of five—four vertical, one horizontal bisecting the group—under the names "Jim" and "Helen." Dad wasn't kidding; he and Helen must have played thousands of games.

He caught me staring.

"She was up two games when she died."

I wondered what the point of keeping score could possibly have been, and then Dad said, "We'll start a new sheet of paper for you and me." The answer was clear: there was no reason to play if we couldn't crown a winner and a loser.

Survival of the fittest in *Sorry* struck me as an absurd notion. The game doesn't require much skill or strategy. Mostly, it's the luck of the draw. If you pull a 2, allowing you to bring one of your four pawns onto the board and get another card, and then pull a 4, allowing you to move back to the mouth of the chute leading home, you can make short work of things. If you draw a 2 and then a 3, you face a longer trip around the board.

I wondered how this game of chance could hold such appeal for Dad, whom I recalled as more of a strategy man. In my youth, his games were poker, *Risk*, and chess, pursuits that played to his agile, tactical mind.

And yet, I quickly found the game pleasantly addictive. The *Sorry* cards—allowing you to move from the starting pod and knock out an opponent's pawn—could fast change the complexion of things. With an 11 card, you could switch places with an opponent, perhaps sending him back to the starting point just as he seemed set to bring a pawn home. After an hour, Dad led four games to three, the last of his victories coming on a huge rally. I'd had three pawns home and one on the board while all of his were in limbo. He still managed to win.

"I'm just better than you," he said.

"Seriously, man?" I said. "You're trash-talking me on a game of chance?"

It wasn't just trash talk. Dad was cheating.

At first, I dismissed the errors as innocent. I would see him take nine spaces on an 8 card, and I would reach across the board and move his man back a square. He complained about the light—"I can't see the board"—or just played dumb.

Then came other transgressions. Instead of taking one card, he would take two, peeking ahead at what I had coming.

"Stop looking at the cards, Dad."

"They're sticking together," he protested.

Once, on a 7—a useful card that allows you to split your move between two pawns—Dad counted five spots, slid down a chute, and then, with the same pawn, took two more spaces and killed one of mine.

"You can't do that."

"Sure I can. Seven."

"Seven spaces between two pawns, Dad. You can't take five and slide, then take two more."

"Yeah, I can."

"You can't. It's against the rules."

"Rules? We're just playing a friendly game."

"Friendly, my ass. You cheat. You keep redundant score. You trash-talk me. There's nothing friendly about it." About ten games in, convinced that I wasn't giving him proper credit for his victories, Dad began keeping score on his own sheet of paper.

"What are you so wound up about?" he said.

"I'm just not letting you get away with a bullshit move."

"It's not bullshit."

"It is bullshit. It's always bullshit with you. You're cheating. You've always been a cheater."

Dad sprang to his feet. "Fuck this," he yelled. He grabbed the board, slinging it off the dining room table into the kitchen. The pawns bounced off the refrigerator and skittered across the floor.

I shook my head, stood, and went to the kitchen. I dropped to my knees and started picking up the pieces. Dad fell back into his chair in the dining room and said nothing.

"I think I should just come home. This is pointless."

I stood outside, well away from the double-wide as I talked with Cindy.

"You've got to hang in there, Mitch. If you come back now, this will be it with him. Your last interaction will be a stupid kids' game. Is that what you want?"

I could say nothing, and that was my answer. The day before had seemed promising; I had hoped that he would open up about Helen, and that I might take such an opening as a chance to talk with him in a deeper way about loss. We both had some experience with that. Hell, I had even allowed myself to dream that he might accept an invitation to spend some time with us in California. Pure foolishness.

"If you'd seen what happened, you wouldn't want to stick around," I said.

"You're probably right. But then, he's not my father."

"Sometimes I wish he weren't mine."

My wife sighed.

"I know. This is your cross. Grin and bear it."

MILFORD | JUNE 27, 1979

THE MORNING AFTER Dad's fight with Marie, our crew fell back into its patterns. Dad waited for Jerry, Toby, and me outside the diner, staring at his watch as we arrived late. We dined on bacon, eggs, and for the most part, silence.

"Mitch," he said, "I don't want you running off like that."

"I don't like getting hit in the head," I said glumly.

Dad kept his head down and stabbed at his breakfast.

"I'm responsible for you."

Jerry slammed an empty coffee cup on the table. I flinched as the room came to a dead halt. Every eye in the place was on us.

"Then why didn't you come get him?" Jerry said. "Shit, even Marie knew where to find him."

Dad kept his voice low. "We'll talk about this later."

"It's bullshit," Jerry said.

Not a word passed among us as we rode to the field. For the first time, I didn't sleep, which was just as well. The tension spilling off the men bracketing me made it clear that my head wouldn't find comfort on either shoulder.

At work, the unspoken rancor between Dad and Jerry came out in obstinate fits. When Dad told Jerry to do something, my brother would do something else, so long as it didn't fundamentally interfere with the operation of the rig. These were small rebellions—shoveling when Dad asked for mud, going to the cooler in the back of the pickup for a soda when Dad sought a crescent wrench. Because they were such insignificant challenges, they made the old man all the angrier, although he tried gamely (and futilely) to hide it. My brother, so like our father in so many ways, knew exactly what buttons to push.

"It's uncomfortable to be around them," Toby said to me when we broke for lunch. Dad took his sack and sat up in the cab of the drilling rig, and Jerry perched at the edge of the pit. Toby and I sat on the tailgate of the pickup. Most days, the four of us would congregate there, cracking jokes and enjoying a rest.

"I wish I had my motorcycle here," I said. "I could just ride off somewhere."

"I'm afraid he's going to punch Jerry out," Toby said. "Jesus, man, he's really pissed off."

I didn't worry about that. The more likely scenario, I feared, was that Dad would invent a reason to go after Toby. Weakness or stupidity—and Toby sometimes seemed to have significant doses of both—were like scrapple to Dad. Tangling with someone as strong as Jerry wasn't likely.

Two years earlier, I saw how Dad's predation worked. A weeklong break loomed, and Dad was antsy to get back to the ranch. The thing was, Dad wasn't like most guys. Most guys on a drilling crew, when they're on the verge of a break, they loosen up, lighten up, and let the anticipation buoy them. Dad's mood grew darker and more erratic as we got closer to shutdown, for reasons I couldn't reach. Did he hate to stop working? Did he miss home that much? Was he anxious to see Marie? Did he dread it? I couldn't hazard a guess.

At breakfast, two days before we shut down, Dad cut off all conversation. One of Dad's hands, Al Moak, shook his head at one point, when another try at morning chatter had been choked off.

"You have something to say, Al?"

"Nope. Obviously."

"Say it."

Of all of the workers Dad employed in the summers I spent with him—a score of faces and names that have been pushed out of my head by more immediate concerns—Al Moak was the friendliest. Too friendly, I would say, at least for Dad's crew. He always had a kind word and a smile, always asked how I was, never seemed too put out to gas up my motorcycle for me. He was the kind of guy you would want as a friend. His manner made him vulnerable to Dad, who hated weakness and couldn't see the difference between that and kindness.

"Say it, Al."

Al kept his composure, which ended up being the wrong move. I wonder still if a right move was available to him.

In the parking lot, Dad cracked a right hand across Al's jaw, dropping him.

I shuddered as I remembered it.

"Just stay away from him," I told Toby.

My advice to Toby, sound as it was, turned out to be unnecessary. Dad dug just two more holes after lunch and then announced that we were heading back to town. We'd done barely a half day's work, but nobody said anything. An early shutdown by Jim Quillen amounted to a gift horse.

In town, Dad pulled off the main drag and dropped Jerry and Toby at their place.

"Jerry, I've got to go to Cedar City for some things tonight," Dad said. "I'll bring Mitch by in an hour or so. I'll need you to look after him."

"Why can't he go with you?"

"I'm going to be late, for one thing, and I need to see some people about business. It's no place for a boy."

I bristled at their talking about me as if I weren't there.

"I can stay at the trailer by myself."

"No, absolutely not," Dad said.

"It's bullshit, dropping this on me without any warning," Jerry said. "I have plans."

"Life's tough, kid. You can miss a night of rutting. I'll see you in an hour."

As we rode away, Jerry shot Dad the universal sign of digital defiance. Dad either didn't see it or didn't care.

After his bath, Dad preened at the bathroom mirror, giving himself the once-over. Standing there, his torso bare, he showed why he could be such a rough customer. Dad wasn't imposing at first glance—he was short and had stubby, drumstick legs. But his midsection and arms looked as though they had been cut from stone, and his hands, thickly muscled from manhandling steel, hung from his wrists like small hams. Hardheaded and hard-bodied, Dad could meet any physical challenge.

He whistled as he slapped cologne on his face. The scent of Aqua Velva curled through the trailer.

"What are you doing tonight?" I asked.

"I've got to see a guy about some drill bits, and I'm going to get a line on some more work from a couple of friends."

"Let me go with you. I'll be quiet."

"No can do."

"Jerry doesn't want me there. I'll just be in the way."

"Your brother needs to learn that the world doesn't always work the way he wants it to. He might as well learn it tonight."

"He's just going to take it out on me."

"Jesus, Mitch, just quit. You're not going."

At Jerry's, Dad didn't walk me in; he just stopped the truck and told me to get out, and then he tore out of there.

Jerry proved about as welcoming as I expected. He opened the door and summoned me inside. I sat on the couch, and Jerry walked back through the living room and into the bathroom. As Dad had done earlier, Jerry put on deodorant and cologne. I still wore my work clothes. We hadn't been out long enough for me to get them dirty or for the dust to cling to my sweaty face.

Jerry called to me from the bathroom.

"Look, Mitch, I know this isn't your fault, but Jesus Christ. This really screws everything up."

"I know."

Jerry walked out of the bathroom and into his bedroom, and then he came back into the living room pulling a velour shirt over his head.

"I don't have a choice, so you're coming with me tonight. Just be cool."

"OK. Where are we going?"

"We're going to have some burgers, then go to Beaver for a movie."

"Just you and me?"

"No, Denise and Toby and his girlfriend will be there."

"What movie?"

"Does it matter?"

I kicked at the carpet.

"Mitch, this will all work out if you're cool. If you're not, I'll kick your ass. Do you understand?"

My brother often threatened to kick my ass without ever actually doing it. What would be the point? He was eight years older. Still, given his agitation, I figured that the best answer was the one that would please him.

"Yeah, I understand."

Denise, Toby, and Toby's girlfriend waited at the burger joint around the corner. Someone else came along, too.

"Mitch, this is my sister, Jennifer," Denise said.

I smiled at the girl next to Denise. She had long brown hair that was pulled back into a ponytail, and little freckles dotted her nose.

"She's ten," Denise said.

"Hi, Mitch," Jennifer said.

"Hi."

Trying to hold back the oncoming blush, I sat down across from Jennifer.

"If you want, we could leave you two alone," Toby said, and his girlfriend threw a french fry at him. That made me think that she was cool, a thought that lasted only until she stood a few minutes later, spread her arms, and yelled, "Who chooses this music? It sucks." Someone had put Dr. Hook's "When You're in Love with a Beautiful Woman" on the juke-box.

"I like this," I said. One of the ways I whiled away the hours in the field was by fiddling with the pickup's radio to intercept whatever signal could reach where we were. I knew every hit from that summer, and I was partial to this song, "Time Passages" by Al Stewart, and "Reunited" by Peaches and Herb.

"You're just a kid. What do you know?" she said.

"More than you."

"Mitch," Jerry said. "I warned you."

I clammed up.

"Give me a little Bad Company, and I'm fine," Toby said.

"All day long, brother," Jerry said, and they slapped a high five across the table.

We rode the thirty-five miles to Beaver in two cars. Jerry, Denise, Jennifer, and I were in Jerry's Camaro, and Toby and his girlfriend rode in Toby's Bronco. I sat in the back-seat with Jennifer. We hadn't exchanged more than a hello.

"Don't you two like each other?" Denise said.

"Sure," I said.

Jennifer didn't say anything. I tried to talk to her.

"What grade are you in?"

"I'll be in fifth."

"I'll be in sixth."

"Where do you go to school?" she asked.

"Garfield Elementary in Olympia, Washington."

"I've never been there."

"It's a long way. I had to fly in a plane to get here."

"I've never been on one."

"It's fun. Mostly." I remembered my throwing-up episode, and I decided not to share that.

It took a little while for us to start talking, but once we did, we didn't stop. She told me about her school and her friends and the things she liked to do. They sounded a lot like the things I did back in Olympia: riding bicycles and playing sports and going to church and having sleepovers with friends. I didn't like Milford very much, and I would never trade all my friends and the places I knew in Olympia for this place—never in a million years would I do that—but I thought I could deal with Milford a little better if I had a bicycle (or a motorcycle) to ride and friends to play with.

When the alien popped out of John Hurt's stomach during the crew's dinner, Jennifer grabbed hold of my arm and squeezed. After the scene, her arm stayed in mine. I had never touched a girl like that, for such a long time. I tried not to get a boner, but the youthful rush was more than I could fight. I was thankful that I was sitting and no one could see it.

Plenty of other scenes scared Jennifer, too. I also felt scared, but I tried to act as though I wasn't.

"I am never, ever, ever, ever eating spaghetti again," Denise said as we walked back to the car.

"Oh man, that was so great," Toby said.

"It was gross," his girlfriend said.

"My favorite part was the end," Jerry said.

"Yeah, when it was over," Denise said.

"No, no, when the alien was inside the control panel of the ship. God, that was freaky. I loved it."

"Were you scared?" I asked Jennifer.

"A little."

"Me too."

We got back to Milford a little after ten, and Denise said she and Jennifer had to get home. Jerry drove up to their house, and Denise leaned in and kissed him. Then she whispered something in his ear that made him smile.

It would have been too much to expect a kiss from Jennifer, though a boy could dream. Sure enough, she only waved.

"Bye, Mitch."

"Bye, Jennifer."

On the way back to Jerry's, he said, "Nice girl, isn't she?"

"Yeah."

"Glad you came along?"

"Yeah."

We watched TV awhile, but neither of us found it interesting. Jerry spent most of the time fiddling with a deck of cards, shuffling and shuffling, and I kept talking but not really saying anything. Jerry would swat my chatter across the space between us, and I would just let his volleys roll to the floor and die.

Around eleven, Jerry stood up and said, "Let's head back to the trailer. He's got to be home by now."

When we saw the empty space in front of the Holiday Rambler, Jerry said, "Fuck" underneath his breath.

"Just drop me off," I said. "I'll be fine."

"Shit no. I'd never hear the end of that. Damn, Mitch. This really messes everything up."

"Come in. There's beer." I hoped the offer might placate my restless brother.

"Yeah, yeah, OK."

He cut the ignition.

Jerry blunted the boredom of the first hour with two Blue Ribbons from the fridge. Then he grew restless and profane.

"Fucking bullshit, man. Where is he?"

I fought my closing eyes. It was nearly midnight, far past the point at which I usually drifted out to sea.

Jerry flipped on the TV and stewed.

The banging of the outside door against the trailer jolted me from sleep. I heard Dad, too loud by half, bellowing through the screen door.

"This will be great," he said. "My sons are here. You'll love them."

Dad lurched up the stairs, followed closely by a tiny blonde wearing about half as much dress as she needed to cover her body. It seemed perversely apropos. I figured her to be half Dad's age.

Groggily, I tried to absorb the sudden change in the room's chemistry. My brother no longer sat beside me, basting in his anger. Jerry stood up, jutting his jaw toward our father.

"Jesus Christ," he said. "Where in the hell have you been? It's fucking one a.m."

"Brenda," Dad said, straining to stay upright as the alcohol played tricks on his equilibrium, "the mouthy one is my son Jerry. And that guy"—he listed left as he pointed at me—"is Mitch. He's the friendly one."

"Hi," Brenda said, to no reply from either of us.

"Boys, say hello to the woman who might become your new mother," Dad said.

I wanted to throw up.

Brenda giggled.

"Are you out of your mind?" Jerry said. "What the fuck did you do all night?"

Dad grinned at my brother. "Isn't it obvious?"

Brenda giggled again.

"Oh man, this is so fucked up," Jerry said.

"Brenda, go on to the bedroom," Dad said, pushing his new friend toward the hallway and giving her a swat on the ass for good measure. She stepped through the door and closed it.

"No, no, no, no," Jerry said.

Dad cut him off.

"Boys, your new mother and I are going to go to sleep now. Let's keep it down out here, OK?"

As Dad bobbed toward the bedroom, Jerry grabbed him by the shoulder and said, "There's no way in hell you're..."

Lightning quick, as if his drunkenness were a mirage, Dad spun Jerry around, twisting his arm behind his back.

Grabbing Jerry by the collar, Dad smashed my brother's face against the refrigerator door.

"No way in hell I'm gonna do what? What have you got, tough guy? You've got nothing. Fuck you, Jerry. Fuck you if you don't like it."

He pushed Jerry to the floor, and then he turned and walked through the bedroom door.

I cried. Jerry sat on the floor, his nose bloodied.

A couple of minutes later, the telltale sounds started on the other side of the door. I had never heard sex, never seen sex, never really contemplated sex, but I knew what it was the moment the sound hit my ears. I cried louder, uncontrollably. For me. For Jerry. For Dad, who didn't deserve my tears. For Marie, who surely did, no matter her faults.

Dad yelled at me through the door.

"Stop that goddamn crying, Mitch."

Jerry pulled himself off the floor and sat down beside me. He wrapped his arms around my shoulders, and I sank my head into his chest, muffling the cries that wouldn't stop, no matter how much Dad berated me.

"It's going to be all right," he whispered, and he stroked my head. "Shhhhh. Shhhhh. It's going to be OK."

BILLINGS | SEPTEMBER 19, 2007

MORNING CAME AGAIN, and once more I awoke before Dad. When I was a child, Dad's anxiousness about work stirred him before the sun arrived, and he had to jab at me to get me moving. Now, no longer burdened by the rigors of a job, he slept soundly, while I lay a room away, cracking open my worries.

I thought about the call I would have to make to change my ticket to something open-ended. My flight home, as it stood, was twenty-four hours away, and I suspected that I needed longer than that to settle things. I wondered, too, what Cindy would think of that. Was she ready for me to come home? Or was she happy to be rid of me?

The old man snoozed. I dressed and left the house.

I drove along Lewis Avenue toward downtown Billings, still stretching from its slumber. I found the way out to the south and crossed Interstate 90, to the patch of ground that I had to visit. It was awfully early to be parking a car in front of a stranger's house, so I continued past our old place and drove to Coulson Park, along the Yellowstone River. A good, brisk walk would get me back to what I wanted to see, and it would do me some good.

I delighted at the beautiful fall day. I saw one hardy jogger out for a morning run, but aside from him, the park was mine. As I stared at the water and Sacrifice Cliff behind it, I could pretend that Billings and its hundred thousand residents—all of them behind me from that vantage point—scarcely existed. A half turn, however, would bring it all into view. The downtown buildings, the refinery, the highway and the city streets, the rimrock that cradles the city.

I recalled how the town had always plucked at my senses. My earliest memories of the place rested not in the visual but in the olfactory. The refineries, the sugar beet factory, the meatpacking plant, now gone—these were things that could push a stench across the city, a foulness that couldn't be moderated by those things that appealed to other senses. In the later years of detachment from Dad, with that wall of anger and grudges standing between us, the thought of Billings would braid my guts. I'd left important things undone here for a long time. My presence demanded that I confront them, if I dared.

Sacrifice Cliff inspired another thought, one drawn by my voracious youthful reading. In 1837, sixteen Crow Indian riders climbed atop their terrified, blinded horses and rode off the cliff to their deaths. To them, it was the price of appeasing the gods and stanching the smallpox that shredded their people. Brought to this land by the white man, the disease killed the Crow in multitudes.

It had always struck me as a heartbreaking story, but on this day, it conveyed needed perspective. The disease that ran through the Quillen family, not near as fatal as smallpox but every bit as insidious, didn't compel me to climb Sacrifice Cliff and launch myself to my death. I just needed to turn around and face what was behind me.

Ten minutes of brisk walking carried me to Charlene Street and the house that I had been born in. Though it sat just sixty yards or so from the interstate, the house enjoyed seclusion, thanks to the four large cottonwoods that buffered it from the street. I looked the house over as I approached, trying to reconcile the haziness of memory with what I saw. When we lived there, the place was the drab white seen in many of the houses of the time. A subsequent owner had splashed it with a pleasing sea foam tint.

I walked past the house a few hundred feet, away not wanting to be the odd guy standing in the street and staring into a home early in the morning. Once I had covered a comfortable distance, I turned around for another pass.

As I approached again, I saw a man in the driveway stooping for the morning paper. He spotted me and gave a wave.

"Morning."

I stopped. "Good morning."

I lingered, fighting with myself over whether to say anything else, and then I plunged ahead.

"I was born in that house."

"Really?"

"Yep. June 4, 1968."

"How long did you live here?"

"Till about '71. My dad was here until around '77, so I came back a few times."

"We bought the place in '94."

"Looks real good. I like the color."

"Thanks."

I gave the man a wave.

"Well, have a good day."

I was five steps away when he spoke again.

"Do you want to come in and see the place?"

Memory is strange. It enlarges places and spaces. Until that morning, standing in my old bedroom for the first time in more than thirty years, I had always pictured it as a much larger room. In reality, it was only about eight by eight, big enough for a bed and a dresser. The owners, Don Newcombe and his wife, Angela, had converted it to storage.

The rest of the place, too, bore little resemblance to my faint recollections. The shag carpet popular in the sixties and seventies was long gone, replaced by Spanish floor tiles ("Did that ourselves," Don said). The living room walls, once a faux-brick vinyl that I remember Dad putting up one day in '75, were stripped back to their original form and coated in soft pastels. Whatever imprint the Quillens had made here had long since been overtaken by others' concepts of home. My pilgrimage to stare at an assemblage of drywall, nails, and lumber suddenly seemed silly. This place held no answers for me, no truths to satisfy my questions.

"Do you still live here in Billings?" Don asked as we said our good-byes.

"Oh no. California. I'm just here for a visit with my dad."

"Well, it was nice meeting you," he said. "Come back any time."

It was a nice but unnecessary offer. I liked the New-combes, but their house was one of thousands in Billings. Nothing more. I knew that now.

I walked to the car, shaking my head at my naïveté.

I found Dad in his recliner, munching on a bowl of cold cereal.

"Where you been?"

"I went for a drive down by the old house."

"Which old house?"

"Our old house."

"That one over by the river?"

"Yeah."

"I haven't seen that place in years," he said.

"I was there a few months ago, too."

Dad seemed startled, and that startled me.

"Why?"

"I think about stuff."

"That's one of your problems, Mitch. You think too much. You always have."

"What do you mean?"

"Nothing. Never mind."

As if I could. As if I would.

"No, Dad, you said it, so come on with it. I think too much. I always have. What does that even mean?"

Dad stood up from the couch and walked into the kitchen to rinse out his bowl.

"I don't want to talk about this," he said.

Typical. He had made a cottage industry out of taking vague shots at me, only to retreat to "I don't want to talk about it" or "I didn't mean anything" when he was challenged. I wasn't going to let this pass.

"Listen, old man, there are a lot of things we're going to talk about before I go home, and this is probably the easiest of them. So let's have it."

Dad bristled, and then he leveled his guns.

"You want everything to have significance, to have some big meaning, and some things just don't," he said. "Some things just happen. I figure you'd have learned this by now, but you're just the same as always, with your head in the goddamned clouds."

"Things just happen?" I mocked him. "Do you think Mom leaving just happened? That Jerry just happened? That all those years you didn't call me and I didn't see you just happened? You don't think there's some reason for all of that?"

"I think you think I'm the reason."

I laughed right in his face.

"Oh God, man. I know you're the reason."

"You don't know shit," he said, flinging his spoon into the sink.

BILLINGS | SEPTEMBER 19, 2007

SILENCE DESCENDED ON US AGAIN. Dad showered and dressed, then left wordlessly, climbing into his pickup and driving away.

I turned my attention to the calls I needed to make.

The first went quickly, and expensively. I ate the return ticket and would have to buy a full-fare one-way ticket when I was ready to leave. (Ready to leave? I was ready when I arrived, I fumed silently.)

The second, to John Wallen, proved more wrenching.

"If you won't be back tomorrow, when will you?" he asked.

"I don't know."

"Huh."

I waited.

"I can't close these deals without you."

"I know."

"But you're not coming."

"No. Not tomorrow."

"Whatever. Do what you have to do."

He hung up.

Finally, I called Cindy.

"I don't know where we are," I said to her first and inevitable question. "What are we supposed to be talking about? I come here, and all I can think about is what's happening back there and what happened thirty years ago with him. But I know the point of it is what's happening now with Dad. How do you get a foothold on something like this?"

"I don't know," she said. "But I know the past has everything to do with why you and he are where you are. I don't think you can talk about now without talking about then."

"We can't talk about then without pissing him off," I said.

I told her about our morning fight. We had glanced off the topics that mattered, like a rock across a pond. And even that had built a taller fence along our border. As I relayed this to Cindy, I realized that it all sounded familiar. That's exactly what she and I had been doing for months, bouncing from grievance to grievance and settling nothing.

"Where is he now?" she asked.

"I don't know. He didn't say anything. He just left."

"So what are you going to do?"

"I guess I'm going to wait for him. Then I'm going to try to talk to him again, this time without pissing him off."

"I like that plan."

So did I, aside from the fact that I had not the first clue how to manage it.

I fell asleep in Dad's recliner, and the images that came to me were familiar. I saw Dad as a young man, just coming off the USS *Hornet* from his Navy hitch in Bremerton, Washington. I saw my mother, young, blonde, and beautiful, a carefree nineteen-year-old, embracing the hippie lifestyle nearly a decade before the term would be in the common vernacular. A coincidental meeting had sown an unlikely union.

Mom had gone with her University of Washington roommate, who was from Bremerton, to that town for the weekend. That same weekend, Dad's ship put in and he walked away from the service. Boy met girl in a waterfront bar.

Figuring out the first, animal attraction was no great trick. Dad was young, vital, and good-looking. Mom was younger still and so beautiful. The part I'll perhaps never understand is how someone like my mother—vivacious and bright, well on her way to a college degree—could find someone like my father appealing intellectually or emotionally. She never bothered to explain it to me, and I never asked, so I'll just have to accept that she saw something in him. For a few weeks, Dad bummed around Puget Sound, spending as much time with Mom as her classes would allow. She took him to Olympia to meet her parents, and by all accounts that was a debacle. Grandpa, a county judge, didn't care for Dad's lack of education or his bawdy, off-the-sea persona. Grandma simply thought that her daughter, her only child, could do better.

Neither judgment mattered a few days later, when Dad told Mom that he was heading back to Montana to join a drilling crew. Mom dropped out and went with him, her parents' objections be damned.

I wished I knew those people as they were then—their motivations, their dreams, their innermost thoughts. My grandparents are dead, and they rarely talked about Mom and Dad to me. Mom is gone too, and she had little to say when the conversation drifted to her life with Dad. She would tell me to look forward, not back, and such counsel frustrated me. Everything I wanted to know was behind me. I could more easily cut out my own heart than ignore it and move on.

I knew only the traces of Mom and Dad's life together: meeting, running away together, marrying, having Jerry, having me, splitting up when I was three years old. For all practical purposes, an accounting of our lives as a nuclear family was lost. So many people took the story with them, and Dad wasn't giving it up.

My dreams of Mom and Dad in their youth—images that I conjured from imagination and the few mementos I had of them from that era—always carried a darkness, a menacing presence that I could not bring into focus or stop from overtaking them.

My eyes fluttered open, and I caught my breath.

The house remained empty, except for me and my fleeting grasp on what had passed through my head.

When Dad returned, I tried to put the fight behind us.

"Hey, Pop."

"Sport."

"Where have you been?"

"Cemetery. I bring her flowers on Wednesdays."

I smiled. I didn't have words for that. I found his tenderness toward Helen endearing and jarring. It challenged many of my assumptions about the man, and although I empathized with his loss, I couldn't help but think that we—that I—had been denied such devotion.

"I wish I could have gone with you."

"I like to see her alone."

"I understand."

He plopped heavily into the couch.

"Do you need anything, Pop? Something to eat or drink?"

"No. Just let me sit awhile."

We watched television for about an hour, and Dad chuckled gently at the situation comedies he preferred. Then he surprised me.

"Let's dig up some flowerbeds."

"Now?"

"As good a time as any."

Outside, I found that Dad didn't have a cooperative effort in mind. He aimed to use my labor to reclaim flowerbeds lost to the year he spent caring for his wife. He put a shovel in my hand and pointed me to the sorry boxes that fronted the double-wide.

"What did you have in here?" I said, looking at the forlorn husks of former plant life.

"Bellflowers. I'm going to put in some columbines in the spring."

Under Dad's watch, I dug out the clumps of dead flowers, which went easily enough. Then I got on my hands and knees to pull up the insurgent weeds, and that was much more difficult. I used muscles that had lain dormant during my office-space years, and they carped at the rude awakening. In the heat of the day, the sweat rolled off my neck, down my back, and into my drawers.

Once, I stood, put my hands on my hips, and swiveled my back, trying to loosen up.

"It's harder than I thought it'd be," I said.

"This is nothing."

"Says the guy sitting on the porch steps."

Dad lit off the stairs, grabbed the shovel from my hands, and started in on the box on the other side, the one I hadn't gotten to yet. He dug viciously and expertly into the sod, sending displaced plants into the gravel of the driveway. What I had taken twenty minutes to do, Dad accomplished with a few turns of the shovel.

"Get the picture?" he said, putting the shovel back into my hands. "I'm not staying out of it because I can't do it, Office Boy. I'm giving you a chance to work, which will do you some good. You haven't worked hard a day in your life."

I bit my lip. I didn't want another go-round. I went back to work.

Once the flowerbeds were clear of vegetation, Dad handed me a key to the shed behind the double-wide, so I could retrieve the hand tiller.

"You do one and I'll do one," he said, pointing at the beds. "I don't want to wear you out."

"No, I'll do both."

I would have loved the help, because I was already worn out. But I wasn't going to give Dad the satisfaction.

I couldn't have won with either choice. The old man looked plenty satisfied, watching with a shit-eating grin as I worked over the second flowerbed.

MILFORD | JUNE 28, 1979

I AWOKE to Jerry's shaking me.

"Mitch."

"What?" The light from the table lamp filled my eyes and cut a bleary path through the darkness of the trailer.

"Take this."

He slipped a folded piece of paper into my hand. "Don't let Dad see it."

I clutched the paper and tumbled back into slumber.

"Motherfucker."

Dad stood at the table.

"That son of a bitch. That goddamned, worthless son of a bitch."

"What?" I said.

"Your brother. He's gone."

I tried to shake the sleep from my head.

"What's going on?" I asked.

"Read it for yourself."

Dad put the paper on the table and headed to the bathroom, cursing my brother all the way.

I picked it up.

Dad—

*I don't know why you did what you did. But that's it for me.
I'm out.*

*I've tried to look past everything, tried to do what was right, but
I can't do that anymore. You beat me up and you scared Mitch. I
can't do anything for him, but I can for me.*

I hope she was worth it.

Jerry

The haze of sleep receded, and I remembered that Jerry
had given me something. I dug the paper out of the tangle
of blankets. When I unfolded it, three twenty-dollar bills fell
out.

Mitch—

I have to leave. After tonight, there's no way I can stay.

*I'm worried about you, but you're just a kid. I don't think he is
going to hurt you.*

*If he does, you call Mom. Call her right away. She'll buy you a
plane ticket, and this money will get you to Cedar City.*

*Dad's calling card number is 40655287679829. Use it any
time you need it.*

*Don't spend this money on candy and crap. Hold it. Use it only
if you have to.*

Don't let Dad see this. Don't let him know you have this money.

Keep your head down and do what he says.

Jerry

I stashed the letter and the money in my back pocket
until I could find a better hiding place.

When Dad returned, he said, "Let's go. We'll find him."

"Where's that girl?" I said.

"What girl?"

"From last night."

"Don't worry about her. She'll find her way out."

At Jerry's place, we found only Toby, who sat in the kitchen in his work clothes, sipping a cup of coffee.

"He woke me up around three, Jim. He said he was leaving."

Dad stalked around the place, throwing open empty drawers in Jerry's room, picking through the newspapers and magazines.

"He took everything," Toby said. He stood in the doorway.

"He didn't say shit about where he was going?" Dad asked.

"Not to me."

"I bet you he told that girl," Dad said. Then he looked at his watch. It was after six a.m., and we were late.

"I'll talk to her later. We've got to get to work. You guys get in the pickup."

I noted ruefully that things had turned out exactly as Jerry had predicted. Dad had run off another hand, and it now suited his purposes that I could pilot the pickup.

"We're just a couple of days from a break," Dad said on the drive out. "I don't have the time to get a new hand. Toby, you're moving up. Mitch, you can drive the pickup and do the shoveling. We'll just push through."

Toby and I nodded but were otherwise silent.

A few minutes passed.

"He'll be back," Dad said.

Nothing Toby or I did was correct—and to be fair, with Jerry gone, our crew wasn't half as efficient as it had been. Toby, having never been the lead guy, moved slowly, mishandling the pipe, not working in concert with Dad on the connections the way Jerry did.

I was even worse. I wasn't strong enough to carry two boxes of explosives at a time, the way Toby could, and when he tried to cover for me, he left Dad hanging. I couldn't shovel fast enough to keep the churned-up earth out of the pit. When I had worked with Toby at shoveling, my effort had been appreciated, in that it lightened the load. As a solo shoveler, I was a disappointment. Dad continually jumped from his perch to augment my efforts, cursing me and his sorry luck to have such an insufficient couple of workers.

Toby and I got lit into something fierce that first day without Jerry, and after four holes had been dug in the time we would usually need for six or seven, Dad announced in a profanity-laced soliloquy that we were "shutting the motherfucker down for the day."

The only person who spoke on the drive in was Dad, and he punctuated vast stretches of silence with a mix of proclamations, intimidations, and lamentations.

"When that son of a bitch comes back, he's in for a surprise, because I ain't taking his ass back on this crew."

Silence.

"You guys better be a lot goddamned better tomorrow than you were today, or there's going to be changes around here."

Silence.

"Two half days of work just before break. It's pathetic."

Silence.

"I should have fired his ass before he could leave. Worth-less."

Silence.

"Mitch, time to be a big boy. I don't want to hear shit about what you can't do. You need to start doing."

Silence.

"Jesus. Why now?"

Dad dropped Toby off and demanded directions to Denise's house. Toby clearly didn't want to cough up the information, but he seemed aware of the consequences of saying no. He spilled it.

Dad burned rubber getting there.

"Stay in the truck," he said.

He got out and walked to the front door, kicking up dust as his boots, caked with dried mud, landed on the gravel driveway.

Denise answered and looked none too pleased with who she found on her doorstep.

Dad talked first, and Denise shook her head violently at his questions. Then, eyes aflame, she started in, jabbing her left index finger in the air toward him.

I leaned into the passenger door and slowly cranked down the window, hoping to catch a few words. I kept my eyes forward; Dad had been looking back at the truck, and I didn't want him to know I was spying.

"Calm down, little girl. I'm just asking if you know where he went."

"No, no, I don't know," Denise said. "He wouldn't tell me. He knew you'd be here. He doesn't want you to know."

"Well, then, you'll tell me when he calls you."

"Not a chance. I'd never tell you."

Dad headed back to the pickup. I cranked the window up.

"Listening in, huh?" he said as he opened the door.

"It got too hot in here."

"Whatever you say, Mitch." Dad smirked at me.

We were back at the trailer before he spoke again.

"She doesn't know where he is. Fuck him then."

I sneaked away after dinner and found a pay phone. I had no reason to be surreptitious. Dad didn't speak to me while we ate. He disappeared into his own thoughts and grudges, and I was just part of the scenery.

"Hello?"

"Hi, Mom."

"Hi, my prince." It was somehow comforting to hear her use the nickname that I otherwise detested. "How are you?"

"I'm doing good."

"How's Jerry? How's your dad?"

"Jerry's fine, I guess. Dad's OK."

"Is Jerry there? Can I talk to him after we're done?"

"Jerry left."

"What do you mean?"

"Jerry quit and left."

"Why?"

"I don't know."

"Why would he do that?"

"He didn't like working for Dad, I guess."

"Is your father there with you?"

"No. I'm at a pay phone."

"This doesn't make sense. Where did Jerry go?"

"I don't know. He just left."

"And nothing happened to cause this?"

"Not that I know of."

"I don't understand this at all."

The call continued along those lines for a few more minutes, with Mom confused about what was happening in Milford and worried about Jerry, and with me playing dumb. If I told Mom the truth, I knew I would have to leave Milford and leave my father, probably for good. The finality of that frightened me, and so I let Mom flop in confusion on the other end of the line.

The decision, or the compulsion, to keep my mouth closed came with a heavy burden. Damned few days go by without my pondering a question I can't answer. Had I told Mom the truth, could Jerry have been found and persuaded to reconsider? Could that have changed things for our fated family?

But to do all of that, you invoke the butterfly theory, where the ripples of one decision change everything else. There's no way to know how things would have shaken out had Jerry stayed. And it's the not knowing that breaks me down a little at a time.

MILFORD | JUNE 29, 1979

THE NEXT MORNING, Toby met us at the diner at five. He looked nervously at me as he walked in. It turned out that my peripatetic father was in better spirits, a development that served only to throw Toby and me further off-kilter.

"Last day before break, fellas," Dad said, toasting us with his coffee cup. "Let's make it a good one."

We dug into our breakfast, happy that the noose had been loosened and not wanting to tempt a fresh hanging by asking Dad what had changed in twenty-four hours.

It didn't much matter, anyway.

I rolled onto my back with the grease gun in my hand, ready to go to work on the water truck. My quarry were little steel outlets on the joints that Dad called nipples—a word that could elicit giggles from a boy. But, indeed, that's what they looked like. I had to find them, pop the extension from the grease gun over them, and pump the trigger until the joint was filled.

I pushed at the brittle earth with my boot heels, wriggling underneath the truck from the back side of it. I found the nipples on the rear axle and transfer case, held the rubber extension in place with my left hand, positioned the metal tubing of the gun against my right side, and cocked the trigger four times. Job done.

I again pushed with my feet, propelling myself nearer the front of the truck. I had moved about two feet when something thumped heavily against my hard hat, knocking it askew.

I tilted my head and nearly dumped my bowels. A rattler coiled against the passenger-side front tire, and it shook the end of its tail furiously.

I froze, resisting the compulsion to roll quickly to my right and out from under the truck. I dared not do it. One move, and it might well strike again. Now that I faced it, it wouldn't miss. Warm water ran down my leg as my bladder released.

"Mitch, get a move on." Dad came around the other side of the water truck to see what was taking so long. He kicked at my foot, and my flinch set the rattler to shaking a fresh warning.

"Oh shit," he said. "Mitch, where is he?"

"Right front tire." I squeaked the words. The snake persisted in its warning. I stared into its night-black eyes, and I waited in terror.

I heard Dad's steps carry him away. I learned later that he walked a wide circle around to the other side of the water truck, so as not to set off the snake. In the throes of my fear, I thought he was leaving, and I silently panicked. The snake and I stayed in staring stalemate. I wasn't going to move, and the snake sensed no safe exit. The thick, aluminum taste of fear spread into my mouth.

Then, out of the corner of my eye, I watched as the blade of a shovel moved in slowly from the other side of the truck. I held my breath and kept my gaze on the snake, which watched me just as intently.

It ended in an instant. Dad dropped the shovel blade onto the snake's neck, and it thrashed wildly. "Now," Dad yelled, and Toby grabbed my foot and pulled me out the other side. My chin bounced against the ground, and my teeth clamped on my tongue, gashing it and sending the tinny blood running into my mouth and throat. I heard Dad pummel the rattler with the shovel.

When he was done, Dad came around to the other side, where I sat on the dirt, shocked, my wet drawers clinging to me. My chin bled heavily, soaking my work shirt. He knelt down and took my chin in his right hand.

"Did he get you?" Dad's eyes widened.

"No."

"I think I banged him up pulling him out," Toby offered.

"Are you OK, sport?"

"No."

My father wrapped his arms around me. I dropped my head into his shoulder and wept.

After Dad patched me up and rounded up a new shirt and a fresh pair of pants, we put in a full day. I was unharmed, at least physically, although I returned repeatedly to the rattler's strike at my head and thought of how a change to the geometry—a strike that found skin instead of hard plastic—would have made the situation dire. It seemed that the episode shook Dad more than me. For the rest of the day, we went quietly about our work, and when Toby or I messed up, Dad simply stepped in to help, with none of the profane barking and belittling we had come to expect.

When the last of the holes had been dug and Dad had tied his report to the stake, he said we would move the equipment to Milford for the break. If it sat out in the back-country for a week, he said, it would be stripped bare before we returned.

I instantly grasped the import of this, at least for me. Three of us and three trucks. I would have to drive the pickup twenty-five miles to town on a state highway, at eleven years old. Adrenaline and fear flooded into my head and my gut. I would be using the upper two speeds of the four-speed pickup, traveling faster than I ever had while bounc-ing across the sagebrush.

Dad saw the faraway look in my eyes.

"Mitch, I want you in between us," he said. "First me, then you, then Toby. You take your cues from me. You got that?"

"Yeah."

That drive was easily my crowning moment as a kid. I settled into the driver's seat, pulled my cap low on my head, slipped on a pair of Dad's sunglasses, which were far too big for my face, and lurched the pickup into gear behind Dad.

We traversed a few miles of rugged country and dirt roads before reaching the Ely Highway, where we turned right, toward Milford. The big rig took a while to dial up to cruising speed, and so I gradually guided the Supercab into second gear, and then third, and then, finally, fourth. I peri-odically checked the rearview mirror and saw Toby plugging along behind me.

As we met vehicles traveling the opposite way, I knew that Dad would give them the standard, understated trucker

salute—a left index finger lifted off the steering wheel—
and so I did the same, and I thrilled every time my greeting
received one in kind. There I was, piloting a pickup, and
other drivers were buying it. I would have stories to tell back
at Garfield Elementary.

The drive to Milford, seemingly endless on most days,
finished far too quickly. Dad pulled into a gas station on the
town's edge, climbed from the rig, and went inside to ask if
we could put the trucks there. When he emerged, Dad sig-
naled that it was the place. I shut off the pickup and got out
to help lock everything down.

"You did good, sport," Dad said as we walked back to the
pickup. He grabbed the bill of my cap and shook it from
side to side.

"You're going to be a truck-driving man yet."

I showered and changed into fresh clothes, then packed up
my stuff. Dad sat at the table, reconciling financcs.

I itched to get outside. The rush from the drive still
coursed through me, and the tiny trailer couldn't contain
my exuberance. I wasn't sure anything could. Maybe I'd just
go to the park across the street and run in circles until I was
spent.

"Dad, can I go out for a walk?"

He glanced up from his work and looked me over.

"You all packed?"

"Yes."

"Go ahead then."

I banged out of the door and ran into the receding day-
light.

I walked the drag toward downtown. At the Hotel Milford—
its glory faded but still the most beautiful building in town—
I turned right and headed up into the heart of town. At the
town park, I saw a familiar face.

"Hi, Jennifer."

Denise's sister was with a group of three or four kids.
One, a kid bigger than me and wearing only cutoff jeans,
tube socks, and shoes, walked toward me.

"Who is this kid?" he said, sneering at me.

"Leave him alone, Damon. He's my friend."

Damon turned back to his friends and started a little chicken dance, chanting, "He's my friend. He's my
friend," as the others broke into laughter. I clenched my
fists.

"You guys are jerks," Jennifer said. Damon and his merry
band of buttholes ran toward the other side of the park,
mocking her. "He's my friend, he's my friend." Damon
turned around and made kissy noises.

"Just ignore them," she said.

After the kids were gone, we started walking.

"What happened to your chin?" Jennifer asked.

I touched the bandage, fresh since my shower.

I told her about the rattlesnake, and she gasped.

"I'm glad you're OK."

"Me too."

"I heard about your brother."

"Yeah."

"Do you know where he went?"

"No. He didn't tell me."

"He didn't tell Denise, either. She's so sad."

"So am I."

We made laps in the park, talking about my brother and her sister. A couple of long silences intruded, but they didn't faze me. I liked being with her.

Finally, she said, "I have to go home for dinner."

"OK."

"Do you want to come?"

"I'll have to go ask my dad."

"I'll come with you."

I expected a no. I knew Dad's feelings about Denise, and I explained that Jennifer was her little sister.

He seemed delighted that I had shown up with a girl in tow. He told Jennifer that she was pretty, and he asked questions about school and her folks.

"Just be home by nine, Mitch," Dad said. "We've got a long day tomorrow."

Jennifer and I walked back through the park and over the hill to her house.

"Denise says such mean things about your dad," she said. "I really like him."

Jennifer's mother made barbecued spare ribs, potato salad, corn, and bread and butter. Everything tasted so good, and Mrs. Munroe encouraged me to have seconds, then thirds. I happily obliged her on each offer.

Mr. Munroe told about working for Union Pacific. He was a second-generation railroad man. Earlier that day, he said, a train had been dead on the line fifty miles outside town. That's railroad talk for a train whose crew has reached the end of its hours. When that happened, the train would shut down wherever it was. Mr. Munroe had to do what he called "dogcatching"—riding out in a shuttle and helping to bring the train in.

I had grown accustomed to the whistle of the trains arriving hourly before heading to Salt Lake or Las Vegas. I reveled in hearing about what it was really like in the rail yard, with all the shift changes and the loads of scrap, coal, new cars, and whatever else you could imagine coming through town.

"It sounds like a fun job," I said.

"It's a job," Mr. Munroe said. "The four a.m. calls to do this or that, I could do without."

"The missed holidays," his wife said.

"Those too."

I told them about Dad's work and how I was helping now. I even told them I had driven the pickup on the highway, although I probably shouldn't have.

"Hell, on a farm, boys come out of the womb driving trucks and tractors," he said, and Mrs. Munroe clucked her tongue.

"Tell about the rattlesnake," Jennifer said, and so I did, but I skipped the bit about peeing my pants, just as I had with her. Mr. Munroe whistled.

"You're lucky, son. Real lucky."

"Yeah. I'm glad my dad was there."

Denise, who hadn't said anything, spoke up.

"I think your dad's a real asshole."

"Denise!" her mother scolded. The table fell quiet. I filled the awkwardness by stuffing bites of spare rib into my mouth. Denise, crying, stood and ran out of the room.

"We sure hated to see your brother go, Mitch," Mr. Munroe said as he watched his wife chase after Denise. "We liked having him around here."

After dinner, Jennifer and I went for a walk.

"I'm glad you came," she said.

"I'm glad you invited me. I like your family."

"Yeah."

We walked on.

"Mitch, are you OK here?"

"Sure. Why?"

"I don't know…never mind."

I stopped.

"Hey, my dad's a good guy," I said. "I'm sorry about Jerry too, but…well, it's hard to explain."

"It's OK."

As we rounded a corner and headed back toward her house, Jennifer slipped her hand into mine.

I intended to walk to the trailer, but Mr. Munroe shot down that plan.

"It's getting dark," he said. "I'll drive you over."

Jennifer rode with us. Nobody talked very much, but when we rolled up behind Dad's pickup, Mr. Munroe told me, "You come see us any time, Mitch. I mean it."

"Thank you, sir."

"Bye, Mitch," Jennifer called out as I walked to the trailer. I turned and waved.

The trailer lights burned. I figured Dad was watching some TV before hitting the hay. Nearly eight hundred miles of driving to the ranch in Split Rail awaited us in the morning.

Inside, I didn't find Dad. Only a note.

Mitch: Be back soon. Go to bed. Dad.

I locked the door and turned off the lights, then fired up the TV.

An hour went by, then an hour and a half. The test pattern came on the TV.

After midnight, I heard Dad walking up the gravel driveway. I flipped off the TV and dove into the covers.

Dad fiddled with his keys, trying to unlock the door. Once he was in, he came over to where I lay, and the stench of whiskey floated off him.

"Are you asleep?"

I kept my eyes shut tight.

"Mitch?"

I didn't move.

He stayed a few moments longer. It was all I could do to keep my eyes closed. Finally, he said, "Good night."

When I heard the bedroom door close, I opened my eyes.

BILLINGS | SEPTEMBER 20, 2007

DAD HAD COFFEE WAITING for me when I came into the kitchen.

"What time is it?"

He chuckled. "Quarter after eleven."

"You've got to be kidding."

He handed me a cup and, when I hesitated, rolled his eyes and fetched me cream and sugar.

"A little hard work wears you out, huh?" he said.

No doubt. It had taken some coaxing to get my legs moving, and a dull burn radiated across my shoulders and in my biceps. Could I really be this far out of shape?

"I work hard, but yeah, physical labor is a bitch."

"You don't work hard."

I looked at Dad, and he grinned. He was picking a fight just to entertain himself, and damned if I didn't give it to him, proving that my brain was as soft as my muscles.

"You ever sell five-million bucks' worth of something, Pop? I've done it in a weekend." A long time ago, I silently conceded.

"That's not so hard."

I took dead aim.

"It's easy to sell bullshit," I said. "You've done it your whole life. But bullshit isn't worth anything."

Dad skittered into the living room, laughing at me.

After I showered and dressed, I came back into the kitchen and shook some cereal into a bowl.

"Don't eat," Dad said.

"I'm starving here."

"No, you're not," he said, jabbing his forefinger into my gut. "We're having lunch at the Elks."

"Why?"

"It's Thursday. I always eat there Thursdays. Don't you want to get out of here for a while?"

Dad insisted that we drive over in my rental. On the five-block drive to the Elks Club, he fiddled constantly with the car's gadgets.

"Satellite radio? What's that?"

"It's beamed off of satellites, hundreds of stations. Anything you want. And you don't have to worry about losing a signal."

Dad whistled approval.

"I don't drive enough to get something like that," he said.

"You can get it for your house."

"No shit?"

"No shit."

"I might have to do that."

Dad's buddies were in the Elks dining room, playing cards. After a round of back slaps and busted balls, he introduced me.

"This here is Pete Rafferty," Dad said, guiding me to a slight, stooped man wearing a USS *Hornet* ball cap.

"You were on the *Hornet*?" I asked.

"Same time as me, too," Dad said. "We met at a reunion in '99 and found out we lived in the same damn town."

"Didn't know each other then, though," Pete rasped.

"Or don't remember now if we did," Dad said. He gave Pete a chuck on the arm.

I cut Dad off on his next introduction. I'd chatted with Ben Yoder, Helen's brother, after her funeral.

"Hi, Ben," I said. "Didn't think I'd see you again so soon. How are you doing?"

"Can't complain."

"You must remember this fella too," Dad said. He guided me to the last figure at the table.

I took a look at the ample gentleman. His all-white buzz cut, round glasses, and weather-beaten face seemed faintly familiar, but I couldn't place him. He looked the way a lot of older men look—a tendency I could see making steady inroads into my own face.

"I'm sorry, I don't," I said, offering a handshake to the man.

"Well, I remember you," he said, wrapping my hand in his bigger, meatier mitt. "You've grown up since I pulled you out of that ditch."

"Charley Rayburn?" I said.

The man cracked a wide smile. "The same."

"Holy crap."

He laughed.

Charley Rayburn. Jesus. Did I ever owe that guy.

We enjoyed a gloriously greasy lunch. I had a bacon cheese-burger and fries, and Dad got liver and onions. I leaned away from him, lest the stench from his meal bring me to full-on nausea. I figured that once Dad's generation passed into the great beyond, liver and onions would disappear as a food source, since I had never seen anyone younger than sixty-five eat the stuff.

For a while, Dad, Ben, and Pete tangled in vigorous conversation—from my brief listening in, I deduced that it involved the absence of desirable women at the Elks—and so I leaned over to chat with Charley.

"You still live in Split Rail, Charley?"

"Yep. Still on the ranch. I'm not much use up there any-more, but my daughter and her husband are letting us lin-ger on while they run the place."

"What's Jeff up to?" My memories rewound to that sum-mer, to the week we spent in Split Rail, and to Charley's son, who had befriended me.

Charley's smile drooped, and then he picked it back up.

"Well, we don't see a lot of Jeff these days," he said. "He's in the prison in Deer Lodge."

"Oh, I'm sorry," I said. "I didn't know."

"It's OK, son."

I scrambled to reset things.

"How often do you get down this way?"

"Once a week, for this little gathering. Wouldn't miss it."

"That's great."

"What about you? You're in California?"

"Yeah. San Jose."

"Family?"

"Yep, I've been married eleven years. We have four-year-old twins, a boy and a girl."

"Congratulations, Mitch. What are their names?"

"Avery and Adia."

"Beautiful."

I ate the remaining fries on my plate.

"What do you do for a living, Mitch?" Charley asked.

"I sell medical equipment."

"Do you like it?"

"Not lately."

He chuckled. "Well, it's work. The enthusiasm comes and goes."

"I guess. Listen, Charley, I don't think I ever took the time to properly thank you—"

He smiled and cut me off.

"No need, son. It was a long time ago."

After the dishes had been cleared, out came the cards again for *Texas Hold 'Em*. I soon learned that I was out of my depth. The stakes weren't high—five-cent smalls and ten-cent bigs. True, it was no-limit poker, but with four guys on fixed incomes and me playing with ten dollars' worth of nickels each, nobody was going to go broke or get filthy rich. That did nothing to rein in the competition at our table.

An hour in, Pete and Ben were wiped out, and I was well on my way to joining them. Dad and Charley sat behind impressive stacks of coins. I had a much smaller stack, maybe two dollars.

Dad dealt a card to me, one to Charley, one to himself, and then he made another pass. I cupped my hand around my hole cards and turned up the corner. Pocket aces, spades and clubs. It was the most promising start I had seen.

I tossed in twenty-five cents.

"Big spender," Dad said.

Charley threw his cards in. "Nothing here," he said.

Dad called.

He burned a card and then set the flop: four of diamonds, four of spades, ace of hearts. There it was, the boat. Now I just had to reel Dad in.

I checked.

Dad smiled and checked behind me. All right, I told myself, you know this guy. What's the buzzard got? Probably nothing. I'm going to see a bluff here.

Then came the turn. Jack of spades. It didn't help me and couldn't help him.

I checked again.

Dad smiled again and said, "Fifty cents." He threw in the coins.

He's bluffing, I thought. He's in too far now, and he's trying to salvage it. I called the bet.

Dad turned the river card. King of diamonds.

I checked yet again.

This time, Dad didn't smile. He pushed fifty more cents to the middle, trying again to buy the pot. It was time to bring the big fish aboard the boat.

I counted out my remaining nickels—a buck and thirty-five cents—and pushed them in.

"All in."

When Dad grinned, I knew it was done. The guy looked like he had just bedded Miss America.

"Here's the thing, Mitch," he said.

I tasted bile.

"You have the aces. I knew that when you leaned forward—that's a tell, sport—but I didn't care much. You see, I have the fours. Oh, and I call."

He turned his cards over. The clubs and the hearts.

I couldn't bear to validate him by showing my cards. I threw them in and said, "Bastard."

"No mucking," Dad said. He reached for the cards. "When you get called, you show your cards. I'm going to see them."

I fixed Dad with a stare, and he stared back. Charley laughed nervously.

Dad flipped the spades. "There's one." Then came the clubs. "And there's two. Pleasure taking your money, Mitch," he said while he raked in the stack.

Pete and Ben howled in laughter. Charley gave me a sympathetic look, and I appreciated that. A half hour later, the old man dispatched him too, and poker was over. What I wouldn't have given to play a game of *Sorry* instead.

As we headed back to the house, Dad again took up his fascination with the satellite radio.

"We could drive around and listen to it," I said.

"Waste of gas."

"Not if we're heading somewhere."

Dad looked at me. "What have you got in mind?"

"I want to go see Split Rail."

"Why?"

I shrugged. "Seeing Charley again got me to thinking. I haven't been up there in years. I'd like to see it again."

"Damn, Mitch, it's a long way."

"It's only eighty miles or so, isn't it? We could go up, look around, have some dinner, and come back. I'd like to go."

Dad shrugged.

"All right. Go."

I turned off Lewis and started slicing back through town to the Rimrocks. Above sat Highway 3, the stretch of road that led us deep into central Montana, and me deep into my memories.

THE ROAD TO SPLIT RAIL, MONTANA
SEPTEMBER 20, 2007

IN BROADVIEW, about halfway to Split Rail, Dad said, "What's up with you and your wife?"

I tried to hide my surprise.

"What do you mean?"

"I've seen you. When you call, you go outside. Like yesterday. You do know that voices carry, right?"

The day before, I stood on the gravel road outside Dad's place and loudly argued with Cindy over the same old topic that I couldn't seem to get past, one that I was ill inclined to share with my father.

"It was a quarrel," I said. "No biggie. It happens."

"Right."

"Seriously, that's it."

"Do you think I'm stupid, Mitch? You're here, and you show no sign of leaving. You're fighting with your wife. What's going on?"

"The reason I'm here, Pop, is you. Don't forget that. You're the one who called and called and didn't say a thing. You want to talk to me about what's going on? Do it. I'll leave tomorrow."

"This isn't about me."

"Like hell. Everything has always been about you. Everything now, everything then. Everything."

"Get some help, Mitch. Jesus."

I drove on a few miles, gripping the steering wheel. Finally, I muttered, "Physician, heal thyself." Dad torqued in his seat, facing away from me, pretending not to hear.

We rode in silence for another twenty miles or so, and I tried to balance what I needed against the ways in which I thought Dad might take advantage of anything I might tell him. I couldn't deny that I needed to talk to somebody about this thing with Cindy. It's just that Jim Quillen was the last person on earth I would choose for my unburdening.

"All right, Pop, here it is," I said. "Cindy and I are in some trouble."

"What kind of trouble?"

"Marital trouble. We've got issues. Some real big issues. I don't know if we're going to solve them."

"So she kicked you out?"

"She didn't kick me out. We agreed that I needed to come see you about this mystery you've been dropping on us, and we also agreed that we could use the absence from one another."

Dad chewed on that awhile.

"So what happened?"

I took a deep breath and expelled it.

"A hundred tiny little things. Inattention, taking each other for granted, a lack of passion."

I paused, not wanting to get into the next part. I was certain I couldn't put the emotions into words.

"Before the kids came, we were tight, Cindy and me. And we had a common purpose. We wanted to build a life together and to have children. Now, this is going to sound bad, and I don't mean for it to, because Adia and Avery are the greatest gifts in my life, but…"

"Yeah?"

"I'm the dad, and Cindy is the mom. But we're not the parental unit. There's her, and there's me, and the kids are between us. So, you know, I threw myself into work for a while. And when work went badly, I soothed myself with nights out with the guys at work. At home, I try to be the best father I can, but I do it independently, just like Cindy does. I paid less and less attention to my marriage, and Cindy knows it."

"What about her?"

"I'm getting to that part. A few months ago, I came home and found some notes on the computer. She and this guy were writing e-mails to each other. She was emotionally involved."

"What do you mean, emotionally involved?"

"Just that. It's somebody she met over the Internet. I found a bunch of their e-mails. They talked to each other intimately, the way she and I used to. It wasn't sex or any-thing like that. It was just stuff you wouldn't want some other man to say to your wife, or your wife to say to another man."

"The Internet, Jesus. What did you do?"

"I confronted her. She admitted it. She didn't have a choice. She couldn't hide it. She ended it. It wasn't about this guy, per se. We've been seeing counselors, and she says she needed attention she wasn't getting from me. But…

I can't get past it. I close my eyes, and I picture her with another man."

"You're sure it wasn't sex."

"Yeah, I'm sure."

"How do you know?"

"She told me."

"And you believe her?"

"Yeah."

"Typical."

I tightened my grip on the steering wheel.

"You have something to say, Pop?"

"You're a dope."

"Great. Thanks. Real supportive."

"Hey, I'm trying to help here. Your wife's screwing around, and you can't see that? Maybe somebody should point it out."

The blood rushed to my face. I swung the car to the side of the road and slammed on the brakes, put it into park, and faced Dad.

"Look here, you asshole. Don't try to tell me what you think you know about Cindy. You don't know her. You've never given her a chance. You don't give other people a chance. You didn't give one to Mom, you've never given one to me, and you damned sure didn't give one to Jerry."

"We're talking about your wife, not Jerry or your mother," Dad growled.

"Maybe we should. You think you know so much about how other people cheat. What can you say about your own? Mom left you because you're a cheating son of a bitch. Same with Jerry. Just because you're an expert, don't act like you know what goes on in my house."

The double-barrel shot of my anger left Dad looking worn down.

"You know shit-all nothing," he said.

"Yeah, I do know," I said, and I steered the car back to the road. Ahead, I saw the turnoff to Split Rail, where I could show him just how much I knew.

THE ROAD TO SPLIT RAIL | JUNE 30, 1979

IT WAS STILL DARK when Dad shook me awake. "Mitch, let's get moving."

I stretched and yawned. "What time is it?"

"Just after five. Come on, sport, get up. Take a shower if you want. I'll load up."

I pulled on pants, socks, and tennis shoes, grabbed a pillow, and stumbled out to the pickup. I climbed into the back and found sleep again.

By the time I awoke, almost three hours had passed and we were nearly to Provo. Dad's cap—emblazoned with "JQ Drilling Co."—rode high on his forehead, almost the opposite of how I wore mine, pulled low with the fabric on the bill pressed smooth by my constant shaping it. The yellow highway lines shot past, and Dad hummed along to a Ronnie Milsap eight-track.

"I'm coming up." I slid over the seat, nearly clipping Dad in the face with my feet.

"Watch it."

"Sorry, Pop."

It was just after eight, and the sun bathed the surrounding mountains, slowly filling in the darkest corners and sparkling off the road ahead of us.

"You hungry, sport?"

"Yeah."

He smiled at me from behind his sunglasses.

"All right. Let's get on the other side of town here and we'll find a truck stop."

Dad went back to humming a Milsap tune—"Let's Take the Long Way around the World"—while I gazed out the window. Provo came into view, tucked into the Utah Valley and lorded over by Mount Timpanogos. Its beauty captivated me in a way that dusty, windy Milford could not. I soaked up the scene, happy to be free of work and worry. I wanted to ride that road, and my father's good mood, as far as it would carry us.

We steered into a truck stop between Provo and Orem and hopped out of the Supercab. I lifted my arms above my head and reached for the sky, enjoying the tingle as my latent muscles awoke. Dad stepped lively over to the gas pumps and started glad-handing. If a trucker showed an inclination for conversation, Dad would oblige him. He spoke the language of the long-hauler, and he would quiz the drivers about their cargo and their destination, offering any information he had about speed traps and accepting any reciprocal wisdom. Jokes he heard would be rewarded with a gut laugh. Those he told would be accompanied by his grasping his newest buddy's shoulder as he delivered the punch line.

You would have thought he was running for office.

After an extended tour of the pumps, Dad ambled back my way and we headed inside. The lady at the cash register got a wink and a "darlin'." The haggard, fifty-something waitress got the same.

Dad asked for eggs over hard, toast, bacon, and hash browns, the breakfast he'd had every morning since I arrived. I went with the tall stack of pancakes.

"Did you have fun last night?" Dad asked.

I should ask him that question, I thought, and then I wisely reconsidered.

"Yeah, it was neat."

"What did you have to eat?"

I told him about Mrs. Munroe's feast and how the food kept coming. He asked what Mr. Munroe did for a living, and I told him that too, as well as some of the railroad stories that Jennifer's dad had relayed.

"They sound like nice people."

"They are."

"Sort of makes you wonder how they raised such a bitch of a daughter."

"Denise doesn't like you very much, either."

"What'd I ever do to her?"

The arrival of food ensured that I wouldn't have to answer his question.

Dad, chipper right up through breakfast, didn't have the energy to keep it going. The road began to wear on him. The morning rush in Salt Lake had pretty well cleared by the time we hit town, but even the slight crowding of the freeway put him on the defensive. He yanked out the eight-track tape with an "Enough of that shit." As we pushed through the gut of the Salt Lake, Dad told me to hush up and let him concentrate on driving. The towns that sat beyond—Layton, Clinton, Ogden, Brigham City—came into view and then dropped back, and Dad seemed to sink deeper into his seat, his gaze growing longer as each mile clicked off. We had covered nearly three hundred of them. Five hundred more lay in front of us.

It became an endurance test, with his patience pitted against my happy chatter pitted against the asphalt.

I punctured silences with futile attempts at conversation.

When Dad whistled admiringly at a passing Peterbilt hauling cattle, I asked him, "Is that a good truck?"

"Peterbilt does good work, yeah."

"How come you bought an International?"

"Deal was right."

"Do you wish you had a Peterbilt?"

"No."

"What about Kenworth, is that a good truck?"

"Mitch, shut up, huh?"

And then later:

"Dad?"

"Huh?"

"Did you play baseball when you were a little kid?"

"A little."

"My team was good. I wonder if they won their last game."

"Don't know."

"What was the name of your team?"

"I don't remember."

"What position did you play?"

"Is there a point to this, Mitch?"

And then, finally:

"I'm going to ride my motorcycle when we get there."

"It'll be late. You can ride it tomorrow."

"That's what I meant."

I waited a few beats and then said, "Dad?"

"Yeah."

"Can I get a new motorcycle this summer?"

He looked at me. "What's wrong with the one you have?"

"I'm a lot bigger than I was two years ago."

"I don't know."

"Please?"

"Don't beg."

"OK, but will you think about it?"

"Maybe."

"I'll—"

"Shut up about it. Jesus. Do you ever stop talking?"

In Pocatello, we gassed up again. Dad slipped me a fiver and precise instructions.

"Buy a magazine or a book, something that will help you fill the time. You need to stop jabbering at me."

"Yeah, OK."

I slunk into the store as Dad handled things at the pump. I should have been happy to have the money—five dollars was a lot of money to a kid my age—but I wasn't. I didn't understand why it made him feel better to make me feel worse.

I returned with my arms full of comic books—Archie and Jughead, Richie Rich, Donald Duck, and whatever else I could lay my hands on. The comics, particularly the back pages, proposed a hundred ways a boy like me could burn his cash. Sea monkeys, selling *Grit* magazine, X-ray goggles, you name it. I had no cash to blow, having spent the money Dad gave me on the magazines (and remembering Jerry's words that the other sixty dollars I had was off-limits to capricious spending). I disappeared into the magazines as we continued our long slog north, and back on the open road, Dad finally loosened up again, popping some Willie Nelson into the eight-track. Blackfoot and Idaho Falls and Rexburg beckoned, and then we would see West Yellowstone, by far the prettiest part of our drive. Soon enough, we would be on the last stretch to the ranch.

In West Yellowstone, we stopped for a late lunch at a drive-in hamburger joint. Dad shoved fries into his mouth. I slurped soda and thumbed through a comic book with greasy fingers.

"What do you have there?" Dad said.

I held up a Richie Rich.

"Richie Rich and his girlfriends," Dad read from the cover. Four girls were popping out of a big birthday cake.

"Those are all his girlfriends?" Dad said.

"Yep."

"Lucky guy. Do you have any girlfriends?"

"No."

"What about that girl from last night?"

My face flushed red.

"Yeah," Dad teased. "You like that girl."

"Dad, I have to go pee."

He looked at his watch. "Hurry."

I didn't really have to go. I jogged into the restaurant anyway and went into the men's room, locking the door behind me. Instead of doing business, I read the walls, which had been well marked by the lavatory's many bored visitors. I could see that the management of the restaurant had made a few losing attempts at stemming the flow of bathroom innuendo. The graffiti apparently reached a critical mass, and there was no more sense in resisting. It wasn't literature, of course, but I could see some merit in the knife-scratched words of someone who proudly called himself the Shithouse Poet:

West to East
East to West
Across This Great Land
Of Fruit and Grain
High and Low
From Door to Door
The Shithouse Poet Rides Again

THE ROAD TO SPLIT RAIL | JUNE 30, 1979

I WALKED OUT of the drive-in doors and saw Dad talking to a long-haired man in tight jeans that frayed at the bell bottoms. Dad spotted me and pointed, and the man turned and waved. Dad jerked his thumb toward the back of the pickup, and the young guy threw his duffel bag into the box.

As I walked to the front of the truck, I got a close look at the guy, who was holding the door open for me. He was in his early twenties, I figured. His freckled face had been darkened by the sun and was ringed by a thin, scraggly, dirty-blond beard. He gave a cheerful smile and ushered me into the pickup.

"Hey, man," he said. "I'm Brad."

I acknowledged his handshake and said, "Hi."

"This fella's going to ride with us for a bit," Dad said.

"OK."

Brad piled in next to me, and I returned to a familiar position—wedged between two men on the pickup's bench seat. The new guy smelled ripe.

We rolled out of town, skirting the stands of conifers on the western edge of Yellowstone National Park.

"Appreciate the lift, Mr...."

"Quillen," I said.

"Jim," Dad said.

"Appreciate the lift, Jim."

Dad nodded. I thumbed at my magazines idly, but I had lost interest in them. I looked up at our guest.

"Why are you hitchhiking?" I asked.

"I was working."

"At what?" Dad said.

"I was with a road crew for a while, a flagger. Now I'm just trying to get back to Bozeman and figure out what's next."

"You looking for work?" Dad said.

"Yeah. Do you know of some?"

"Maybe."

I didn't like Brad at first. He had intruded on us and was trying too hard to be liked, plus he stank to high heaven. Soon, though, I was happy to have someone who would talk to me. He said he had dropped out of college in California the previous fall—"I missed Montana really bad," he said—and had moved home and hooked a job with a road crew. It ended in West Yellowstone.

"What happened?" Dad asked.

"Didn't get along with the boss. Personality conflict."

Dad grunted. I knew he wouldn't see such a thing in Brad's favor. Dad had fired a whole lot of guys, and it had never been his fault. And personality conflicts? The only personality that counted was Dad's.

Once I figured out that Brad would lend an ear, I spilled loads of chatter on him. I told him how my parents had met, that we had lived in Billings, that she had left. I told him about Jerry. I told him about Marie. I told him about my driving the pickup. On and on I talked, with no revelation too personal or trivial. My loneliness was such that any listener, even one desperate for a ride, represented a chance to unload.

"I don't think your dad wants you giving out family secrets," Brad said, sending a nervous glance in my father's direction.

I turned and looked at Dad. His jaw clenched hard, but he said nothing. I'd put him in a hell of a spot. I knew he wanted me to pipe down, but I also knew he wouldn't berate me in front of a stranger.

I turned away and started chattering at Brad again.

We reached Bozeman at dusk, and Dad pulled over at a gas station. Brad would have to cover the last stretch on his own.

Before Brad left, Dad said, "If you're serious about work, we'll be here a week from today, around ten in the morning. You can come with us back to Utah and work on my drilling crew."

"Seriously?" Brad said.

"Serious as a heart attack."

"Ten a.m. next Saturday. I'll be here."

"Make sure of it. If I get here and don't see you, I'm gone. On this crew, you're on time."

"You can count on it."

Brad gave a wave and started walking. Dad put the pickup in gear.

"About next week," he said to me. "Your endless talking is over with. You got that?"

I averted my eyes.

Dad eased the Ford onto the road in front of the gas station, then barreled down the ramp onto I-90 eastbound. I rode in silence for ten minutes or so and then drifted off to sleep.

It was dark when I woke up. Dad had stopped the pickup, and I watched the headlights illuminate him as he fought with the lock on the steel gate to the ranch access road.

"You were dozing pretty good," he said when he climbed back into the cab.

"We're here?"

"We're here."

We bumped along on the pockmarked route, until I saw the ranch house. Every light in the place was on, and the beams cut gouges into the dark.

Dad eased the pickup into the driveway, and when he saw that Marie's car wasn't in its place, he punched the dashboard. I flinched.

"What the hell?" he said.

I sat still, waiting.

Dad sighed.

"Well, grab your things," he said. "Let's go in."

SPLIT RAIL | SEPTEMBER 20, 2007

I CLUTCHED THE STEERING WHEEL hard, relenting only after the pain hit my shoulders, and Dad sat indignant in the passenger seat of my rented Ford. We rode in silence those final few miles after the turn toward Split Rail. The well-worn state highway dropped behind us, and we climbed a sandstone butte, stacked layer upon layer like a wafer cookie. The deeper we pushed into the country, the angrier the road to Split Rail became.

"How long since you were out here?" I asked. As the curtain of silence fell, I exhaled.

"Long time."

"I don't remember the road being this bumpy."

"People here don't pay their taxes," he said. I smiled. All my life, that had been his stock answer for anything that wasn't right with the world. Roads in bad shape? People don't pay their taxes. No emergency clinic in the neighborhood? People don't pay their taxes. Dropouts plaguing the high school? People don't pay their taxes. For everything I wished were different about the old man, I found comfort in just as many things that never changed.

We fell silent as I chewed on whether to push the question. I decided to risk it.

"No, seriously, how long since you've been here?"

I held my breath.

"It's got to be three years, at least. Helen and I came out and saw Charley once in a while, but that didn't last after she got sick."

"Charley looks good."

"Yeah."

"He told me Jeff's in prison. What happened there?"

"I don't really know, Mitch. He doesn't say, and I don't pry. Maybe you shouldn't, either."

My ears singed. I doubled back to the topic of Split Rail. "Three years? Who knows, maybe the place has changed."

"Split Rail never changes," Dad said.

I hadn't been to Split Rail in twenty-eight years, not since that last summer with Dad. I soon found, though, that Dad was right. We rounded a bend and started down the back side of the butte, and Split Rail lay out before us, the same as I remembered her. The tripod water tower with the red top, the block letters spelling out "Split Rail." The main drag that took in a gas station, the Livery bar, a small grocery, the farmers' credit union, the Tin Cup diner, a grange hall, Split Rail School, and the weekly paper, the *Standard*. Of the four hundred or so residents, just a handful lived in a smattering of clapboard houses in town. The rest spread out across the country like cattle. Literally and figuratively, Split Rail sat at the end of the road. The dusty lanes that shot off the main strip led to farms and ranches of various shapes and sizes. Those who wanted to get goods to market would have to look south to Broadview and the railroad. For a night on the town or to load up on supplies, Billings was the ticket.

Living in Split Rail wasn't easy, and from what I recalled of the people who called the place home, they liked it that way.

There were rewards for the hardy few, though. On a clear day, like the one gracing us, you could scan the horizon and see many mountain ranges—the Snowys, the Little Belts, the Castles, the Crazys, the Bulls. I took in the scene as I nudged the car into town.

"Beautiful," I said.

"Yeah." Dad sounded as awestruck as I did.

I cruised up the main drag until it petered out, then turned the car around and made another pass. The diner was still an hour from opening for dinner. We saw a couple of cars at the grocery. Other than that, Main Street kept quiet vigil.

"I've forgotten the way," I said. "You're going to have to give me some directions here."

"The way to where?"

"To the ranch."

"We're not going to be able to get in there."

"Let's go take a look anyway."

Dad didn't fight me. As we passed the Standard, he pointed to his right, and I turned onto the gravel road. Soon enough, Split Rail proper was behind us, and we headed into the maze of ranch roads that ringed town. For the first time since we had started our little day trip, my stomach began churning.

I thought about Dad and his ranch, and how bittersweet it must have been for him to think of it, much less see it.

Dad lost it in 1983, six years after he had bought it in a fit of joy and a cascade of cash.

Mom had predicted that ending a year or two earlier, though I don't think she was particularly proud of her perspicacity. Her signal that things had turned badly for Dad came when my child support checks stopped in 1981. He ran late for a few months, rallied, and then stopped altogether. Mom and I badly needed the money, but she wasn't the sort who would have withheld his right to see me over it. That mattered little; the plug had already been pulled on my visits. I had never come back this way.

Years after Dad lost the ranch, when Mom was gone and a bit of long-distance détente set in between him and me, we talked about it during one of our semiannual phone conversations, and Dad had sloughed it off as his decision. The ranch, at two sections and more than twelve hundred acres, was too big, he said. He wanted a life closer to town, he said, and so he sold out and moved to Billings. The public records I sought later suggested something different: bankruptcy. When the energy crash came, he had stayed on top of the ranch mortgage for as long as he could, trying to patch together a living with water-well work. Eventually, though, he succumbed to the wave of creditors who took his rig, his ranch, his boat, his life's work. He limped out of Split Rail with a failing Ford and that old Holiday Rambler.

When we got the news about Jerry, Dad lived in a trailer park in Billings, subsisting on unemployment and odd jobs. Mom offered to buy him a plane ticket to come out for the funeral—a gesture she didn't need to make and one she couldn't afford. I told her as much, but she said she and Dad made Jerry together and that they ought to see him off together. In any case, her offer was moot. Dad declined. He might have sat there in squalor until the end of his days had he not met Helen, who lifted him up and gave him another shot at prosperity—or at least comfort.

I thought of all this as we bounced along the gravel road. It always seemed to me that Dad had gotten a fairer shake than any he had offered to the rest of us, but now I wasn't so sure. We were coming up on the access road that led to the old ranch house, and I felt sorrow for this man who had once had so much and now had so little. Feeling sorry for him pissed me off. It wasn't why I'd come.

The steel gate, put in by Dad to dissuade trespassers during his long absences, was locked up tight. We climbed out of the car and rested our arms on the gate as we started across a newly tilled field abutting it.

"Looks like they're getting it ready for wheat planting," Dad said.

"Yep."

We looked a while longer.

"Do you miss it, Dad?"

"This?"

"Yeah."

He chewed on the question for a few seconds. I wondered if I would be sorry that I asked.

"I do. Sometimes."

"I think about this place a lot."

"Why?"

"A lot of things happened here. This is the last place I ever saw Marie."

"That's no big loss."

"True. But it happened just the same. Don't you ever think about that stuff? Think back to what happened and wonder what might have been?"

Dad scoffed.

"Things work out the way they work out. I've told you that before, Mitch. You live with your head in the clouds. There isn't anything that fixing the past can do for you now."

I kicked at the ground and turned toward him.

"It's not fixing I'm talking about. That's not what I said. I'm talking about trying to figure it out, to see what can be learned. I guess it's easier to be dismissive about the past if you don't care. Well, I care."

He wheeled around and faced me.

"It sounds like you've got something to say. Why don't you unburden yourself and say it."

Maybe it was that word, *unburden*. It was so similar to what Cindy had said before I left: "The man has some sort of burden." Maybe it was the years of carrying my memories around, alternately trying to sort them out in my own head and fighting with myself over whether to drop them all on Dad and make him account for the things he had done. Whatever the case, I decided right there, on that dirt road, that if he wasn't going to own up to whatever was bothering him, to this great mystery that had brought me out here away from my home and my family, I'd damn well spill my grief. Split Rail, to my mind, was a poetic scene for the confrontation.

"OK. I hate you for what you did to us, to Mom, to me, to Jerry. I hate you for a few weeks from twenty-eight years ago that no matter what I do, I can't get out of my head. I hate that she's gone and he's gone, and you're the one who's left. I hate that for all the time I've carried this around, you won't even see me, won't let me in, won't help me deal with this. Even now, you're doing the same old thing. You're jerking me around, because that's what you fucking do."

Dad quaked. He balled his fists. His eyes bore in on me.

"Are you fucking done?" he hissed.

"Not even close. I can't forgive Marie. She drained you. But you deserved it. You deserved to lose what you lost."

"Fuck you."

"Fuck you right back, Dad," I said. "I can't blame you for Mom, but I'm glad for every day she never had to see you, never had to be with you. I'm happy that when she died, she died free of you."

"You don't have a fucking clue what you're talking about," Dad said. His body twitched.

I kept going.

"But Jerry," I said, and I saw my father's jaw drop, "you didn't plant the bomb. But you killed him, just as sure as if you'd put a gun to his head and pulled the trigger."

Dad swung a right hand that grazed my neck as I bobbed out of the way. I dropped my shoulders and rammed his midsection, and the breath blew out of him as his back hit the steel gate. He wrapped his right arm around my head and pounded my back with his left hand, but I ended that by wrestling him down. He moaned as his back hit the ground. I scrambled on top of him and pinned his shoulders under my knees. He kicked wildly but couldn't dislodge me.

"You're going to listen to me," I said, spittle hitting Dad in the face. "Mom and I watched Jerry's coffin come off that plane. We took him back home. We watched him get buried. Why couldn't you have been there, you piece of shit?

Why couldn't you have owned up to what you did, to making him leave us? You're such a coward. You have no idea how many times I've wished you were dead."

"Fuck you," Dad said.

"Fuck you back."

He strained beneath me, his face burning crimson. I dropped my ass into his chest to further restrict him.

That's when I heard the pump of the shotgun.

"What the hell is going on?"

I whipped my head around. A man stood on the other side of the gate, looking down the barrel at me.

"This is my dad," I said.

"You ought to treat him better than that."

"You don't understand."

"Nope, I don't. Don't want to. Also don't want any trouble. So how about you climb off the old man, get into your car, and get out of here?"

I clambered to my feet. I offered Dad a hand, but he slapped it away. While he slowly rose, I dusted off.

The rancher kept the gun on us and watched as we made our way to the car and climbed in. I thought about telling the guy that Dad used to own his place, but that would have been even more absurd.

I fired up the car and we left.

Silence again carried us along, back to Split Rail and over the butte to the highway. The bumpiest part of the ride— and our day, I hoped—behind us, I said softly, "I'm sorry."

"About what?"

"All of it. But mostly about the fight. Are you OK?"

"You can't hurt me."

I had no stomach for another go-round. Not now. What had Cindy told me? Don't take the bait. What had I done? I took it.

Besides, he could hurt me. I could match him "fuck you" for "fuck you," but that didn't matter much when they were the only words we knew. I'd said it behind his back for years, and now I'd proved that I could say it to his face. A useless skill. Our words expended, we remained poles apart.

We slid past Broadview and the diner where we had planned to stop on the way home. Hunger wasn't part of our reality now. Shared solitude was.

I stole glances to the side. Dad sat stoic and stared ahead, his face contorted in a fist.

"I'm trying to find a place where I fit in with you," I said.

He kept his eyes and his voice low.

"I don't want to talk about it."

I lowered my own voice to a soothing tone. "I'm not talking about Mom here. I'm not talking about Jerry. I'm talking about you and me."

"What do you want from me?"

"Your time. Your thoughts. Your ears. I think if, just once, I could talk to you about these things, I might be able to put them away for good."

Dad at last looked up, and I swear to God, he was crying.

"Why does it matter now? What good will it do?"

"Because twenty-eight years of being quiet hasn't worked. Do you ever think about Marie and what she took from you? Do you ever get mad about that?"

"Yeah."

"Well, something was taken from me, a long time ago, and I've never been able to get it back. Do you understand?"

"No."

"If I promise not to yell at you or to accuse, will you listen? Will you let me explain it?"

Dad rubbed his eyes.

"I'll think about it."

"When you're ready, you let me know."

"I wish you didn't hate me so much, Mitch."

The last of my energy spilled out, as if I'd been gut-punched.

"It's not hate. I wish you could see that."

He said nothing else. I stared at the coming bend in the road and waited for Billings to return to our sights.

"Jesus, Mitch. You actually hit him?"

"No, he hit me. I knocked him to the ground."

"Oh, well, that's something entirely different," Cindy said.

"You know, this doesn't help."

"Well, Christ. You think you're making progress?"

"I'm aware of how stupid it is, OK? I just spent eighty miles rethinking every move I've made since I arrived. Don't need you to do a recap, you know?"

"OK, OK."

"I'm in deep shit here. I don't know what I'm doing."

"I know," she said.

"And Wallen is about to lose it. This trip is going to cost me everything."

"It's not. We're right here. We're on your side."

"Yeah, but for how long?"

"That's not fair."

"I'm here, you're there, your little boyfriend is there. I'd say you've got things set up just right."

"Mitch…"

A voice broke in on us.

"Hi, Daddy."

How long had Adia been listening in? We had done little right, but shielding the children from our meltdown had been one thing we agreed on. My mind raced with fear at what Adia might have heard, and what questions she might have.

"Adia," Cindy said, "hang up the phone."

"How are you, sweetie?" I cooed.

"Good. When are you coming home?"

"Just as soon as I can. What's your brother doing?"

"He's playing."

"You better go play with him, huh?"

"OK. I love you, Daddy."

"I love you too, baby."

The phone hit the cradle.

"Oh no," Cindy said.

"I think it's OK."

"I hope so. Listen, Mitch, you don't need to worry—"

I cut her off again.

"I know. I'm just lashing out."

"OK. But it's getting old, Mitch."

I ran my fingers through my hair. I had no words to corral the entire mess. The problem between us, so insurmountable before I'd even arrived here, had only grown.

"I'm sorry. Look, what am I going to do, Cindy?"

"Whatever you can. For however long it takes."

"And if I lose my job?"

"We have money. You have contacts. There will be another job."

"You sound rather confident."

"Well, I'm not. But what else can I say?"

"And what if I lose you?"

"You're doing the right thing. I said I'd wait. I'm waiting."

Dad stood waiting for me in the living room.

"What'd she say?"

"It's between me and her, Pop."

"Are you going home?"

"When we're done here."

"When do you figure that'll be?"

"The outlook is cloudy, old man," I said.

Before he could stop me, I wrapped him in a hug. For a few seconds, he hung limp in my arms, so I hugged tighter. Finally, he patted my back. So quietly that I barely heard it, he said, "I'm sorry about today, too."

Goddamn. It was a start.

SPLIT RAIL | JUNE 30–JULY 1, 1979

DAD STALKED INTO EVERY ROOM. He looked around corners and turned off lights as he confirmed that Marie wasn't there. I stood in the living room with my bag and watched.

"Mitch, put that stuff away," he said.

I trudged down the hallway to the first door on the left and flipped on a light that Dad had just shut off. Any hint that this space belonged to me had moved out when Jerry moved in the previous year. Now, Farrah Fawcett tossed her hair and smiled winsomely at me. Kiss, The Cars, and Bad Company struck rock-star poses and stared back from magazine clippings. I unpacked and found an empty drawer for my clothes; then I carried my dirties into the utility room.

I heard Dad on the phone.

"Every light in the place was burning. ... No, she's not here. ... Did she say anything about where she was going? ... Has she been spending much time out here? ... I've got Mitch with me. Can you come out and sit with him? ... I don't know. ... OK, I'll wait for her."

"Who was that?" I asked after Dad hung up.

"J.C."

J.C. Simmons and his wife, LaVerne, owned the next ranch over. When Dad had bought his place, the Simmonses were in danger of going under a sea of debt. Dad saved them by buying a passive interest in their place. Their end of the deal was that they looked after his ranch while he was away. They brought in cattle, spread hay, cut the ice in winter. Good people, J.C. and LaVerne were, and after Dad had saved their place, there was nothing they wouldn't have done in return.

"Where are you going?" I asked. "Can't I come?"

Dad stood in the kitchen, rummaging through drawers and papers in search of anything to indicate where Marie had gone.

"No, Mitch, you can't come. It's been a long day."

"I'll be good. I'll—"

Dad slammed a drawer. The silverware crashed violently.

"Goddammit, no! Somebody in this house, by God, is going to do what I say."

I ran to my room.

I was still there when LaVerne arrived. I rose from the bed and crept to the door, cracking it just far enough to hear what she and Dad said.

Dad sounded agitated, and I couldn't blame him. We had come a long way, our nerves were shot, and Marie had left the meter running while she went off to who knows where. Dad told LaVerne to let me watch television until I fell asleep, and he added that she should feel free to send me to bed if I gave her any lip. LaVerne told him that she expected no trouble.

"Yeah, yeah, yeah," Dad said.

"Jim, I'm sure it's nothing," LaVerne said. "Marie's probably just out with some friends and lost the time."

My father expelled a heavy sigh.

"She knew I was coming. I called her from Pocatello."

I waited for the close of the door and Dad's boots thudding across the porch in his short, angry gait, then for the pickup to fire up. When the sound of the engine grew faint, I opened the bedroom door and walked out.

"You're really growing up," LaVerne said, admiring the height I had tacked on in the two years since she had last seen me. "You're nearly as tall as your dad."

"I guess."

I saw no similarly transformative change in LaVerne. She had to have been in her mid-forties, and she had a deep, natural beauty that didn't need burnishing. There's a saying about ranch women: when they're thirty, they look fifty, and when they're eighty, they look fifty. That was true of LaVerne. She wore no makeup. Her long, brown hair was pulled into a tight ponytail. Ranch work in all sorts of weather had carved deep lines into her face, giving her an appearance that wasn't haggard so much as experienced. Her deeply tanned arms rippled with muscle and sinew. There was no ranch job LaVerne couldn't do. I couldn't help but contrast her with Marie, who was so meticulous in primping herself. I was one of the few who had seen Marie before she'd had a chance to put on her face and do her hair, and the difference could take your breath away. LaVerne, I suspected, rolled out of bed looking like this.

"Where's J.C.?" I asked. LaVerne's husband had a good twenty years on her and was a jolly soul.

"He's got matters at home demanding his attention. It's you and me, kiddo. What would you like to do?"

"Can I call my mom?"

LaVerne glanced at the clock. It was coming up on nine. "It's getting a little late," she said.

"Not in Washington. It's an hour earlier."

"So it is. Well, go ahead then."

Mom seemed happier than usual to hear from me.

"My prince! Where are you now?"

"We got to the ranch tonight."

"A week off, huh?"

"Yeah. I get to ride my motorcycle tomorrow."

"Mitch, be careful on that thing. I don't like them."

"I will."

Because she insisted, I always wore a helmet. It had saved my hide a time or two. Dad's ranch was full of ruts and uneven patches of ground, all capable of setting my bike down or sending me over the handlebars. What Mom didn't know about this, like so many other things when it came to time spent with Dad, didn't hurt her.

"I heard from Jerry yesterday," she said.

"Really?"

"He called at dinnertime. You're not going to believe this. He joined the Marines."

"The Marines? Really?" I wondered what Dad, the strident Navy man, would think of that.

"That's exactly what I said. He enlisted in Salt Lake, and he's down in San Diego for boot camp."

"Why the Marines?"

"He said the job there with your dad toughened him up and he was ready for it."

"Did he say anything about why he left?" I knew the answer to this, of course, but I wanted test her knowledge. That she hadn't screamed bloody murder and demanded that Dad send me home posthaste was a good sign that she had no idea about what took place in Milford.

"He just said it was time to get serious about something. He said drilling with your Dad isn't a good career. Having lived that life, I agree with him."

"You sound glad."

"I'll worry about Jerry. That's what I do. But I think he made a good decision. He's smart. He'll do well."

"OK."

"What's your Dad up to?"

"He went to get Marie."

"Where?"

"I'm not sure."

"You're there all alone?"

"LaVerne is here."

"Who is LaVerne?"

"She's a neighbor. Do you want to talk to her?"

I looked over at LaVerne, who raised an eyebrow.

"No, that's OK. ... Mitch, one other thing. Your baseball team won their last two games. I was there for the last one. They gave out trophies. Yours is here waiting."

"Neat. Did you put it in my room with the others?"

"Of course. Your coach said they loved having you on the team and to say hello."

"Thanks, Mom."

"You bet, sweetie. Be good. Call me next week, OK? I love you."

"Bye, Mom. I love you too."

Mom's nonchalance about Jerry's decision to join the Marines confused me. On one hand, I was happy that she seemed OK with it; that would certainly make it easier for me to tuck away the details about why he left. On the other hand, I couldn't help but wonder how she might feel if she knew about that night. This was clear: I wouldn't have been in Split Rail had she known. That being the case, discretion seemed the only sensible play.

I pulled out my wallet and thumbed the three twenty-dollar bills Jerry left me. They had become a security blanket. When I was sure Dad wasn't around, I would open my wallet and touch Jerry's money. It was my connection to him.

I hoped like hell I'd never have to use it for the purpose he intended.

SPLIT RAIL | JUNE 30–JULY 1, 1979

LaVerne and I settled into the den to watch TV. Isolated as Dad's ranch was from the big stations in Billings and Great Falls, the reception was poor. Dad eased that a bit by installing a monstrous antenna, but still we watched through the electronic snow drifting across the screen.

I stayed alert through *Alice* and *The Jeffersons*. After that, my eyelids grew heavy. I slumped against LaVerne, who wrapped me in an arm as sleep and dreams washed over me.

We stood in a semicircle, the five of us: me, Jerry, Mom, Dad, Marie. We were in the middle of a dry lakebed that stretched in all directions to the horizon. Our bare feet sank into the parched white sand.

Each could see the faces of the other four. Everybody else stood perfectly still, but I didn't. I craned my neck around at each of them, and my mouth formed words—"What's going on?"—but no sounds.

Mom said, "I have to go," and she peeled away from the group. She looked beautiful—luminous and sunny, wearing her favorite blue spring dress. Finally, my mouth worked. "Mom, where are you going?" She continued a few paces, then turned and waved at me, as if urging me to join her. She looked as though she were saying something, but I couldn't hear it.

"Mom!" I yelled.

She turned and kept walking. Soon, she was a dot in the distance.

Then Jerry said, "I'm gone too."

He set a hand on Dad's shoulder as he left, and I watched with incredulity as Dad's shirt and muscle crumbled, leaving a gouged-out crater.

"Where are you going?" I called to Jerry. My brother never turned around, disappearing into the haze just as Mom had done only moments earlier.

Marie stepped through the distance toward Dad and stood before him. She pushed her sunglasses atop her forehead and dug into him with her brown eyes.

"Good-bye, Jim," she said, and she slapped his face, shattering it. I shielded my head as pieces of my father rained down.

My father, whole and beside me just moments earlier, was now just a stump of sand, no more than a foot high. And then he wasn't even that. Marie kicked away what remained of him as she headed for the horizon, like Mom and Jerry before her.

I tried to scream, but my lungs expelled no air. I tried to move, but the sand swallowed my legs, rendering them useless.

Tears running down my face, I saw with dread the coming darkness and the desert's yielding to the chill of night…

The slam of the front door pulled me from sleep. Beside me, I felt LaVerne jump too.

I rubbed my eyes and tried to make sense of where I was. The TV signal, now a test pattern, broke a hazy trail of electrons through the dark. My heart thumped in relief that I was in the ranch house, not mired on a dry lakebed in God knows where.

Marie's voice clacked like a typewriter, but I couldn't make out her words. Dad shushed her.

LaVerne and I climbed to our feet and made our way to the front room.

The tension was palpable, something LaVerne picked up on right away.

"Well, I see you folks are here in one piece, so I'll be saying good night," she said, and she scooted for the door.

"Thank you, LaVerne," Dad said.

He turned his attention to me.

"It's one in the morning. Why are you up?"

"I fell asleep in front of the TV."

"Hi, Mitch," Marie said.

"Oh, no, no, no. Don't start making nice," Dad said.

"Screw you, Jim. I can say hello to my stepson."

Dad wheeled on her.

"Screw me? What do you know about it, whore?"

Marie dashed away, cutting across the room. I watched this unfold as if on the fifty-yard line at a football game. The whole sickening scene played out in front of me.

Dad pivoted in the direction she had skittered and kept moving toward her.

"Don't touch me, Jim." At the back wall, Marie grabbed a figurine from the mantel and flung it at Dad. The piece shattered against the floor at my feet. I watched the pieces of it skitter across the wood. Out the window, I saw LaVerne's pickup disappear down the lane.

I screamed. "Stop it, stop it, stop it!"

For the first time, the adults in my life did as I demanded.

"You're being stupid," I said. The totality of the day—the long ride, the cowering at Dad's scoldings, the dream—sent tears down my face. I was angrier than I was scared, and I was plenty scared. Time apart had done nothing to mend the fray between Dad and Marie.

Marie stared daggers at Dad and then walked back across the room and knelt in front of me. She tried to hug me, but I pushed her away.

"No."

"Mitch, I'm sorry," she said.

"I don't care."

Dad came over, and he set a hand on Marie's shoulder. She bristled.

"Settle down, sport."

My chest heaved as I fought with my breath. My tears, which I hated, fell in open defiance of my desire that they hold back.

"I'm sick of it," I said.

He reached for me, and I slapped at his hand.

"Leave me alone."

An edge crept into his voice. "Now, Mitch."

"I'm sick of it!"

Marie clasped me by the shoulders. I grew tense at her touch, but I didn't resist.

"We're done," she said. "You shouldn't have seen that."

"You shouldn't have done it."

"You're right. It's done. It's over."

I slowly gained control of my tears and sniffling. I wiped my nose with the back of my hand.

"I just want everybody to get along."

Dad said softly, "OK, sport. We're working on it."

We played nice for a few minutes, and then Dad suggested that I go to bed so I could get an early start.

"No chores tomorrow," Dad said. "You can ride all day."

I plodded down the hall. I wanted to cry but couldn't find the energy for it. Dad and Marie could tap a limitless well of conflict, but I could take only so much. I'd had my fill.

I kicked off my shoes and set them by the closet. Off too came my socks and my T-shirt, and I shimmied out of my pants. A few minutes after my head hit the pillow, just as my eyes grew heavy, I heard Dad and Marie turn their guns on each other again, this time in the bedroom opposite mine.

The words were quieter now, delivered in low tones so as not to rouse me. It was a senseless consideration. I lay in the dark, my eyes open, and took in every syllable.

"I hate it here," she said. "I hate being with you out there. I deserve better."

"This is the deal," Dad said. "You knew it when you married me."

"I didn't know it would be like this."

"That makes two of us."

"What do you mean?"

"I can't keep up. You're bleeding us dry, gallivanting around. I come home and find you in Billings—"

"I was just having fun."

"It looked fun, you and that guy."

"He's just a friend. Not that you'd know—"

"He was friendly, that much was clear. He can be friendly with a busted nose."

"Oh yeah, big man Jim. You can't understand it, so you've got to hurt it."

"Whore."

"I didn't do anything that you didn't do first."

"Lying whore."

I turned over, wrapped the pillow around my head, and said a silent prayer that it would end soon. It seemed to me, as I lay there in the dark, that Jerry had made the only sensible decision.

He had gotten out.

BILLINGS | SEPTEMBER 21, 2007

HOURS AFTER THE STORM, morning came and brought an air of uneasy consideration to the way Dad and I dealt with each other, one that hadn't existed until after we had rolled around in the dust in Split Rail.

I'd seen enough violence in my life to know that good things rarely come of it, but in our case, the scuffle cut through some of the deep divisions between us. Dad knew I wasn't going anywhere until I was satisfied with where I stood with him. Perhaps for the first time, I knew it too.

I awoke the way I had all those years earlier, with Dad shaking me from slumber.

"Mitch, let's get some of those doughnuts," he said.

I blinked my eyes to chase away sleep, and there he stood, a floppy grin stitched across his face.

We rode in my rental while Dad fiddled with the radio again. At the grocery store, I held the box open while Dad counted out six doughnuts from the self-serve bin. At the coffee kiosk, he poured two cups, and unprompted, he added my cream and sugar, looking up and smiling at me.

It was like we were normal people or something.

"What's your plan for today, Pop?" I asked between bites of jelly doughnut.

"Errands."

"Yeah? You need some company?"

"Nope." He looked at me. "I could use your help here, anyway. You know how to use a lawnmower?"

I gave him a quick look to gauge his intent. He twinkled.

"I'm pretty sure I can figure it out."

"There's a push mower and a rake in the shed. Can you whip this yard into shape?"

His patch of lawn ran as long as the double-wide and about ten feet deep. It wouldn't be much of a job.

"You pay overtime?" I asked, and Dad laughed.

Just before nine a.m., Dad left. "I'll be back pretty soon," he said on his way out.

"Sure you don't need company?"

"The mower and the rake are in the shed," he said.

I chuckled. "I'm on it."

I listened as Dad's little pickup sputtered to life and he sent it rattling down the lane, and then I turned back to the morning's newspaper and my third cup of coffee. The yard could wait.

The cutting duty, like so many things, had gotten away from Dad, and I had to make three passes with the push mower to saw down every long blade of grass. My back took umbrage at the raking and bagging of the cut grass, but that was my own damned fault. At this stage, I lifted more drinks than weights, and my body merely told me, in a language I could understand, that I had been an idiot.

I finished in an hour. The cuttings were bagged and tied and sitting out with the trash bins. I dragged the rake back to the shed.

I was about to lock up when a box in the rafters caught my eye. In marker, in Dad's jagged hand, was written *Letters/ papers.*

I peeked outside, gazing along the entry road. The assumption that I was being surreptitious made me feel foolish, but the more I contemplated what I was about to do, the more on-point caution seemed. I asked myself a question: if Dad were to walk in and catch me digging through this box, would he be upset?

Despite the answer, I stepped inside the shed and dragged down the box.

Forty-five minutes later, I stood in the darkness of the shed, trying to get my head straight.

I had known only the faintest outlines of Dad's upbringing. He was born in Havre, Montana, the only child of Raymond and Luetta Quillen. When he was eighteen months old, his parents died in a car crash, hit head-on by a farm truck. Dad, in a bassinet in the back seat, survived. With no siblings and no one stepping forward to claim him, Dad ended up in the St. Thomas Home orphanage in Great Falls, where he stayed until he was of legal age. Then the Navy took him. That was Dad's story, although he never talked about it with me. Details came to me in scraps of conversations I wasn't intended to hear. As I grew more curious about him, Mom filled in a few details she knew. What I found in the box changed everything.

There, underneath his discharge papers and information on long-ago bank accounts and old payroll stubs, I found a stack of envelopes, bound together with rubber bands. Each had the same return address, from someone named Kelly Hewins, from a post-office box in Havre, penned neatly in cursive.

December 11, 1963
Dear Jimmy,

 I hope you don't mind that I tracked you down. I don't want to bother you if you don't want to be bothered, and so I'll just write this letter and hope that you respond.

 It's been a long time since I've seen you, and I want you to know that you're missed. Dick—you remember him, right?—and I got married eight years ago. We have two little girls, Kathy and Kelly (after me!), and another on the way. It would be so nice to see you again and catch up and find out what you've been up to all this while.

 Have a merry Christmas and a happy New Year.
 Please call or write.
 Love,
 Kelly

June 13, 1968
Dear Jimmy,

 Dick and I were in Billings over the weekend, and we saw the birth announcement for your little boy in the paper. We didn't even know you'd gotten married. It's so wonderful that you have a son. And Mitchell is a beautiful name. Congratulations to you and Leila.

I keep hoping that someday I'll answer the phone and you'll be on the other end, or I'll reach into the mailbox and pull out a letter from you. I'd love to talk to you, to see you, to know you again. I also know why you might not want that.

We're in the place we've always been, if you ever change your mind. We have four kids now. Our oldest, Kathy, is 11—how did that happen? There's also Kelly (9), Coby (8), and Charles (6). We're done, I think. I hope.

Love,

Kelly

August 4, 1976

Dear Jimmy,

We don't get to Billings very often, but it seems like every time we do, we get a piece of news about you. You're remarried? We wish you much happiness.

Kathy is a year into college in Missoula. Kelly will soon be next. The other kids will be coming up behind them soon enough. Time sure flies. Your boy is growing up too, I would imagine. It all happens fast.

I realized today that it's been 22 years since I've seen you or heard from you. I hope not too much more time will pass before your heart softens. I miss you.

Love,

Kelly

February 9, 1980

Dear Jimmy,

You're hard to track down. The past couple of letters I sent to your house in Billings came back here.

I just thought I'd let you know. We buried Dana yesterday. She'd been sick for the past year and she finally passed on.

I know how you felt about her and him, and maybe even me. I guess I don't blame you much.

I half expected to see you at the funeral, though I know that's silly. Anyway, I thought you'd like to know.

Love,

Kelly

December 21, 1982

Dear Jimmy,

Merry Christmas! The whole family is back together for this holiday. Kathy and her husband Dan and their two kids are here. They live out in Portland. Kelly came out from Boston. Coby and his wife and their little baby are up from Billings. Charles, who's in his sophomore year at MSU, will be here too.

You know, you're only a few hours away. If you decided to show up for Christmas, we'd love to have you here.

Love,

Kelly

June 2, 1986

Dear Jimmy,

This will sound silly, but I've been going to the library and reading the papers from all over the state, looking for a graduation announcement for your boy. Mitchell would be 18 now, wouldn't he? I'd like to send him a card. It breaks my heart that I've never met him. It breaks my heart even more that it's been more than 30 years since I've seen you. I wonder how much longer I should even bother sending out these notes, since they're never answered.

I'm sorry about what happened to you. I would give anything if I could somehow make it better. You'll recall that I was there too. I suffered too. I don't know what good it does to keep the whole world out, Jimmy.

Love,

Kelly

April 14, 1991

Dear Jimmy,

I'm sorry it's been so long since I've written.

Dick died last year. It was very hard. He collapsed there at work, and he was gone. I miss him so much. He was a good man and a good husband and a good father.

I was depressed for a long time. Charles was working for an accountant in Denver, but he moved back here to Havre and opened his own office. He lives down the street and looks after me, though I'm slowly getting into the swing of things again. I have good friends and good kids, and I'll be all right.

I hope life has been treating you well.

Love,

Kelly

June 1, 1994

Dear Jimmy,

Does this date have any significance for you? It does for me. This was the date you left Havre and entered the Navy. The last time I saw you, 40 years ago. When will this silence end?

Love,

Kelly

March 3, 2002
Dear Jimmy,

I can't do this anymore. I've given you as much room as I can give you, in the hopes that you'd meet me somewhere in the middle. I can see now that you never will. I will adhere to your wishes, then, and not contact you again.

I love you. I always have, and I always will.

Kelly

I pawed at the letters, and I read them all again. Kelly? Dana? Who were these people?

The pain that dripped from the letters gnawed at me, too. Kelly, whoever she was, found herself stuck on the other side of Dad's wall, where so many of us who cared about him did our time in silence.

I was set to dig deeper into the box, but I looked up and saw the old man's truck turn into the trailer park. I jammed everything back in and hustled the box back to its resting place.

SPLIT RAIL | JULY 1, 1979

WHEN I THINK ABOUT THE AFTERNOON when everything came apart for Dad and Marie, the fight rarely registers much significance. I don't think about how knockdown, drag-out, let's-call-the-whole-thing-off battles flare from the smallest of kindling. I don't wonder how two people, ostensibly grown up, can grapple over who can more effectively use a boy as a pawn, all in their zeal to hurt each other. I know all of that. I saw it. I was there. But I don't fixate on it.

No, I remember that at last, after pining for it for weeks, I had spent the early part of that day riding my motorcycle. It was a bit too small for my frame by then, two years after it had been purchased for me, and my elbows rested lazily on my drawn-up knees. I looked ridiculous, hanging on that bike, all arms and legs and right angles. I didn't care. Of far greater import was that I had all the acreage I wanted with trails cut into it every which way by trucks and tractors, I had a full tank of gas, and I had no chores.

The day belonged to me. Then, quickly and without mercy, it didn't.

Dad rolled the motorcycle out early, before I awoke, and he gassed it up and changed the oil. It was a rare anticipation of what I would be eager to do, one perhaps inspired by the previous night's row with Marie and done, perhaps, in an effort to placate me, or at least distract me.

I bounded outside after breakfast and found the motorcycle in the driveway, looking as new as the day Dad bought it for me two summers earlier. I ran a finger along the gleaming red tank.

"You remember your way around this thing?" Dad asked.

I pulled down on the helmet straps and squeezed the shell over my head. It fit, only barely.

"Of course."

"OK, then. You be careful."

"I will."

I climbed on and pushed the Honda up, booting the kickstand into riding position. I grasped the clutch and gave the kicker my full weight. After two years of sitting idle, the Honda almost caught on the first kick. The second one set her to purring.

I looked at Dad and grinned. He pointed back at me.

"Drive by the house every so often," he said. "If I have to come out looking for you, you'd better be dead."

I nodded, set the bike in gear, and released the clutch. If he had anything else to say, he could tell it to my dust.

The ranch presented enough changes in topography to keep me entertained. I happily carved new lines in trails cut out of the country long ago. My standing orders were to give a wide berth to the cattle—Dad ran about fifty cow-calf pairs on the ranch—and to the cultivated fields. The rest was free for exploration.

I headed first for the original house, at the opposite end of the property. The old place enchanted me. Built partly out of sandstone cut from the rims, the little house stood on the edge of the property like a ghost, sturdy far beyond its years and yet obsolete. Hunters stalking the property during mule deer season would occasionally use it, either overnight or just as a place to grab a few winks before continuing the hunt. Time and vegetation had encroached on the place, but still it stood, keeping watch over the land, holding fast to whatever secrets it had gathered.

The only other time I had been there, I had unearthed some of its history. In what remained of the kitchen area, I found an old silver spoon, small and delicate, and shards of china. I brought those things back to the house, and Marie claimed them. The spoon got a shining, one that nearly made it look like new, and ended up in a shadow box on the wall. The china pieces were put on the mantel. Sometimes I looked at the artifacts and wondered about the people who used them. I would contemplate what their lives must have been like as they made their stand in a bountiful but unforgiving land. The people who had come here first and whittled a life out of this place had none of the conveniences I took for granted, and I marveled that through hard work, wits, and fortitude they were able to build an existence from the ground up. It led me to approach their place—and theirs it was, much more than Dad's or Marie's or mine—with something bordering on reverence.

As my motorcycle crested a small hill and the old house fell into view, I saw that little had changed. The old structure looked ready for another century of what man and nature could throw at it. I pulled up where the door would have hung and powered down the Honda. I took off my helmet and stepped inside the old place for another look, another visit to a time and place I could see and feel but had to imagine to bring to life.

I cut along the back side boundary of the ranch, taking a loop around the grazing cattle. As I turned the nose of the motorcycle toward the house, I stopped. Ahead, a rattlesnake slithered across the double-rutted road and headed for the rocks beyond.

I gunned the Honda and tore out after him, and I thrilled at the sickening collapse of his head as my tires hit it. At the end of the lane, I whipped the bike around for a look. I stopped several feet away, giving the snake a healthy respect despite my surety that he was dead. I watched his body for a few minutes until I was fully satisfied. I was all too mindful of my earlier tangle with one of his brethren in Utah. This snake was smaller, a young prairie rattler with a dusty brown color that, had I encountered him somewhere else, would have made him hard to see. That was good for snakes but not so good for unwitting intruders.

Slowly, I moved closer. The snake was dead as dead could be, and still my stomach churned. I knew it was dumb, but I feared that he was feigning death, waiting for me to draw near so he could flash his fangs and exact revenge. This was silly. Man's fear of snakes is exceeded only by snakes' fear of man. Had I given him an out, he surely would have taken it. I had read that some rattlesnakes, when forced to strike people, delivered dry bites, saving their venom for their actual prey. When you get right down to it, snakes show far more sense than people. They spend energy looking for food, they keep to themselves, and they go to great lengths to avoid a fight.

As these thoughts competed for space in my head, a pang of remorse that I had so blithely ended this fellow's life hit me. He was doing what a snake must do, and I had come along and killed him. The least I could do was offer him dignity. I climbed off the still-running motorcycle, walked the final few steps to his body, and kicked him off the road.

As I rumbled into the main yard, I waved at Dad, whose head was jammed into the guts of a tractor. I shut off the bike and flew up the porch stairs two at a time.

I was downing my third cup of water when Marie perched off my left shoulder.

"What happened to Jerry?" she asked.

"He's in the Marines. That's what Mom told me."

"The Marines? Why?"

"It's something he wanted to do, I guess."

Marie frowned.

"That doesn't make any sense. One day he's working for Jim and he's got a girlfriend there in Milford. Then the next he's in the Marines. What happened down there?"

"Nothing. He and Dad weren't getting along, and he quit."

"I don't believe that."

Had I thought concern for Jerry inspired Marie's questions, I might have given her more to go on—certainly not the full story, but something that nudged closer to truth. I knew she was digging for ammunition against Dad, and she could find enough of that without my help.

"Believe it or don't. That's what happened."

I set my glass down and headed for the door.

I rode to the end of the ranch access road, about a mile from the house. I gazed past the gate to the road that led into Split Rail. It moved away from the ranch to the south and west. Hundreds of miles beyond, my brother sat in San Diego, getting on with his life.

I wished he were with me, so I could hug his neck.

When I returned, I found Dad sitting in his recliner, nursing a beer and a cigarette.

"How's it going, sport?"

"Good."

"Do you need more gas?"

"Not yet." I called into the kitchen. "What's for lunch?"

"Hot dogs," Marie said.

"We're eating like kings now," Dad said, and that brought a peek around the wall and a cold stare.

After all the diner fare and slapped-together, meat-in-a-can lunches in Utah, I welcomed hot dogs. And Marie had undersold it. Potato chips, fruit, and pasta salad rounded things out. Kings, indeed. Sensing that the tension between Dad and Marie had eased little, I told Marie how good it all tasted, in the hope that some kind words might send the tenor of the house in a new direction.

"Thank you, Mitch," she said. Then she looked at Dad, who wordlessly shoveled forkfuls of food into his mouth. "It's nice that someone noticed."

Dad looked up at her. "I noticed," he said. "I didn't realize you expected a parade."

Marie dropped her fork, and it clattered onto her plate. "See, Jim, it's telling that for you, it's either silence or a parade. How about just a simple nice word? How about some kindness?"

"You mean the kind you were showing that guy?"

"Jesus, Jim."

"I'm going outside," I said, standing up. Marie put a hand on my shoulder and gently eased me down.

"Mitch. I'm sorry." She glanced at Dad. "We're sorry. Help me clear this stuff away, OK?"

Dad looked up and gave me a nod.

"OK," I said.

I had just shoved the leftover pasta salad into the fridge when we heard the thump on the hardwood floor in the living room.

"Ah hell."

"What is it?" Marie said.

"Mitch, come in here, would you?" Dad said.

I walked into the living room, Marie on my heels. In front of Dad's chair, I saw the overturned ashtray, with dozens of cigarette butts and ash sprayed out in all directions from the tumble.

"Grab the broom out of the hall closet and sweep this up," Dad said.

"You do it, Jim," Marie said.

"Excuse me?"

"It's your mess. You clean it up. He isn't your slave."

"I don't mind," I said.

"I mind," she said. "You're not responsible for the messes your father makes."

"Are you fucking kidding me?" Dad said. He stared at her.

"Not at all. You think you just can order everyone around. Well, you can't."

"I just asked the boy to help me clean this up."

"You didn't ask. You told. Somebody has to start sticking up for people against you, Jim."

I watched the fight flare toward a fever pitch, and I couldn't move my mouth or body. I didn't believe that Marie had chosen this incident to make her stand. I half-relished and half-dreaded seeing where it would go.

"This is bullshit," Dad said. "The only reason you're making a big deal out of this is because of last night. You fucked up, big time, and now you're trying to pin blame on me."

"That's not it. I'm standing up for Mitch. He deserves better from you."

"I asked him to clean the goddamned floor."

"You told him! You told him to clean the floor. Are you so pathetic that you can't do it yourself?"

Dad reached down and picked up the glass ashtray, and then he rose, holding it in his thumb and forefinger. "You're right," he said. "I'll clean it up."

He dropped the ashtray, and it shattered on the floor.

"Oops," he said.

Dad jab-stepped at Marie, and she flinched. Instead of going at her, he crossed the living room to the fireplace. A wedding day picture of them hung on the wall.

"Here's another mess," he said, and he slammed his fist into the picture, shattering the glass. He grabbed the wooden frame and flung it to the floor.

"Don't worry, honey. I'll clean it up."

"Just stop," I yelled. "Just stop." It was useless. This was the unspooling. They weren't listening to me.

To Dad's right was a picture of Marie and her mother, who had died some years earlier. Dad moved on it.

"Don't you dare, Jim."

"Sweetheart, I never would. I know how much this means to you."

He punched that picture too. It fell to the floor in a twisted heap of frame, photo paper, and broken glass.

I turned and looked at Marie. Tears started down her face. She wasn't broken, though. Her eyes blazed, and she was almost…God, she was. She was laughing.

"Oh, Jim, you've really lost it," she said, her voice a cackle. "I'm glad you finally showed who you really are, and I'm glad Mitch is seeing this. I don't want there to be any doubt when they come for you."

Dad took two hard steps toward her, and she met him in the middle.

"Come for me? Nobody's coming for me," he said. "They'll be coming for you when I throw your ass out. It's over. All of it. I'm sick of it. You're gone."

"I'm glad," she said. "Another minute with you, and I'd have killed myself. That's how much you repulse me."

Dad raised his hand as if to hit Marie. Blood dripped from his knuckles. She didn't shrink. I thought she must be crazy. She said, "Do it. Do it. I'm begging you."

Dad lowered his hand. A grin surfaced.

"It's not too late," he said. "I'll get the shotgun, and we can all be done with this."

I found my legs, and I dashed down the hallway. Tears filled my eyes, and I was dead certain that my father was on my heels, heading off to find a gun to end the misery for all of us.

I slammed the bedroom door and turned the lock. Then, in a panic, I realized I had boxed myself in. I couldn't shimmy beneath the bed. I actually considered a movie-style run at the window but couldn't envision breaking through the glass and coming out all right on the other side. I climbed into the recesses of the closet and pulled the sliding door shut. In the darkness, I bit my lower lip, and I prayed that Dad wouldn't hear my breathing. There was little chance of that; the fight raged on in the living room, the angry words growing ever sharper as Dad and Marie unfurled the last of their marital complaints against each other, ensuring that there would be no going back.

I sat amid shoes and Jerry's clothes and waited, and I wondered if the storm would ever end.

BILLINGS | SEPTEMBER 21, 2007

"JUST FINISHED HER UP," I said as Dad emerged from his truck. I swept my arm across the mown yard. Dad nodded and headed for the stairs, and I fell in behind him.

Inside, we wandered around each other. I had my preoccupation, and he seemed to have his. No matter how hard I focused on what was in front of me, I returned again to those pleading letters.

Kelly Hewins. I had never heard the name, not from Dad, not from Mom. Who was she?

If Dad noticed my detachment, he didn't let on. He sat in his favorite chair, watching the afternoon television shows slide by.

Around six p.m., my cell phone rang. I looked at the display, saw who was calling, and exhaled.

"Hi, John."

"Mitch."

"What's up?"

"I'll get right to it. I need to know if you're going to be here Monday."

"I can't say, John. Maybe. I doubt it, though."

"Why?"

"Things are a little…well, they're fluid right now."

"I see. Here's the deal: I've been patient, Mitch, through this thing and through your slump. I figured you would bounce back. You always do. But I don't know how much farther I can go."

I glanced at Dad, who was now looking at me.

"I can't answer that question for you, John."

"Perhaps we've reached a point where we should talk about whether this is still a good situation, mutually."

"I'd be happy to do that when I get back."

"But you don't know when that will be?"

"That's correct."

John paused, and I didn't move to fill the gap.

"By then, it may be too late," he said.

There it was. Oddly, I wasn't as thunderstruck as I imagined I would be.

"I understand."

John hung up. I closed my flip phone.

"What was that all about?" Dad said.

"I think I just lost my job."

Dad shot out of his chair.

"What? Why?"

"It's been coming for a long time." I sat there, amazed at the feeling that coursed through me. It wasn't sorrow over the loss of my job. It wasn't fear of finding a new one. No, it was relief. It was as if someone had snapped his fingers and made a burden disappear. That John Wallen had been the one to do it, I thought, was just one of life's funny little twists. For all those years, I had focused on pleasing him and building my career. It turned out that he was my jailer and my liberator.

"Well, can you get it back?" Dad's voice was pitched, and his pacing amounted to his biggest burst of energy of the day. "Fly home, tell him it's all a big misunderstanding."

"You never struck me as the groveling type."

"Screw that. I'm not the type who would let someone who worked for me drag ass for a week in Montana when he should be at his desk doing his job."

I smiled. He wouldn't find an opponent in me. "Well, I'm not asking for the job back. I don't want it."

Dad shook his head. "You think your wife is going to be OK with that?"

"You know," I said, "I think she just might."

I pushed up from the couch and headed outside to find out the answer.

Though John hadn't said, in so many words, "You're fired," Cindy agreed that I could be certain my job wouldn't be waiting for me. I asked if she would be.

"You know I will," she said.

"It's hard to know what I know anymore."

"What do you mean?"

I told her about the letters I'd found in the shed, recounting the cryptic passages where Kelly had said things like, "I was there too."

"Is she talking about the orphanage?" Cindy offered.

"Maybe. But who is this Dana that she mentions burying? That doesn't track."

"I don't know. Maybe this Kelly is an old girlfriend."

"I thought of that, but I'm skeptical. Why would she profess love for him years later, while she's talking about her husband and her kids?"

"You're just going to have to find out, I guess."

I shook my head.

"You know, this thing is expanding far beyond what it was intended to be. I came here to find out what's eating Dad and to set things straight with him, not to unearth some mystery from his past."

"Well, Mitch, that's not entirely true. You went there to get to the bottom of something, and this is where the trail has taken you. You can't stop now."

I breathed in. The autumn air filled my lungs and tickled my nose.

"I know," I acknowledged, exhaling. "And if I stay here and eat Dad's food, it will save us money there."

My wife chuckled. "I didn't think of that."

"All right, honey, I love you."

"I love you too, baby."

A simple, lovely moment, so long in coming, carried me back into the house.

I stabbed at my steak as I considered how to approach Dad with my questions. I was half-tempted to just spill things onto the table and hope for a straightforward answer. Instead, true to history where Dad was concerned, I stayed on the periphery.

"Dad, when did you go into the Navy?"

He looked up from his plate.

"Let's see…I was born in '36, and so seventeen years after that…it must have been '53 or '54."

"So you went in when you were seventeen?"

"Yep."

"What were you doing before that?"

"What's with the questions?"

"I'm just curious. I figure we've talked enough about all that other stuff."

"In the orphanage, going to school."

"You stayed in the orphanage until you joined the Navy?"

"Yep."

"Did you have many friends there?"

"At the orphanage?"

"Yeah."

"A few, I guess. It was a long time ago."

"What were their names?"

"Come on, Mitch. What's going on?"

"I'm just asking."

"I don't remember. It's been a lot of years."

"But they were your friends. You must remember—"

Dad cut me off.

"Let's just eat, huh?"

He filled his mouth with steak and mashed potatoes, all the better to keep the words from spilling forth and to force me to keep my queries to myself.

I tried a new tack after dinner.

"Where did you and Mom live after you came to Montana?"

"Right around here."

"Billings?"

"Well, no, I went to work for a driller in Joliet."

"Where is that?"

"Out toward Red Lodge."

"Where did you live?"

"What's going on here? You sound like you did when you were a little kid, a million questions."

"I'm just interested. I've never really heard too much about the early days with you and Mom. She never talked about it."

"Probably because there wasn't much to talk about."

"Humor me."

Dad shook his head. Using his feet as pistons, he turned his easy chair around so he could face me.

"We lived in an old bunkhouse on this guy's property. There wasn't much to it. No kitchen, barely a bathroom."

"Mom must have hated that."

"She never complained, not about that at least. We ate in the main house, with the driller and his wife, and your mom toted the laundry into town once a week. That guy and me were hardly ever there. Always out on some job. And your mom, hoo boy."

"What?"

"She really hated that woman. Whenever I'd come back on a break, that's all she'd talk about. So, eventually, we moved to a small house there in town, so your mom could feel a little better and have some space that belonged to her."

"Why did she dislike the woman so much?"

"Oh, she was a busybody, always telling Leila what to do and where to go, and she always had a better way. Some people just grate on you, I guess."

I smiled, remembering Mom's independent streak.

"It seems weird," I said. "I never knew Mom to say any-thing bad about anybody."

"She probably didn't, except to me. Leila was a good lady."

I smiled again. "I've never heard you say that."

"What?"

"That Mom was a good lady."

"Well, she was."

"I know. But I always figured you disliked her."

"Why?"

"You never talked about her, and she never talked too much about you. What else was I going to think?"

"You think silence means something. Sometimes, there's just nothing to say."

The night churned on. We watched a prime-time cop show—*NUMB3RS*—that I enjoyed, much to my surprise. It occurred to me that I never watched anything anymore that wasn't some kids' show. Imperceptibly, my knowledge of TV pop culture had been reduced to *SpongeBob* and *Bob the Builder.*

During a break in the local news, I said, "Dad?"

He grunted.

"Dad, I need to ask you something."

"What?" He turned again and faced me.

I sucked in a deep breath.

"Who's Kelly Hewins?"

He turned away and faced the TV for a long stretch. When he finally found words, he didn't look at me.

"Where did you hear that name?"

"I didn't hear it. I saw it."

"Where?"

"I was in the shed today, and there was a box—"

"That box is not yours."

"I know."

"So what were you doing rooting around in it?"

"I don't know. I was intrigued."

"So you just opened my stuff and went through it?"

"Well, yeah."

Dad pushed up from his chair and headed into the kitchen. I stood and followed him.

"Dad, who is she?"

"Somebody I knew a long time ago."

"That's it?"

"That's it."

I kicked at the floor. "Come on, man. This woman writes to you over the course of forty or so years, and that's what you give me? I read the letters, Pop. A casual acquaintance doesn't say the kinds of things she said."

"You had no right to do that." Dad shook with fury.

"You have no right to keep secrets from me."

"It's my stuff. It's my life," he boomed. "I decide what gets told and what doesn't."

"It's my life too, Pop."

"Not this. This has nothing to do with you."

I dropped my face into my left hand and massaged my eyes. Jesus. I considered the possible responses to that and decided to sidestep a deconstruction of the flaws in his logic, though I knew that this notion that his life existed separate from mine explained so much about how fucked up we were.

"If it has to do with you, it has to do with me," I said.

Dad set his hands on the kitchen counter and pushed weakly against it. Then he looked up at me.

"What all did you snoop through in that box?"

The question rocked me back.

"Your Navy papers and the letters. What else is there?"

"Nothing."

"Right."

"You just stay out of it."

"Dad, just tell me who she is."

"Somebody I used to know. There's nothing else to tell."

"Who's Dana?"

"Who?"

"One of the letters mentioned a Dana."

"That was her mom."

"Did you know her?"

"Yeah."

"The letter suggested that you knew her pretty well."

"I don't know. It's been a long time."

Dad looked drawn. I had turned this into an interrogation, and that wasn't my intent. I softened my voice and tried again.

"Look, Dad, I'm sorry about the box, OK? I didn't mean to rile you up."

"You should have left it alone."

"OK. But I didn't. Are you going to help me with this?"

"I've told you what there is to tell."

"But that's not anything."

"Exactly."

He made a circle around me and headed for the bed-room.

"I'm not going to let this go," I called to the back of his head.

He replied with a closed door.

SPLIT RAIL | JULY 1, 1979

I KEPT TO THE CLOSET long after I heard the angry words die down. I was half-afraid to come out because of what I might find and half hoping that if I held out long enough, we would wake up the next morning and the unpleasantness would be forgotten.

Marie knocked on the door.

"Mitch."

"Leave me alone."

"Mitch, come on out. It's over."

I sat still.

I held my breath ten seconds. Fifteen. Twenty. Twenty-five.

I blew it out and sucked a fresh mouthful of air.

"Mitch, come on."

I pulled back the sliding door and emerged, then crept toward the bedroom door.

"I don't believe you."

"No, Mitch, it's done. Come out. I want to say good-bye."

I opened the door. Marie stepped to the back wall, giving me plenty of room. A suitcase sat at her feet.

"Where are you going?" I asked.

"I'm going to stay with my sister in Billings for now. I don't imagine I'll see you again before you guys head back to Utah."

"OK."

"Mitch, are you all right?"

"Yes."

"I'm sorry about all this."

"OK."

"Come out to the living room. I'm sure your dad wants to apologize too."

She held out her hand, and I took it.

Dad sat in his recliner, his face drawn into a faraway look.

"Sport," he said.

I settled into the seat opposite him and said nothing. On the outskirts of our silence, Marie kicked up a storm of activity. She grabbed letters and bills and knickknacks and tucked them into her purse.

"You'll be there Friday, Jim?" she said on one pass through the living room.

"I said I would."

"Where?" I asked.

"Billings," Marie answered. "We're going to see a wise man about something."

"What?"

"Something that's been coming awhile."

"A divorce," Dad said. It was as though he were spitting out a hair. Marie shot him a hard gaze.

"Is this because I didn't clean up the mess?" I asked.

"Mitch, no," Marie said, sitting down on the couch. "Please don't ever think that. It just happened. It's nobody's fault."

Dad scoffed.

"It's nobody's fault," she repeated.

I don't think she was trying to convince me.

We sat there awhile longer, three islands of solitary thought, before LaVerne arrived. She helped Marie tote things to the waiting pickup, and when she met eyes with Dad, LaVerne smiled. Dad nodded slightly in acknowledgment.

"I'll come around and check on the place tomorrow, Jim," LaVerne said.

Dad waved her off.

"No need, LaVerne. Mitch and I have her covered. You'll be back on the job soon enough. Enjoy the break."

Marie made a last pass and plucked a few books off the shelves.

"I'll come back after you've gone back to work and get the rest of my stuff," she told Dad.

"Yep." He didn't look at her.

"Bye, Mitch," she said, offering a hug. I stepped into Marie's arms. I breathed in her fragrance and tried not to cry. I couldn't believe it.

After Marie walked out, I went to the window and pressed my face against it. I heard the pickup fire up, and then I watched it head down the access road, spitting dust in its wake. I lifted my hand and waved. I don't know if she saw it.

I heard Dad in the kitchen, digging into the refrigerator for another beer.

"It's just us men now," he called out.

"Yeah."

"We're going to have fun now."

I didn't answer. I hoped so.

I wasn't inclined to lay a bet on it.

Dad didn't object when I made a move toward the motorcycle, so I stuck to trails away from the house for much of the afternoon. Every now and again, I would cut through the main yard and down the access road, the longest, most uninterrupted stretch on the ranch. I rode until stopped by the steel gate, and there I lingered. I cut off the engine and stared down the road that led into Split Rail. Maybe Marie would turn around and come back and we would just try again. That would be nice, I thought. Couldn't we just do that?

Alternately, I grew agitated at myself over my weird longing for Marie. I knew well enough that she was as responsible as Dad for the way things had gone to pot, and I knew that if she came back, things wouldn't be better. I winced at the fresh memory of Dad's suggestion that he could get his gun and end it all for everybody. Terror welled inside me. If Marie came back, I thought, we might well find out if Dad could turn declaration into deed.

I whispered a prayer for all of us and hoped Marie stayed gone.

Dad had chased Jerry away. He had chased Marie away too. He and I were the only ones left.

As the sun beat down on me through the afternoon, I found it difficult to put off a return to the house. I grew thirsty. A sunburn clawed at my neck. I had eaten more slow-flying bugs than I cared to count.

I went back in. When I removed the helmet, the perspiration popped inside my ears. I rubbed at my neck, massaging the dust and sweat into grimy balls that I pressed and rolled, repeatedly, between my thumb and forefinger as I went up the steps and slipped into the house.

Shadows, enlivened by the late-afternoon sunlight, played on the walls. I skirted through the living room and headed to Dad's room. I opened the door and looked in. He wasn't there.

Back down the hall, I cut to my left at the dining room and pressed beyond it to the den. A cartoon played underneath the static on the set. Dad lay on the couch, blasting a baritone snore. I knelt down and retrieved a half-drained can of warm beer from in front of the couch. I carried it into the kitchen and poured the rest into the sink, and then I counted the empties. The one in my hand made eight. It was just before five thirty. I retreated to my room.

Dad's rapping at the bedroom door woke me.

"You in there?"

I sat up in bed, and the haze fell from my eyes.

"Yeah."

Dad came in. He looked like hell.

"Are you hungry?"

I shrugged. "A little, I guess."

"Come out and help me with some chores, and we'll go into town."

"I have to take a shower."

Dad belched.

"Chores first. Then shower. Come on."

I smelled the beer on Dad, but he gave no outward indication that a six-pack and beyond had impaired him. I followed him from the house, and he walked a perfectly straight line, right up to the pickup.

"Can I drive?" I asked.

"Nope."

I climbed in and barely managed to close the door before we were moving.

"Where are we going?"

"Got to find that herd."

Dad charted a course for the back side of the property, where I had spent the early part of the day, when Marie was still part of our lives. We hit the top of the hill, and the swale dropped below us. Cattle dotted the landscape.

"There they are," I said.

"Yep."

"What are we going to do?"

"You'll see."

Dad drove a half circle to the other side of the herd, drawing a bead on a calf standing apart.

He shut off the engine and popped open his door.

"Hop out, Mitch."

I did as I was instructed. While Dad dug around in the cab, I watched the Hereford. It walked toward us.

"It's coming."

"I know," Dad said. "Come over here."

When I got to the other side of the truck, Dad handed me a quart bottle with an oversized rubber nipple atop it. What looked like soapy water sloshed back and forth inside.

"Shake that up and give it to the calf. Hurry."

I shook the bottle like a maraca. "Like this?"

"Harder," Dad said. "Shake it up good."

The calf was upon us. He nudged his anvil head against my stomach and pushed.

"Hey!" I protested.

Dad laughed. "He knows it's dinnertime. Better give it up."

I presented the nipple, and damned if he didn't take it down to the nub. I wasn't ready for his prodigious sucking, which nearly pulled the bottle from my hands. I pulled back too hard, taking the nipple from the calf. He aggressively reclaimed what was his.

"Hold it steady, Mitch," Dad said. "He'll be quick."

In about a minute, the youngster drained the bottle. He sucked for a few more seconds, until he was satisfied that nothing remained, and then he ambled away.

"What did you think, sport?"

"That was pretty neat."

"Glad you think so," Dad said. He put an arm on my shoulder. "That's your chore for the week. Morning and evening, you feed that calf."

On the ride to the house, I asked Dad, "Where's his mom?"

"Oh, she's out there."

"Why do we have to do her job?"

"Because she won't."

We sawed on our chicken-fried steaks at the Tin Cup. I hadn't been terribly hungry when we came in, but when the huge platters were dropped in front of us—loaded with crispy steaks, mashed potatoes, sawmill gravy, and corn on the cob—I found my appetite.

I looked across the table at Dad. He looked good, for the first time all day. He wore his favorite shirt with little blue checks and mother-of-pearl snaps, a crisp pair of jeans, and his going-to-town boots. His Elvis-inspired hair had been sprayed into perpetuity; only a sledgehammer could crack it. His face, drawn and colorless earlier in the day, radiated. It was amazing what a shower could do. Both of us were testament to that. I had wiped away my grit and grime. The Quillen men cleaned up nicely for an evening in town.

Then, my overtaxed mouth unraveled our progress.

"Dad, why did she go?"

He frowned. "I'm trying to enjoy dinner."

"I know. But…"

"What?"

"I miss her, I think."

Dad gazed at his food and started eating again. "Yeah, well," he said. "You're just a kid. You don't know any better."

"Don't you miss her?"

"No."

"I thought since you were drinking so much that—"

"Look here," Dad said, pointing a finger at my face. "I don't want to hear about this from you."

"Quillen!"

Dad's head popped up, and he scanned the room.

"Jim, over here."

Dad turned to his left and smiled at someone behind me. I turned around to get a better look. A man in a cop's uniform waved.

"Come over here," Dad said, and the cop pushed up from his table and lumbered over.

"I didn't know you were back," the cop said. He towered over our table. I couldn't look him in the face. Instead, I stared at his meaty forearms and, under the left one, his gun.

"Just last night," Dad said. The cop dipped his head and made eye contact with me.

"Who's this?"

"This here's Mitch, my younger son."

"Pleased to meet you, Mitch," the cop said, extending a hand that swallowed my meek offering. "I'm Charley Rayburn."

"He's the police chief," Dad said.

"Yeah, yeah," Charley said. "And the dogcatcher. And the mayor. And a piss-poor wheat farmer, it seems."

I squeaked out a hello in return.

"So where's Jerry?" Charley asked Dad.

"Marines. He couldn't take the work."

"He's in for a surprise, isn't he?" They both laughed.

"And Marie?"

"She's gone too," I said.

Charley slapped Dad on the shoulder. "You're losing people left and right. Better keep a close eye on this young fella."

"You can bet on it." Dad bit off the words.

"Well, I'll be seeing you guys," Charley said, putting his hat atop his buzz cut. "Got to make my rounds."

Dad watched as Charley weaved through the restaurant and out the door. Then he turned to me.

"Eat up, Mitch, and keep your mouth full. I don't want any more words spilling out of it."

BILLINGS | SEPTEMBER 22, 2007

WHEN I CAME into the living room, Dad stood up and cut across my path to the kitchen. I followed him to the refrigerator. He turned away toward the dining room table. I poured a glass of orange juice and walked a line toward the seat opposite him. Dad stood up and glided back to the living room.

We chased each other around that house until midmorning, wordlessly, without circus music to highlight our movement. Only when I jangled my keys and reached for the door did Dad speak.

"Where are you going?"

"Grocery store."

"You need any money?"

"I've got it covered."

At Pioneer Park, I settled in at a picnic table away from the walkers and the din of the playground and the steady thumping of tennis players drawn by a sunny day. Given what I had come to do, I needed whatever solitude I could grab in such a public place.

I'd scrawled the number, fetched from directory assistance, on my left palm: 406-794-1978.

My phone sat in my right hand, open and ready to go.

I couldn't bring myself to punch in the numbers.

I closed the phone and stood up. I needed a walk first, if not a stiff drink.

I tried to noodle the situation out logically, even though the circumstances defied logic. The park fell behind me as I crested the hill. I played point-counterpoint the entire way.

To an extent, Dad was correct when he said it was his life. If there were things he wanted to keep close, what business was it of mine to contradict him?

And yet nearly everything that was screwed up about my family—the one I was born into, and the one I was raising— traced back to secrets. Some things need to be dragged into the light. This, I was certain, was one of those things.

OK, but what about this Kelly person? She bowed out years ago and said she was done. What if she had moved on with her life? What if it were an intrusion to bring this up now?

"Just stop," I said, aloud. She didn't step away because she lost interest. I needed only to think back a couple of days to remember that I was the guy who stared at a house I barely knew in a flailing hope that I would find a deeper understanding of not just my own life but also the lives of people I loved. Did I really think she had let this go?

I heard my own voice in my head. "If you don't make this call, you leave, right now. You go back, you give your old man a hug, you pack up your stuff, and you haul ass out of here. This is where the trail forks. Keep going, or go home. Do you think you will ever find peace—with him, with Cindy, with the rest of your life—if you do that?"

I jogged back to the picnic table.

Despite my resolve, I stared at the phone for twenty minutes more, rehearsing what I'd say and how I'd retreat if back-pedaling were needed, cataloging my questions (many) and my answers (few). Finally, I punched in the number.

The call was picked up on the first ring. A friendly sounding female voice, crinkled with age, beckoned with "Hello," and I nearly hung up.

"Hello," she said again.

"Kelly Hewins?"

"Yes."

"My name is Mitch Quillen. Do you know me?"

Silence came back at me. Four, five, six seconds of it. I pulled the phone away from my ear to see if the call was still connected.

"Hello?"

"I know who you are." The clear voice diffused. She said, "I always hoped I might hear from you."

"I found your letters to my father."

Her voice faltered. "Is Jimmy gone?"

"Oh no," I said. "He's still here in Billings."

"Oh good. Do you live in Billings, too?"

"Mrs. Hewins, I don't mean to be rude. But who are you?"

"Jimmy didn't tell you?"

"No."

She paused. "I'm your aunt. Jimmy's sister."

"What?" I said.

"I'm Jimmy's sister."

I scrambled to slow the scattering of my thoughts.

"His parents died in a wreck. He was an only child."

"Yes, I know. He and I were adopted out of the St. Thomas home in Great Falls."

"I've never heard of this. He said he lived at the orphanage until he joined the Navy."

"Well, I'm sorry to tell you that's not what happened. Jimmy and I grew up on a farm up here."

"Why wouldn't he tell me that?"

"Well, Mitch, I don't know. But I have some ideas."

This struck me as more than just another Jim Quillen lie. I was talking to my aunt, a relative I had discovered only by intruding on Dad. Time and circumstance had taken so many people from me, and here was someone I had found. I fumed that Dad, alone, had decided that I didn't need to know her.

Kelly's words filled my ears, and I watched the people in the park through a long gaze, one that rendered their movement in slow motion. They stepped through the minutia of their lives, oblivious to the fact that a fresh hole had been shot through mine.

"OK," I said. "What are your ideas?"

"Mitch, I'll tell you everything I can, after."

"After what?"

"After you tell me all about Jimmy. I haven't seen him since 1954."

I drew the outlines of the father I knew, a task beyond my means, given how scant my knowledge seemed to be. I gave Kelly the broad outline of how he and Mom met. I told of Jerry's arrival in 1960, mine several years later, the divorce, the rich years, the lean years when he and I never spoke, the years when he married Helen and the frost between us melted into a stormy spring of occasional phone calls.

Kelly proved a good listener and questioner. She expressed sympathy where I expected to hear it, such as when I told her about losing Jerry and Mom, and at other points she pressed for details, some that were beyond my grasp.

"Did Leila ever say anything about us? I sent all those letters through the years, and I half hoped that she or…what was the second wife's name again?"

"Marie."

"That she or Marie would press the issue with him."

"I couldn't say. Mom knew what Dad told her, but she never talked about it with me. Marie, I don't have a clue. I haven't seen or talked to her in almost thirty years."

"It doesn't matter, I guess," Kelly said. "I never heard from them. Or him."

Finally, I told Kelly about the phone calls that had drawn me to Billings—leaving out the bit about my own marital discord—and how I had found her letters.

"I have to tell you something," I said. "It's damned frustrating to try to figure out what his problem is now, why things happened the way they did all those years ago and now having this new stuff. I keep trying to get close to him, and I keep ending up farther and farther away."

Kelly laughed, but not in a manner suggesting that she found what I said to be funny.

"You're not alone," she said. "When Jimmy left the farm, he told us he would never come back and that we would never see his face again. I went down into the basement after he walked out, and I cried until I didn't have any tears left."

"Why?"

"Because I knew he meant it. Because I was happy for him."

"That doesn't make any sense."

"Have you got a little while, Mitch?" It was an odd question. We had been on the phone more than an hour.

"Yeah, sure."

"I'll tell you why."

Tears spilled down my face, driven by something so beyond my ability to rein it in that all I could do was turn at the picnic table and hide my eyes behind a hand lodged against my forehead.

Homer and Dana Elspeth chose a boy and a girl not to give lost children a home but with the craven hope of doubling the labor force on their tiny dairy farm. They got their wish through a legal transaction. They enforced it with threats, coercion, and beatings.

"I got it bad," Kelly said, recounting how Dana grabbed her long locks and pulled her to the ground when housework wasn't satisfactory. "Jimmy got it worse."

"Worse how?"

"He got whipped with straps. He got whipped with chains. I saw Homer bounce a horseshoe off his head one time."

"Jesus."

The taste of tin seeped into my mouth, and I realized that I had bitten my tongue.

"I saw Jimmy kicked face-first into cow manure. One time, he dropped a basket of fresh eggs, and Homer clubbed him with a two-by-four until Jimmy screamed for mercy."

"Just stop, OK? Please, just stop."

"I'm sorry," Kelly said.

Orphanages, scheming adoptive parents, a house marked by abuse and neglect—these things smacked of a century earlier. I knew nothing about it, of course, having not even a hint of it until that day, and still I reeled at the notion that Dad, just a generation older than me, would have known such horror. The naïveté he always accused me of harboring? Apparently, I was guilty of it.

"Didn't you go to school? Church?" I asked her.

"Sure. We both went."

"And nobody found out? Nobody did anything?"

"Who would find out? I can't speak for Jimmy, but I was too terrified to say anything. Who would have believed us? We were just poor farm kids. The families we knew, even if they knew what was going on, none of them were going to tell other people how to raise their kids."

I shook my head. "I don't know. I guess…God. I always figured Dad was so closed-off because of his folks dying in that car crash and growing up in an orphanage. I never imagined that it was because he was getting the shit knocked out of him by people who were supposed to love him."

"They didn't love us."

I reminded Kelly of the letter about Dana's death and burial. "Why did you bother? Why didn't you get away after you grew up and got married?"

"Mitch, I'll tell you something. She was a wretched woman. But…I don't know. I cared about her. That sounds strange, and maybe I can't really explain it, but she was as much a prisoner in that house as Jimmy and me. She got beat on just as much as we did. After Homer was gone, she was just an old, lonely woman, pining for this man that she knew she shouldn't have loved, but she did anyway. She didn't have anybody else."

"I guess I understand why Dad would run away from it all and never look back."

"That's why I never pushed him. We didn't have choices when we were kids. Later, he made a choice and left. I wanted to respect that. But I missed him, you know? I loved him. I still do."

On and on we talked, about happier times, too. I got details on her kids and their families, and her nine grandkids. I told her about Avery and Adia and our frustrating, joyful arrival at parenthood. We agreed that we owed it to our kids to be better examples of family than we had been given in our own lives. Long after we hung up, those words lingered in my ears. I knew that I had some work to do at home, just as soon as I could get back.

"Mitch," Kelly said, "are you going to tell Jimmy you talked to me?"

By way of answering, I first told her about his reaction to my finding the letters, and she wept again.

"I'm in the doghouse already, but yeah, I'll tell him. It's not going to matter much if I dig a deeper hole."

"There's something you should know, then."

"What's that?"

"I know why Jimmy won't talk to me. He's ashamed."

"I understand being ashamed. But I can't understand fifty-something years of silence."

Her voice cracked.

"It's bigger than that."

"Bigger how?"

She grew silent.

"Kelly?"

"Mitch, you need to know. Homer did bad things to him out in that barn."

My muscles went slack.

"What? What kind of things?"

"Jimmy would come into the house sometimes and he'd just walk past me as if I wasn't there. I'd look in his eyes, and it was like looking into a pit. He wasn't in there, you know?

"We would buck each other up. When things were bad at the house, we'd give each other a pep talk and try to keep our spirits up. But then there were other days when I couldn't reach Jimmy, when it was like I was all alone, because Jimmy had gone vacant."

She wept.

"I did the wash. Sometimes I found blood in Jimmy's underwear."

"Jesus Christ."

She whispered. "Yeah."

"Jesus Christ."

"Once," she said, "Jimmy told me, 'I'm going to kill that son of a bitch.' That shook me to my bones, because I knew there was a chance that he'd do it, or get himself killed trying."

I swallowed, clamping down on the bile in my throat.

"Remember how you said it didn't make sense, me crying for both sides when Jimmy left?" Kelly said. "It makes sense now. You can see that, right?"

I could. On the last warm day of the year, a chill blew through me, propelled by all the things I once yearned to know and now wished I had never heard.

SPLIT RAIL | JULY 1, 1979

DAD PAID THE BILL, and we stepped into the dusk. The summer evening, like a magnet, had pulled the people of Split Rail into town. Dad tipped his hat to old ladies who scooted past us on the uneven, weather-beaten sidewalk. They offered quick smiles and then turned back to their clucking. We walked on.

From the direction of the small town park—a strip of green with a swing set and a basketball hoop—I heard children laughing and smelled burgers grilling. I started toward the park, but Dad had other ideas.

"This way," he said, squeezing my right shoulder and turning me. In the wake of a passing pickup, we jogged across the asphalt to the front door of the Livery.

A good number of the town's men, and some of the hardier women, found their way to the bar that night. When Dad ambled in with me in tow, I saw that he had managed to make friends in town, judging from the hands raised in acknowledgment.

"Jim."

The proprietor came around the bar and headed our direction. He was a short man, with stubby legs that worked in double time to bring him to us. His eyes, tiny and intense, twinkled, and he mopped at the beads of sweat forming a conga line on his bald pate.

"Jim, great to see you. But he can't be in here." He pointed at me.

"Nick, this is Mitch," Dad said. "Mitch, Nick Geracie."

I nodded at the man, who twitched nervously.

"Pleased to meet you, young man," he said. "Jim, he can't be in here."

My father gripped Nick by the shoulder and pulled him in. "We've had a hell of a day, Nick, just a hell of a day. Wife's gone"—the cowboys nearest us tuned in—"and it's just us men now."

"Yes, well…"

"Your wife ever left you, Nick?"

"No."

"Well, I'll tell you something. It ain't too much fun."

"I guess not, but…"

"I came in to get a liquid remedy, if you know what I mean."

"Jim, the boy can't be in here."

Dad's eyes widened. I had seen this before. Nick didn't know that the joke was on him.

"Well, Nick, what do you think I ought to do here? This is my son."

"I don't know, Jim."

Dad cupped his hands around his mouth. "Anybody here want to buy a kid? He ain't much of a worker, but he'll talk a blue streak. I'll cut you a hell of a deal."

THE SUMMER SON

Laughter pealed through the room.

Dad shrugged.

"No takers, Nick."

"Very funny."

Dad leaned over to me. "You still want to go to that park?"

"Sure."

"Get going. I'm going to have a couple of beers, and then we'll head on home."

The fullness of night dropped on Split Rail. The last of the picnickers doused the flame in the grill, and the smaller children I'd heard zipping back and forth across the park had wound down. Now they sat in the grass or had already headed home.

Illuminated by a street light, three boys, all of them looking to be about my age, took turns flinging a basketball at the hoop.

I approached slowly. One by one, they became aware that I was closing in.

"Hey," I said.

"Hey back at you," said a skinny boy a few inches taller than me. He was stripped down to cutoff jeans and wore knee-high tube socks that left visible a chunk of thigh. His white hair, drenched with perspiration, flopped across his forehead and down his neck. The other two looked at me but didn't speak.

I stepped onto the blacktop, keeping my distance.

"Can I play with you guys?"

"Think fast," the skinny boy said, and he rifled the ball in my direction. I batted it and started dribbling. After I got a feel for the size and the texture of the ball, I lined up a shot from about fifteen feet. The ball ripped through the rim and settled into the chain net with a metallic snap.

The skinny boy retrieved the ball.

"All right, two on two," he said. He pointed at me. "Me and this kid against you guys."

My teammate—he introduced himself as Jeff—and I made short work of the game. Playing make-it-take-it basketball, we put a 15–2 loss on the other two boys. I'd played a lot of basketball in my life, and I made an instant connection with Jeff. We ran picks, made extra passes, and chased down rebounds. It was damned fun, at least for us. The other two, after absorbing their beating, said they had to go home.

"What about you?" I asked Jeff as the two boys cut opposite paths across the park.

"I can shoot baskets for a while."

I bounced a pass to the free-throw line, and he swished a shot. He slid to his right, and I gave him the ball. Another swish.

"Where'd you learn to shoot like that?" I asked.

"Right here."

His next shot caromed off the rim, and I gathered the ball, then dribbled backward and let my own shot fly. It clanged loudly off the backboard and into Jeff's hands.

"Where are you from?" he asked. "It sure ain't here."

"Nah, my dad lives here. I'm just visiting."

"Who's your dad?"

"Jim Quillen."

"I know him. Him and my dad are friends."

"Who's your dad?"

"Charley Rayburn."

"The cop?"

"The police chief."

"I met him tonight."

"Cool. He lets me hang out in town while he works."

He passed me the ball, and I sent it soaring toward the hoop. The sweet jangle of the chain net heralded my accuracy. Swish.

Split Rail's coming slumber could be seen across the town with each doused window light. Under the cover of the moon, my friend and I whipped through the dark, two boys without tether exploring the underside of town.

First, we headed to the Livery. I wanted to make sure Dad knew where I would be—and, just as important, that I knew where he was. Jeff suggested that we cut in behind the bar, up the alley. There, we slipped into the open back door, through the stockroom, and to the entryway to the bar proper. I peered around the corner and picked out Dad. He stood with two ranchers, his arms slung over their shoulders.

I waved but couldn't draw his attention. Mindful of Nick, whose back was to me, I took a step into the bar and flagged with vigor. Finally, one of the cowboys tapped Dad and pointed toward me. Dad sauntered over, and I could see in his uncertain steps that he had taken on a fair bit of alcohol in my absence.

"What's up, sport?"

"I'm going to be hanging around with Jeff."

"Jeff who?"

My friend stepped up, and Dad's face registered recognition.

"Where at?" he asked.

"Just around town."

"OK. Be good."

"I will."

Dad lurched back toward the bar.

"OK, let's go," I said to Jeff.

We beat a hasty exit back to the alley.

"Here," Jeff said. He plopped a warm can of Budweiser into my hand.

"What the—"

"Hey, the opportunity was there."

Before I could object, or decide if I wanted to, Jeff was off and running up the alley. I gave chase as best I could, the stumpy legs my father saddled me with rat-a-tat-tatting up and down on the gravel. Jeff's longer, graceful gait put steady distance between him and me, until I saw him only in silhouette, half in and half out of the street light when he came to a stop at the far end of the town's main drag. He waited for me to catch up.

Our evening was a smorgasbord of skulking, sneaking, and small-time crime. After I caught Jeff, he wrenched open a back door on the building and beckoned me to join him inside. I looked down the alley, making sure that I wasn't being watched, and then I slipped through. The darkness fell across my eyes as I stepped from half light to full-on dark.

"Jeff," I whispered. "*Jeff.*"

I rubbed my eyes. I dared not move until I could make out a crude outline of what was around me.

"Baaaaaaah!" When the hand hit my back and the sound hit my ears, I leapt from my skin and sent my can of beer rocketing skyward. It crash-landed in front of me and split a seam, spraying my pants with warm foam.

"Oh shit."

Behind me, Jeff exploded into giggles.

"You jerk," I said.

That aggravated his laughter, so much so that I had to join him, despite my best intention of being pissed off.

"That was hilarious," he said.

"What is this place?" I asked.

My eyes made the inevitable adjustment, and I could see Jeff and the outlines of the room. Just beyond Jeff, I saw something that looked like a staircase. To my right was a long, tall table, like a bar.

The sense that came most heavily into play, though, was smell. The air hung heavy, as if it had been trapped there a long time, and the acrid combination of must and mildew assaulted my nose.

"It's the old hotel," Jeff said. He knelt and rooted through what I figured to be the front desk. He stood up with a flashlight. He flipped it and put the bulb end under his chin, giving a wicked illumination to his face. He cackled.

"Knock it off," I said.

Jeff swept the flashlight across the room. The beam cut the darkness and brought ghosts to life, if only for a moment. It had been a long time since anyone had lingered here, and the items of value had long since been taken.

The carpet had been pulled up, the telltale padding left to rot. The railing from the stairway had been wrenched off. A few chairs sat scattered around the place, many missing a leg or two.

"How long has it been empty?"

"Forever," Jeff said. "My dad remembers coming here when he was a little boy, but I never saw it while it was open."

I pointed at the stairs. "You ever go up there?"

"Hell no," he said. "Those things are shot."

"It's so…spooky."

"Yeah, I know. I like coming here when Dad lets me hang out in town. It's why I have the flashlight. I'm going to cut it off, though, so nobody sees us."

Darkness dropped on us again.

"Let's have our beer," Jeff said.

"Mine's gone."

"I'll split mine with you."

Jeff pulled back the tab, dropping it through the open hole to the bottom of the can. He took a hearty swig, used his shirt to clean around the mouth of the can, then handed it to me.

The beer diffused when it entered my mouth. I hated the taste but thrilled at the sin. After I choked down a swig, I took another.

"Slow down," Jeff said. "Half of that is mine."

I handed it back. He chugged about half of what remained.

"You can have the rest," he said, handing the can to me. "I didn't backwash."

I downed the suds in two gulps. They tasted like turpentine. I wanted to wring out my tongue with a clean towel.

It was the coolest thing I'd ever done.

We returned to the heart of town by the sidewalk. Jeff pulled some breath mints from his pocket and gave me a couple. "Just in case," he said.

Ahead, Dad emerged from the Livery and came to a halt on the sidewalk. He put his hands on his hips and pushed his pelvis forward, stretching.

"Time for me to go," I said.

"Me too," Jeff said. He cut across the street to his father's office. Charley stood at the window, looking out on his seemingly quiet town. I wondered how much went on that he didn't know about. His own son could probably account for a good chunk of it, from what I'd seen.

I jogged up to Dad.

"Ready?" I asked.

The pickup sat a half block down the street, in front of the Tin Cup.

"All right," I said. "Walk straight. Charley's watching you."

"Aren't you a sneaky little bastard?" Dad said. He put an arm around my shoulders—for balance, from the weight he shifted to me, but also as a misdirection should Charley have been following us down the street.

"Get your keys," I said. "Are you OK to drive?" I worried what we would have to do if he said no.

"Yeah, I'm fine." Leaning more heavily on me, he fished the keys out of his pocket and tried to spin them around on his index finger. Only my quick hands kept them from hitting the ground.

Dad opened his door and climbed in. He popped the lock on the passenger door for me.

"Slow and easy," I said after he started the Ford.

"I know, Mitch."

He jammed the stick shift into first and eased the Ford into the street. I looked back through the rearview mirror, and no lights flashed on behind us. As the last of Split Rail fell away, I knew we were home free. I expelled my pent-up breath in a long whistle.

"I smell beer," Dad said. "Have you been drinking?"

I feigned surprise. "No. But you have."

A couple of seconds later, Dad jerked the Ford off the road, pushed his door open, dropped his head out, and leveled a blast of vomit at the ground. He scrambled out of the truck and staggered behind it, and I listened to the spasms as his stomach rebelled. The pungent scent of beer and stomach acid floated into the cab, and I slipped my mouth and nose into my shirt.

I jumped when Dad rapped his knuckles against the passenger-side window.

"Slide over," he said. His skin looked almost olive in color, and sweat pooled under his eyes.

I was driving after all.

BILLINGS | SEPTEMBER 22, 2007

I DUMPED THE STORY on Cindy as I sped back to Dad's place. Her reaction traced the arc of mine—first confusion, then intrigue, then sorrow, then horror.

"Mitch, this explains so much."

"What does it explain? I have more questions than ever."

"Don't you think this tells why he is the way he is? He never had an example of love in his life. It's no wonder he never let you in. He didn't trust anybody."

She was right. But this was big—bigger than anything I had seen. The canyon between us, always treacherous, was now laced with land mines. I yearned for closeness with this father of mine who refused to give it to me. Now I could see him more clearly than ever, and still I could not bridge the distance. What was I supposed to do with that?

"I don't even know where to start," I said.

Billings sped by as I waited for my wife, wiser than I in such things, to speak.

"I don't either, Mitch. I really don't."

"Shit."

"What?"

I rolled into an empty driveway at Dad's.

"He's not here."

"Mitch," Cindy said, "slow down and think this out. It's just as well, because you're not ready for him yet. You can't mess this up by charging in on him. Not now."

"I know. I'm going to be bouncing off the walls until he gets back. And then what?"

"Well, call me tonight and tell me how it goes."

"I will."

I found a note waiting for me on the kitchen table.

Mitch—

That's the longest shopping trip I've ever seen. Waited as long as I could. I'll be back in a few hours. We need to talk.

Your dad,

Jim

I had been gone awhile. A few hours from when? I had no way to know. I took my wife's advice and settled into the recliner and examined my meager options.

I'd promised Kelly that I would tell Dad we had talked, but the simple fact was that Kelly's fifty-some years of lighting a home fire was, at best, a secondary concern. I would tell him that I had spoken with her, but I had big questions about how to do it.

How much of our conversation would I reveal? How much should I reveal? It was a cruel twist to find that a life of yearning for a way to get from me to him could be sold out once I learned what that meant. I had known about Dad's burden for an afternoon, and it had pushed everything else out of my head. I wondered how he could have borne it for so long.

I began to peel back through the years, pulling out scraps of memory and holding them to the light, to see if I could spot lost truths hidden in the scenes and sounds I'd stashed. The images and the moments had my fingerprints all over them, so commonly were they retraced by me, and still I flipped them over and looked at them from new angles, hoping I would see something that had eluded me before.

Were I inclined to rationality, I would have conceded that it was pointless. I could find little instructive in what had gone before, at least as it pertained to my life. I also knew that I couldn't trust the pictures in my head. The moments weren't frozen in time; they changed, sometimes imperceptibly, as the years dragged on and my sensibilities shifted. Whatever came to me as I put down my time on earth affected my inward and outward views of the circumstances of my life and the lives around me. I was older, wiser, less tolerant, less motivated, more distant—and so was my lens. I could no longer trust my interpretation of long-past events. I could only try to do my best with what came at me now.

My thoughts turned to my mother, and to Marie. Did they know what I now knew about Dad's life? Had they too carried his secrets? If they had, what difference did it make now? Neither one could tell me so, or tell me what to do.

The move was mine, if I dared make it. I was pretty sure I had it in me, but first, I had to get rid of something. Before I was ready, the tears came, and as I sat there, my chest and shoulders heaving for this man—this beautiful, fucked-up survivor of a man—I knew that my tears fell also for me. I had wasted so much time in anger, holding a grudge for what he had done to me. It's not that I didn't have reasons, but my reasons didn't make much difference at such a distance.

I slipped the key into the lock on the shed and tried to turn it clockwise. The mechanism didn't yield. I jangled the key and tried again, and then in the other direction. Nothing.

"He changed the lock," I said, to no one.

The tools that could sidestep this problem lay inside the shed.

I took two steps backward, then lunged toward the door and kicked. The first shot from my ramrod leg rattled the building. The second loosened the bottom hinge. The third knocked out a screw. The fourth tore the little piece of brass from the plywood. Five more kicks higher up the door took care of the top hinge, and I was in.

SPLIT RAIL | JULY 2–6, 1979

DAD'S FEET COULDN'T FIND purchase once we reached the house. I grew weary as he shifted weight to me to compensate. His left arm hung heavy around my neck, and I held tight to his wrist and slipped my right arm around his backside as I guided him to the stairs.

"Come on. Five steps."

He flopped his right foot onto the first step. I strained to push him forward so the left foot would follow. Then we did it again and again and again and again.

Inside the house, I flipped on the living room lights to show him the path to bed.

"Just a little ways more."

We hurtled down the hallway as if we were running a three-legged race in an earthquake.

At the finish line, the bed, I gave Dad a shove and let inertia carry him the final few feet. He landed face-first on the mattress, crawled until he found a pillow, and then lay still. For all I cared, he could sleep in his clothes and wake up in his stink. I wrenched his boots off and nearly retched at the stench of sweat and leather steaming off his socks.

I knelt near his head and listened to his wispy breathing. He looked serene—unfair, considering.

"Good night, you old goat."

The next few days were stultifying in their sameness. I woke up early, grabbed the keys to the truck, and rode out to find the herd. The shunned calf needed only a day to associate me with the bottle. When he saw the truck, he came at a half run, hassling me until I offered him the nipple.

I named him King. I didn't consider him particularly regal, and I knew that his destiny lay in somebody's freezer, which was about as ignoble a fate as there was. But the name stuck, and he didn't mind. As he gulped down his morning meal, I scratched his head and talked to him because I had no one else.

After the feeding, I circled back to the ranch house and had my own breakfast—cold cereal, mostly, since I was fending for myself—and then cleared the house of Dad's empty beer cans. I found them everywhere—the floor, the bathroom, the yard. His consumption grew as each day fell off the calendar, and my worry grew with it. His days started with a beer and ended at the Livery. The in-between hours were soaked in alcohol, too.

After that first night in Split Rail, and for a few days afterward, I didn't see Dad up and moving until around noon. On my passes through the house, I sometimes crept to the brink of his bedroom to see how he was doing. He sawed on sleep, sometimes lying on his stomach, sometimes on his back. He would shed his clothes during the night, although not always fully. The first morning, I found him half in and half out of his pants—one leg free, the other hopelessly tangled in denim. I stifled laughter and left him to his mess.

Once he was up, his presence did little to stanch my loneliness. He grumbled through the day and the tasks he felt up to, mostly minor maintenance around the ranch— replacing fence posts, cleaning the barn, fiddling with the tractor, an ever-present beer at his side. We ate our meals together but in isolation, neither of us speaking very much. I staved off hunger with canned ravioli. Dad subsisted on cheese sandwiches. We passed through each other's days but didn't make much of an impression, at least not until night came and delivered us to our respective downtown mischief.

Mostly, I rode my motorcycle as long and as far as it could take me. I always found a fence, though, whether put there by a rancher who had come before or by my own heart. I yearned to set a course—any direction would do—and ride for the horizon, but I also knew that I could never catch it, and that I would miss Dad once I left.

I always returned to the house.

Friday morning, Charley Rayburn rolled up into the driveway in his patrol car. He and Jeff climbed out.

I saw them from the living room window. Dad, up early, was in the bathroom, getting ready for his trip to Billings.

My heart raced as I heard their footsteps on the stairs. Had Charley found out about our mischief from the few nights earlier? Briefly and stupidly, I considered running out the back, but where would I go? The knock came, followed by Dad's admonition to open the door.

Charley smiled at me through dark glasses.

"Hey, Mitch. Is your dad around?"

I looked at Jeff. His face was a blank slate.

"He's in the back. I'll get him. Come on in."

They stepped inside, and Charley doffed his hat.

"Who is it?" Dad bellowed.

"Charley and Jeff," I said.

"Just a sec."

Charley scanned the living room while Jeff fidgeted next to him. I looked across the room too, to see if anything revelatory had been missed in my daily cleaning up. The tension choked me.

"How are you, Charley?" Dad stepped into the room wearing his Sunday best: a button-front shirt, slacks, and his stepping-out boots. "What are you doing here?"

Charley said, "I figured since these two young guys hit it off so well, maybe they could hang out together. I've got some business up in Judith Gap, so I thought I'd drop on by before I left."

I exhaled.

"I'm headed down to Billings," Dad said. "But LaVerne Simms is coming by to watch Mitch. If you're OK with her looking after Jeff, it'll be fine, won't it, Mitch?"

"Yeah, absolutely," I said.

Dad and Charley chatted at Charley's patrol car. I turned to Jeff in the living room.

"I thought he'd found out about the beer."

"Nah, he doesn't know," Jeff said. His blithe surety set me only slightly at ease.

"Where's your dad going?" he asked me.

"Him and my stepmom are getting divorced."

"Wow, really?"

"Yeah."

"I don't know anybody whose folks are divorced."

"Mine are. This will make two for Dad."

"So you live with your mom?"

"Yeah."

"Where?"

"Olympia, Washington."

"Wow. I think that would be weird."

Jeff made me feel self-conscious. It's not like I could do anything about divorce. I was just a kid. Besides, it wasn't that weird. I lived with my mom and I went to school, just like other kids. Every other summer, I saw my dad. It was no big deal. I knew a lot of kids whose parents were divorced. I wasn't used to someone making a federal case out of it.

"What do you feel like doing?" I asked.

Jeff carried my pellet gun as we skulked through tall grass at the base of the buttes. I fell in behind him as we walked diagonally across the incline. I had no idea what we were tracking—I don't think Jeff did, either—but it was fun to pretend like we were trailing a mountain lion or something equally terrifying.

We rode on my motorcycle after saying our good-byes to our fathers. The ride had been ridiculous. Alone, I was too big for the Honda. With Jeff—older, taller, and heavier— riding behind me, the bike groaned under our bulk. We left the motorcycle sitting on the road.

"Hey, city boy, are you ready if we see a mountain lion?"

"I don't think our gun is big enough," I said.

"Forget the gun. It won't help. You know how you get rid of a mountain lion, right?"

"No."

"You throw a handful of shit right in his eye."

"Come on."

"No, seriously, that's how."

"Where am I supposed to find that?"

"Just reach into your pants."

Jeff cackled. He had put one over on me and had a laugh at my expense, but it was pretty funny. Still, I hoped I wouldn't have to find out if he was right.

We decided to head back when we saw the lightning crack down from the gathering dark. It looked like a Montana summer cloudburst, a brief, thunderous drenching, was galloping our way. I sure didn't want to be far from shelter when it hit.

We'd just started down the hill when Jeff came to a halt.

"Don't move," he whispered. I stopped, and I ran my eyes across the hillside in front of us, trying to pick up what he saw. A snake, maybe? Another mouse?

Then I saw the bird, about ten yards in front of us, perched on a green ash tree.

I watched Jeff raise the barrel and sight it. Before my protest could well up in my throat, he pulled the trigger and dropped the bird. Its body toppled from the branch and fell to the ground.

"One shot!" Jeff squealed. He took off on a run to see what he had done. I followed, amazed that it had unfolded so quickly.

The pellet hit the bird below the eye, exploding the feathers in blood and rendered skin. The eye remained open, staring back at us.

"That was great," Jeff crowed. "Did you see what I did? One shot."

"Why?" I pushed Jeff in the chest, and he dropped the gun.

"What do you mean?"

"Why would you shoot a little bird like that?"

"Why not? We've been shooting at stuff all morning."

"Yeah, rodents. Not birds. Look at him."

"Jeez, man, settle down. I didn't mean anything by it."

I pushed him again. "It was stupid."

"OK, man, take it easy."

I pushed him again, and Jeff got mad.

"Stop pushing me, Mitch."

I went to push him again, and as soon as my fingers touched his chest, Jeff belted me across the left jaw. It didn't hurt at first, but my legs went rubbery as the tingle radiated across my face. Jeff grabbed me by the shirt and shook me. "I don't want to fight with you, Mitch, but stop pushing me. I'm sorry I killed the bird. OK?"

"OK," I said.

As soon as he let go, I took off down the hill. When I kicked the motorcycle to life, Jeff figured out what I was up to. "Hey!" he said, but by then, I was spitting up dust on the way back to the house. A walk would do him some good. Jeff said he was sorry, but by the time he walked all the way back in what was coming for him, I could be sure that he really was.

LaVerne Simms looked at me askance when I came in.

"Where's Jeff?"

"He's coming. He wanted to walk."

She looked at me with a smirk, one that suggested she wasn't satisfied with my explanation.

"I hope he hurries. It looks bad out there." She turned back to her book.

I crept deeper into the living room.

"What are you reading?"

She held up the book, and I read the title aloud. "*A Woman of Substance*, Barbara Taylor Bradford. Do you like it?"

"It's good," she said. "Intriguing."

"Would I like it?"

She laughed. "Maybe. But I doubt it."

"I like to read," I said.

LaVerne peered at me over her glasses.

"Yes, Mitch. So do I."

I got the message. I sat down opposite her and massaged my throbbing jaw.

Jeff dragged in about fifteen minutes later. His hair lay flat on his head, held down by the residue of the rain that had hit him. His T-shirt and pants were soaked.

"Good lord, boy, get in here," LaVerne said, standing up and fussing over him. "What happened to you?"

"Got caught in a gullywasher," he said, gulping for breath.

"Why did you walk? Couldn't you see it coming?" LaVerne, like any rancher, knew what a storm in summer could bring. The rain fed the land, but woe be unto those who had nowhere to hide when the lightning came cracking down. I knew from experience that a cowboy looked skyward not just to tell the time but also to be vigilant against a storm. The cloudbursts appeared and moved on quickly, but they could wreak damage in so short a stay.

"I told you, he wanted to walk," I said, shooting a look at Jeff.

"Yeah, that's right," he said. "I just wasn't thinking."

"No, you weren't," LaVerne said, clucking her tongue as she headed off to see if she could find some dry things for Jeff.

LaVerne cooked hamburgers and homemade french fries, and I tore eagerly into the first decent lunch I'd had all week. Jeff wasn't talking to me, which was just as well. He'd gotten his.

Jeff had been lucky; he came out of the storm with nothing more than wet clothes and hurt feelings. The longer we sat there, the more I regretted abandoning him, even though I was pissed at what he had done. He must have been terrified, hopscotching all the way back to the house as the thunder and lightning roiled around him. I watched him glumly eat lunch, and my smugness over my revenge lost its luster.

After lunch, Jeff offered me a handshake and a single word: "Truce?" I accepted. There was no reason not to.

The storms rolled in all day, pinning us down in the house. I hauled out board games—*Yahtzee, Battleship, Connect Four*—and Jeff and I lay on the floor in the den and played.

We were restless, though, and the afternoon slogged by. I began looking for excuses to get outside, the weather be damned.

"LaVerne," I said, "what am I going to do about that calf?"

"We'll keep an eye outside," she called back to me. "When we see a break, we'll go get him fed."

Later, back in my room, Jeff suggested another game.

"Do you have a pencil in here?" he asked.

I dug through the drawer in the desk and found one.

"Is the eraser good?"

"Yeah," I said. "Why?"

"I'll show you."

Jeff called the game *Man or Mouse*, and it involved neither skill nor strategy. It was simply a test of tolerance. Jeff flipped the pencil upside-down in his right hand and began rubbing the eraser on the back side of his left hand, right on the long bone that leads to the middle knuckle. Rubber flakes left the eraser and drifted across his hand.

"You just do this to the other guy," he said. "You just keep rubbing and rubbing, for as long as he can take it."

"That doesn't look so bad."

"You can go first, then," he said.

Put off by Jeff's enthusiasm, I offered my right hand, and he grabbed hold of my wrist and pushed it down to the table.

"Hold it still," he said. Then he started to work the eraser. At first, it kind of tickled, but after a half minute or so, I began to understand how the attrition worked. The eraser built up friction against my skin, and the small area where Jeff insistently rubbed began to grow warm. Not long after that, the pain set in. I winced and turned my head a bit.

"Ready to give up?" Jeff asked.

"Not even close."

He bore down hard, shortening the strokes with the eraser and digging deeper. I watched the thin outer layer of skin peel off. Pain shot to my hand as the eraser tore at the exposed flesh.

"Had enough?"

"Nope." I spat out the word through a grimace.

As the blood began to flow, I heard Dad's pickup roll up.

"Stop," I said.

"You're a mouse," Jeff taunted me.

"No, my dad's here."

My hand felt as though it were on fire. I pushed open the door and hightailed it across the hall to the bathroom to find a bandage. Behind me, Jeff laughed and called me a pussy.

We stepped into the ethereal light that followed the summer storm. Sunrays punched openings in the gray clouds overhead. The world smelled clean—its odors washed away and the air shocked into neutrality by lightning.

"Come on, boys," Dad said. "Let's go on in to town."

I remembered something.

"What about King?"

"Who?" Dad said.

"The calf."

"We'll get him tonight when we come back."

"It'll be dark. I think we should do it now."

Dad looked at me, and I gave him a pleading look back. "Fine. Hop in."

I piled into my usual place when three rode in the truck: the middle. As I sidled up to Dad, I smelled alcohol. Maybe LaVerne had smelled it too. She had taken a hard look at him when he sent her home.

"Where is he?" I asked Dad.

"He's got to be around here somewhere."

Dad looped around the herd, and we scanned the pasture, our searching eyes looking for the lone calf. He wasn't there.

Dad pulled the truck to a stop.

"You guys hop out and fan out across here and see if you can find him."

Jeff and I walked diagonally away from each other, tromping through the high grass that had been baked to a golden brown. Water from the storm soaked my shoes and pants. A few hundred yards out, I reached the edge of a draw. I scanned the gulley until my eyes settled on a lump of black.

I didn't need a closer look to know.

"Dad!" I screamed.

As Dad and Jeff came on a run from opposite directions, I clambered into the draw and pushed through the grass to my calf.

I reeled in horror. The crack of lightning that got him singed his legs and blasted a fleshy, charred hole in his side. King's thick tongue hung from his mouth, and his dead eyes stared at me. I stood and stared back.

"Jesus," Dad said.

"Look at that," Jeff said.

Dad backed the pickup to the draw's edge while Jeff waved him on. When Dad had told me what we were going to do, I said I was staying with King. Dad tossed a length of rope down to me.

"Get it tight around his leg," he said. "You know how to tie a double knot?"

"Yeah," I said.

King smelled of burned hair. I looped the rope around his leg and tied it. I gave Dad the thumbs-up, and he went back to the cab and fired up the truck again, then set it in gear.

The leg didn't move once the rope went taut; rigor mortis had set in already. King's carcass made a sickening sound as it slid up the wall of the draw. Once it crested, I scrambled up behind it. Dad was already untying him.

"It's one big lift, boys, into the bed of the truck," Dad said. "I'll get the ass end of him. You guys hold his head."

King's black eyes stared at me, accusing, as we hoisted him. I looked away.

Dad broke the quiet of our ride into Split Rail.

"What happened?" he said, nodding at my fresh bandage.

"Snagged my hand on a tree," I said. I was becoming quite the inventive liar.

Jeff jabbed me in the ribs. I jabbed him back, harder.

In town, we saw that Charley was back. Jeff asked to be let out at the police station.

"You want to come, Mitch?" he asked.

I didn't, but Dad made the choice for me. "He'd love to," he said, pushing me toward the door. "I'll be over at the Livery."

I nodded and then followed Jeff inside the redbrick corner building, where we saw Charley fiddling with paperwork at his old Corona.

He looked at us over his bifocals when we entered.

"Hey, if it isn't the Hole in the Head Gang," he said, chuckling. "You fellas have a good time?"

"Yeah," we answered in dishonest unison.

I scanned the room. It was the first police station I had been in, and it was scarcely bigger than my living room in Olympia. There was room for Charley's desk, a small kitchen area with a sink, a bulletin board (there really were wanted posters), and against the north wall, a single cell. A gaunt, haggard man peered at me, and I jumped a little when I spotted him. He was maybe forty years old, his thinning hair askew, with gray stubble that ran down his neck, nearly to his collar.

"Who's this?" Jeff said, walking toward the cage.

"Just leave him be," Charley said. "That's who I was getting in Judith Gap."

"What did he do?" Jeff asked. I was embarrassed for the guy, being talked about where he could hear it.

"Never you mind."

"I don't mind talking to 'em, Charley," the prisoner said. His lumpy words fell from his mouth like oatmeal.

"Suit yourself, Pete," Charley said, not looking up from his paperwork. "Just keep it clean."

Jeff stepped closer to the cage, and I wandered over, staying a bit behind him.

Pete stared at his feet for a few moments as he considered what he would say. Finally, he looked up at us.

"Boys, I been bad pretty much my whole life. Didn't care about school. Never could hold down much of a job. Drank too much." At that last bit, he licked his lips. "Anyway, I guess what I'm sayin' is, I messed up a lot. So take it from me and don't mess up like I do. Ain't that right, Charley?"

"Yeah, Pete, that's right."

"That's it?" Jeff said.

"Pretty much," Pete said.

"Great," Jeff said, rolling his eyes. "Thanks a lot."

"All right, step away, boys," Charley said. He stood and put on his hat. "Pete, I'm gonna scoot over to the Tin Cup and get you some dinner. Don't go anywhere."

Outside, I asked Charley, "What did he do?"

"Beat the hell out of his wife and took off. Made it as far as Judith Gap before he decided he needed a drink. They picked him up after he got into a fight."

"Man," I said.

"Yeah, well, if they weren't dumb, we'd never catch 'em."

SPLIT RAIL | JULY 6, 1979

RAIN DRIBBLING ON MY LIP brought me around. My eyes opened, and I saw Charley Rayburn's face staring back at me. A fat droplet slid off the brim of his cowboy hat and shattered against my face.

"Are you hurt, Mitch?" Charley asked.

"I…I don't think so. What happened?"

"You crashed."

Water slid past on the windshield. The strobe from Charley's patrol car lit the scene in alternating blue and red.

"Stay put," he said.

I turned my head to the right, and a dull ache spread through my shoulders. Dad sat next to me, staring straight ahead, with blood flowing from his nose, across his mouth, and onto his shirt.

Charley appeared at Dad's side and pulled open the door.

"Put this on your nose, Jim. It will stop the blood," Charley said, handing Dad a handkerchief.

Charley stood outside the truck, staring into the truck at us. His sopping uniform clung to his body.

"Jesus Christ," he said. "What were you guys doing?"

When Jeff and I left the police station, we renewed acquaintance with Split Rail, whipping through backyards by scrambling over chain-link fences and then lighting out across the landscape, without fear (or suppressing fear) of what awaited us there. The adrenaline surged through my body as I hit the ground on a dead run past children, families gathered around a grill, and more than once a territorial dog. By the time anyone figured out what the hell was going on, we would be over the next fence, trailed by a "Hey!" It was thrilling, and it got my mind off what had happened to King.

Then the storms moved in again, short-circuiting our fun. Jeff and I hightailed it back to the bar and sneaked in through the alley. We stayed low as we moved into the main area of the bar, and I crab-walked to where Dad stood talking with three cowboys I didn't know. Jeff fell in behind me.

"Sport, what are you doing?" Dad said, pulling me in close and mussing my hair.

"Just getting out of the rain."

"You boys sit down here."

We did as we were told, seemingly to the irritation of Dad's friends. It didn't take Nick Geracie long to sniff us out.

"Absolutely not," he said, walking to the table and wagging a finger. "You guys get out of here. Jeff, you ought to know better. Get out of here, or I'm telling your father."

"But, Nick," Dad protested. "It's raining outside."

"Yeah?" Nick said. "Maybe you ought to take yourself and that boy home."

Dad looked at me and shrugged. We wouldn't be going home. That much was clear.

On the front stoop of the bar, protected from the rain by the awning, Jeff and I debated what to do. He wanted to head back to the police station, but I had no interest in seeing Pete again. As we thumbed through our ideas, I watched Marie's Skylark pull up in front of the Livery.

When she stepped out, Jeff whistled. She wore a black dress cut to here that was entirely inappropriate for the weather or the place. Not that anybody was going to complain, least of all two boys still a few years away from being in the presence of raw sex.

Marie scooted down the sidewalk toward us as fast as her four-inch heels would allow. She brushed past me to Jeff.

"How have you been?" she said, wrapping him in a hug. "It's been so long since I've seen you."

"Fine, ma'am."

"And your dad?"

"He's fine too."

"Well," she said. "I better get inside. Too stormy out here."

She slipped through the door, never giving me a glance. Jeff stared after her.

"What was that?" I said.

"I don't know. It was pretty cool. She smells great."

Jasmine. I had smelled it too—that night, as it mingled with the scent of rain, and many times before.

Jeff bailed on me and headed back to the police station. I cut through the raindrops to the alley and breached the storeroom. I hid behind some stacked pallets and watched through the doorway.

Marie flitted around the bar, not spending too much time with anybody and yet managing to be the center of attention. Dad made a concerted effort not to acknowledge her, which of course everybody noticed, making his denial of her all the more futile. He moved to the other side of the table, putting his back to her. He abandoned that when the dances of his buddies' eyes—in concert with Marie's migrations—enraged him.

Marie upped the ante by draping herself across some rancher, and Dad called. He walked over to the table and slammed his fist on it, hammering silence across the bar.

"Get your fucking hands off of my wife," he growled at the guy. Marie cuddled in closer and fixed Dad with a wicked grin.

"Get your hands off of my wife," Dad said, "or get your ass outside."

The rancher stood, ready to oblige, and Dad stepped aside to let him pass. Once the rancher's back was turned, Dad cracked a chopping right hand into his kidney. The rancher, a tall drink of water, crumpled. As the man curled on the floor, Dad spat on him.

Nick Geracie and most of the bar patrons converged amid a tangle of pushing and angry words.

"I told you already to go home, Jim," Nick said. "Now go, or I'm calling the cops."

"But..." Dad sputtered.

"But nothing. You go. You're not welcome here."

Nick wheeled around and faced Marie.

"You go too, Mrs. Quillen. I don't need the kind of trouble you're bringing to my place."

She stood up and pointed at Dad.

"I'm not going until he's gone."

Nick looked at Dad and pointed him toward the door. The rancher, the pawn in Marie's game, was just climbing to his feet as Dad walked past. Every eye in the place watched his exit.

I caught up with Dad on the sidewalk, and we did our usual gig. I walked with him to the pickup—quickly, for fear that Charley Rayburn would be upon us. Dad got in and drove until we were outside of town. I slid across the bench seat to the driver's side, and he walked around the front of the truck. Halfway around, he stopped and screamed, and I flinched. He slammed his fist on the hood, then came to the passenger side, opened the door, and fell into his seat. "Go home," he said.

Charley returned to my side of the truck.

"Mitch, can you climb out of there?"

"I think so." I looked over at Dad, who was already out.

Gingerly, I pushed off the seat and out the door. I saw Dad at the front of the pickup, which sat nose-first in the gutter lining the road. He was assessing the wreck. I went over to take a look. The grille was pushed in, but there was no sign of internal damage.

"It's OK to drive, I think," I said.

Dad turned. The rain had diluted the blood from his nose and spread it across his face.

"You think?"

He backhanded me across the jaw, and the force of the blow knocked me into the mud.

"You goddamned idiot," Dad said. He reached down to grab me by the shirt. I braced myself for another blow, but it never came. Charley pulled Dad away and threw him against the pickup.

"You stay there, Jim," he said. "You put your hands on the hood, and don't move."

Dad did as he was told.

"Here's what I want to know," Charley Rayburn said as he paced our living room floor. "Why the hell was Mitch driving?"

Once Charley had ascertained that we didn't need a hospital, and once he had bulled Dad into submission, he folded us into the back of his police cruiser and led the tow truck to the ranch. The drive had been filled with his telling us how lucky we were. Now, he started the interrogation.

"I was drunk," Dad said. Dried blood caked his face, which had slammed across the dashboard, turning loose a gusher from his nose.

"And is this a regular occurrence, using your minor son as a chauffeur when you tie a few on?"

Dad said nothing. Charley looked at me.

"It's happened before," I said.

"When?"

I looked at Dad. He didn't look back. I figured a little more truth wasn't going to make a difference.

"Every day this week."

Charley leaned in on Dad and put a stare on him that Dad couldn't find the gumption to return.

"I'm going to ask you just one time," Charley said, "and you better give me a straight answer. Had you been drinking when you drove my kid back to town tonight?"

"No," Dad lied.

"You're sure of that, are you?"

"Yes."

Charley turned to me. The throbbing in my head grew more pronounced.

"Is he telling the truth?"

"Yes," I lied.

Charley stared at me for a few uncomfortable moments, and then he turned to Dad, whose eyes fixated on the ground. Finally, he came back to me.

"OK, Mitch. Tell me what caused the wreck."

I took a deep breath and started in.

"Well, I was driving, and it was hard to see with all the rain. I saw a deer run out in the road, and I slammed on the brakes. The truck started sliding in the mud. That's what I remember."

"That's it?"

"Yeah."

"So let me make sure I've got this straight," Charley said, his voice rising. "A boy has been driving on my roads at night all this week, and tonight he wrecks the pickup because he can't see and can't drive in the conditions because he's eleven goddamned years old and shouldn't be behind the wheel in the first place. Is that about the size of it, Jim?"

Dad slumped in his chair.

"Yes."

Charley took off his hat and ran his fingers through the stubble of his crew cut.

"I ought to lock you up. Between what happened at the Livery and what happened out there, I really should. This could have turned out so much worse than it did, for both of you. So listen up, Jim. I want you to stay out of that bar. You got me? If I see you in there, I'll put your ass in the clink in five seconds flat, and you know me well enough to know I'll do it. You need to stay up here and take care of this boy. He shouldn't be in these kinds of situations. This is not his fault, do you understand? It's yours. If you hurt this boy, I'll make you wish you were never born. Am I clear?"

"Crystal," Dad said. "It doesn't matter. We're hauling out for Utah in the morning."

Charley ran his fingers through his hair and then slipped his hat into place.

"Well," he said, "that's probably for the best."

BILLINGS | SEPTEMBER 22, 2007

DAD'S SECRET HAD NOWHERE TO HIDE. I had kicked in the door of its sanctuary, and now it lay bare for anyone to see. The audience for this lie consisted of just one man, and I waited silently for his arrival, even as the rage boiled inside me.

I had almost missed it. At the bottom of Dad's box, I found pictures of me spanning my school days. Not just the early years, when Dad was still in my life, but later, too, after we'd lost Jerry and Dad and I had retreated into silence. On the back of a photo, Mom had jotted the year and the grade, and a taste of bittersweet filled my mouth. My heart brimmed at the realization that he'd had these pictures of me even as I denied him my attention. Seeing Mom's handwriting where I didn't expect it took my breath. I lingered over the photos, and her words, remembering.

I was closing the box when I saw the corner of the envelope peeking from the fold of the cardboard, a wisp of paper gone yellow with age.

Mom's perfect cursive script crossed the envelope, inscribed, simply, "Jim."

July 3, 1971
Dear Jim,

I think we both knew this day would come, and I think we both know it's for the best. The cuts and unkindnesses have come from both of us, and for a long time, but it would not be right for me to leave without apologizing. I will spend the rest of my life regretting what I did to you, and that is without regard to anything you've done to me. It was wrong, and it never should have happened. I am so sorry.

This may be difficult for you to believe, but I do not consider this marriage a failure, even though divorce is where it is going to end. Every time I look into our boys' eyes, I see pictures of you and me. Jerry is so like you, it makes me laugh. Mitch, I'm afraid, isn't like either of us, and maybe that's a good thing. He has a beautiful spirit. We made that together.

Somewhere, at the very core of all of that, there is still a 19-year-old girl who thought you were just about the most amazing thing she had ever seen. She's buried under a lot of years of struggling and fighting, and she's weary now, but she's still there. I hope to rediscover some of her once I get to Washington. I've missed her. Maybe you could find him again, too.

I'll miss you. I love you.
Your wife (at least for a little while longer),
Leila

I waited for him. Three o'clock came and went, and I had long since expected him to roll up, to find the letter sitting on the kitchen table. I had pushed everything off to make sure he didn't miss it. The porcelain salt and pepper shakers rested on the floor, shattered and spilling their contents on the linoleum.

I was placid, at least outwardly. I could wait all day. I could wait longer than that. I already had.

Dad had called me some variation on "candy ass" more times than I could begin to remember, but it wasn't until his pickup hit the driveway that I gave honest consideration to the idea that he might be right. In that moment, my afternoon of defiance—a pose so easily struck when I was in the house alone—turned to deep dread. The shed doors, blown off their hinges by my angry feet, lay in a heap in the yard. He would surely see that, surely know what I had done and what I had found, and there would be no more dodging what we had spent this week, and years before it, dancing around.

That's what I wanted. A showdown. A let's-lay-our-cards-on-the-table, free-flowing exchange of invective. Like a petulant child, I had pointed and pouted, and I was about to get what I asked for. In that moment of certitude about what was coming, I also found unwanted clarity. This thing between Dad and me—this rock that we couldn't roll off the only road between us—was going to blow sky-high. Only in that moment did I consider the collateral damage, and when I did, my heart seized up.

Dad came through the door slowly.

"Why, Mitch?" he said when he saw me. "Why can't you just leave it alone?"

My legs buckled. I steadied myself and grabbed the letter from the table.

"Why did she apologize to you? What reason in the world did she have to apologize to you?"

With trembling fingers, Dad took the letter from me and reacquainted himself with the words that he surely knew. They had been important enough to him to keep all these years, just like the letters from his sister.

Finally, he sighed. The long, heavy release did nothing to cut the tension.

"What do you think you know about your mom and me?"

I took a hard step toward him.

"I'm not doing this answer-a-question-with-a-question bullshit. You answer me first."

"Goddammit, Mitch, I'm going to tell you what you want to know. Just answer my question."

I took time to consider my words, even though my tongue had been pregnant with them for as long as I could remember.

"I know that you were awful to her. I know that you cheated on her. I know that you disregarded her. I know that when she finally had enough and left you, you didn't give two shits about us. You just let us go."

Dad didn't flinch.

"Your mother told you all of this, did she?"

That stopped me cold. If she had, I didn't remember it. I fast-forwarded through my memories and was hard-pressed to think of a time that she had ever bad-mouthed Dad. Mom saw the possibilities in everything and the best qualities in everyone—even the people she had no reason to trust. People like Dad.

"Not in so many words, no, but I know what I know."

Dad sat down in his recliner, and he waved me to the couch. I took a seat and kept my eyes on his.

"I was a bad husband. You're right about that. I worked too much, I was gone too often, I took Leila for granted, and I spent evenings in bars that I should have spent at home, with you and Jerry and your mom. But I never cheated on her."

I didn't believe him. "OK," I said. "Even if that's true, why did she apologize to you?"

He waited an uncomfortable while to answer.

"Because she cheated on me."

I wanted to punch him in his lying face. I reeled at the gall of his dropping such a scurrilous lie on me about my mother, one he knew I couldn't refute now that she wasn't around to shame him for what he had said.

I sat and I listened as he followed with a bunch of platitudes about the woman he had just called a whore.

"Now, don't get me wrong, I'm not knocking Leila. I didn't give her much to hold on to, and she got lonely. She was a young woman with a lot to offer and a husband who wasn't giving her the attention she needed. Hell, as much as it bothered me, I understood it."

My bile bubbled over.

"You're a fucking liar."

"I'm not, not about this."

"You're the cheater."

"Nope."

"You are such an asshole. You act like I don't know what I know. Do you remember the night before Jerry left? I was fifteen feet away while you fucked that girl. She wasn't your wife. Don't you sit there and tell me you're not a cheater."

"Hell, that was years after this. I'm not talking about that, and I didn't do anything that Marie wasn't doing herself. I'm talking about me and your mother."

"And I'm saying that once a cheater, always a cheater."

Dad threw the letter at me.

"Read it again, Mitch. Does that sound like a woman who's been cheated on? Use your goddamned head."

"Fuck you."

He pushed the letter at me. "Read it."

I grabbed it from his hands and read it again. And that sinking feeling came back, the same sensation that cascaded through me when Dad pulled up. Much as I wanted to believe otherwise—I had built my identity on believing otherwise—I knew he was telling me the truth. I could internalize it. But I couldn't acknowledge it. Not then. Not there. Not to him.

Instead, I took the offensive. This scene in my head had played out in my head so many times. Not once was I rocked back on my heels. I strained to avoid it now, even as the earth shifted under my feet.

"So why the divorce? If you're saying that she was a wonderful wife, this thing aside, why did you run her off? Why didn't you come for us?"

"Mitch, I'm not dodging you, but I don't know. I wanted to try. Your mom was so embarrassed by what happened. I think she saw that the writing was on the wall. We didn't have much of a marriage. I wanted her to stay. She felt like she had to leave. And that was my fault. I felt like I had to let her go, if that's what she wanted."

We didn't speak for a long time. Dad sat in his chair, I sat in mine, and we were together, but alone, with our thoughts. Mine flowed in a flood of contradictions.

Why had Mom never told me what happened?

What would she say? "Mitch, I cheated on your father"? Come on.

It's unbelievable. How could she have been the one to do that?

She was human. She wasn't infallible. It's a disservice to her for you to suggest that she was, because you know better.

How could she have let me think otherwise for so long, to blame it on him?

She never did any such thing. You reached your own conclusions about your father's infidelity and your mother's purity, and you did so on the basis of some hard-earned evidence. Don't slough it off on her when reality doesn't look like the fantasy.

I can't believe it.

Look at your own life, at your own marriage. It's sliding sideways, and you both set that in motion. There are no white hats and black hats in these things. Everything's a shade of gray. Your mother at least had the integrity to recognize that the marriage was broken and move on of her own volition.

I looked out the window to the west, at the sinking sun. A brilliant orange, dappled with yellow, settled over Billings.

"Dad?"

"Yeah."

"Your note said we needed to talk. About what?"

"It'll keep."

I leaned forward and clasped my hands in front of me.

"I called Kelly."

Dad betrayed neither emotion nor motion. His eyes never left the television screen. He thumbed the remote, flipping through the cable directory, just as he had done before I spoke.

"Did you hear me?"

"I heard," he said.

I waited.

He studiously avoided my stare as he spoke, finally.

"I wish you hadn't done that."

"I wish you hadn't kept it from me."

He said nothing, so I pushed on.

"I know who she is. I know why you left. I know why you want to just ignore it. I also know that she loves you and misses you, and—"

"Mitch, just shut up. OK? We're not talking about this."

"We have to."

"No, we don't. No matter how new and wonderful this seems to you, it's ancient history to me. I'm not going back there."

"Wonderful?" I said. "How could I call this wonderful? It's horrible. It breaks my heart. I just think…God, you know, I'm the only one left, Dad. It's you and me. I wish you trusted me enough to let me in."

"I wish you trusted me enough to let me say that it's a place you don't want to be."

"You've got to open the door to someone. You didn't with Mom, you didn't with Marie, and I bet you didn't with Helen. Well, Pop, you have one person left."

"They all knew about Kelly."

"What?"

"Your mom, Marie, Helen. They knew."

My assumptions again twisted into something I didn't recognize. I couldn't have expected Marie to say anything about anything, and I didn't know Helen well enough to talk beyond the surface of a topic. But Mom?

"Mom never said anything to me."

"Of course she didn't," Dad said with irritation in his voice. "She was decent enough to keep things to herself, especially things like that."

"How much did she…I mean, what did she—"

"She knew what she needed to know." He hadn't answered, but my questions were moving faster than my ability to dissect his answers.

"Well, what about Kelly? Dad, she's haunted by this thing. She misses you. She wants to see you. Don't you think it would be good to have a relationship with the one person in the world who was there?"

Dad looked at me. His face hung haggard.

"I'm an old man. I haven't seen her in fifty-something years. The past is best left where it is."

"All the time, in every case? I don't believe that."

"In this case."

"Let me ask you something. Why did you keep those letters if you don't care? Why would you keep them tied together and put away in a box? That doesn't make sense."

He didn't answer. He couldn't without conceding my point, and I knew he would never do that.

"Why did you come here?"

The question hit me like a rifle shot.

"To see you. To find out what was going on. You're the one who kept calling. Not me. Remember that?"

"But you also came because you're in a bad way with your wife. And it seems you've got some other things digging at you too."

"Don't make this about me."

"I'm making it about us. You know how you told me on the drive back from Split Rail that you just wanted to get some things off your chest?"

"Yeah."

"Well, go ahead."

"Why are you doing this?"

"Isn't it what you want?"

"Yeah, but what's in it for you? Why now?"

"It's time."

I found his serenity—or at least his projection of serenity—to be at once disconcerting and inviting. I made the snap decision to set my reservations adrift and dive in.

"Why didn't you come to Jerry's funeral? Why have we never been able to talk about him?"

Dad massaged his eyes. I waited.

"I had no money. I was just scraping by."

"Mom offered to pay your way."

"I couldn't have done that."

"Why?"

"I just couldn't."

I lost it. I stood and began shouting.

"Don't hold out on me now. Mom and I, we picked him up at the base. We rode with him to the cemetery. We watched him go into the ground. We did all of that. We found the strength. Why couldn't you? Forget about Mom and me. You owed Jerry that."

Dad hung his head. The words, when they came, had nothing behind them, and they dissipated into the space between us.

"I know."

"You know what?"

"I know it's my fault. I know he left because of me, and I know that he died because of me."

Dad looked up. His eyes floated in tears.

"I've lived with it every day since. If I hadn't done what I did, he might be still with us. I couldn't face it. I couldn't face Leila. Why she even wanted me there, I don't know."

"Dad, she didn't know."

"What?"

"I never told Mom about that night."

"God, Mitch. Why not?"

I shrugged.

"Maybe some things are best not revealed."

We sat quietly for a few minutes.

"It was a terrible day," I said, finally.

"What?"

"The day we found out about Jerry."

On that October day in 1983, I watched through the living room window as the car pulled slowly through our cul-de-sac and stopped in front of the house, and I knew. When two grim-faced men stepped out, I had the most preposterous thought, that if I just dashed out the door and met them, ushered them back into the car and sent them away, we wouldn't have to hear it, and it wouldn't be real.

Instead, I croaked out "Mom," and my mother, who was cutting vegetables in the kitchen in a desperate effort to draw her attention away from two days of deep dread, knew it too.

Then came the two crisp raps against our oaken door, and Mom and I walked wordlessly to the entryway and let the Marines in out of the rain.

We had feared the worst on that Sunday, when the bombing of the Marines barracks in Beirut had been all over the news. We knew Jerry was there, and we hoped against hope that he had been among the survivors or hadn't even been in the area at the time. But I could tell from the way Mom talked that she had a sense that our news would be crushing. I guess I had the same sense, given the knot that kept growing in my gut. Still, we wouldn't know anything for sure until the government was good and ready to tell us. With men still being accounted for and rescues still being attempted under sniper fire, who knew when that would be?

Mom made phone calls but no headway. Whom do you call, anyway? There's not a dead-Marine hotline. You wait. You worry. You wonder if life is ever again going to be what it was before the uncertainty set in. And then, if you have a soul, you wonder how even the news you want to hear could be considered good when the families of two hundred and forty-one men were about to find out that their son, their brother, their husband, their father would be coming home in a box.

I stayed home from school on Monday and Tuesday. It's not as if I could have concentrated on my studies, and I wanted to be home in case our worst fears came knocking. I didn't want Mom to absorb that news by herself. Mom had the same idea, calling in sick. We spent two days sequestered in our small house, not speaking beyond the perfunctory, daring not to give words to our worry.

"You think it only happens in the movies," I told Dad. "But it was real. We let the Marines in, and they hung up their raincoats and followed us into the living room. Then they told us that Jerry was gone."

Dad looked at me.

"How did Leila take it?"

"It was...weird," I said. "Mom never took her eyes off the Marines. She looked almost serene. I know that sounds weird, but that's what I saw. I listened, and I heard the part about the nation's indebtedness to Jerry, and I almost laughed."

"Laughed?"

"Yeah. I mean, we were the ones with the debt. Jerry wasn't ever going to get married, have children, or grow old. Who could pay us back for that? Nobody has pockets that deep."

Dad looked hollow.

Ten days after the Marines visited, we met the plane. We stood in the rain, watching the flag-draped coffin as it was off-loaded. We rode beside Jerry those seemingly endless miles down Interstate 5 to Woodlawn Cemetery.

I sat beside Mom for the service, flanked by Jerry's high school friends, his coaches and teachers, people from the neighborhood, and a contingent of Marines. When the rifle volley echoed against the leaden Washington sky, Mom flinched beside me. The scent of the guns' discharge found my nose, and nausea bubbled in my gut.

I watched as my brother was consigned to the earth. The flag was presented to my mother, yet another gesture that could not begin to account for our loss.

"I hated you," I told Dad. "I thought about how you were sitting back here in Billings, in that Holiday Rambler where it all was set in motion. You beat him up over a girl, and he was gone. And you couldn't even be there."

"I'm sorry." Dad's voice was a whisper. "I wish I had been."

Tears ran down my face. I hadn't cried for my brother in a long time. Then I realized I wasn't crying for him at all, but for the man across from me.

The good-byes you refuse to say must be the hardest of all.

Time had stopped for Dad and me, but the world continued spinning on its axis. I watched the march of commerce proceeding on the TV, faintly illuminating a living room otherwise gone black.

"I'm going to see him again," Dad said.

"You're going out to Olympia?" I hadn't been back in years, not since I lost Mom. "I'll go with you."

Dad looked up. A smile tugged at the corners of his mouth. A shiver went through me.

"No, Mitch. I'm dying."

I listened as Dad at last put the puzzle pieces into place, filling in the picture of what had compelled me to come to Billings.

A routine checkup. A marker in Dad's blood that attracted the doctor's attention. Then came the unraveling of a life.

An exam found swelling in Dad's lymph nodes. That's when he started calling me. He needed to talk, but he couldn't find the words.

A couple of days after I arrived, he had gone not to Helen's grave but to a hospital for a CT scan. The verdict: pancreatic cancer marching throughout his abdomen. The diagnosis was as grim as it could be. The doctors saw no chance at cutting it out or blasting it with chemotherapy. Dad was advised to get his affairs in order and to prepare for what was to come. He had spent two days figuring out how to tell me, and I had spent those days ripping his life apart.

I had finally reached my father. Soon, he would leave. How much could one family be expected to give, I wondered? Jerry, gone. Mom, gone. Dad, going.

"I won't have anyone left," I said softly.

"Bullshit," he said, and I half laughed and half cried to see my gruff father return. "You have a wife. You have two kids. You love them, don't you?"

"I do."

"You hang on, then. You hang on, and don't let go."

Silences weaved among our short bursts of conversation. It was as if only a few words could knock the breath out of us again. When the decades unspool into the dusk of a single day, it's hard to know what to grab hold of.

"Dad?"

"Yeah?"

"Can we talk about Milford?"

"We just did, didn't we?"

"We did. But I'm wondering."

"What?"

"You sent me away. Why did you do that?"

"Mitch, it was a long time ago."

"I know."

"It was a bad time."

"I know. But, Dad, I've never gotten past it."

"It was just a mistake, Mitch. Just a mistake."

He yawned.

I let him off the hook.

As darkness settled into Dad's house, he headed for bed.

"How long?" I asked.

"Three months. Six months. Hard to say. Not long."

I walked over and hugged him. I held on until he hugged me back.

A few minutes later, I heard snores slipping under the closed door of his bedroom. Exhausted as I was, I had no desire for sleep. I had too much to reconcile, and not nearly enough time to do it.

I also knew I couldn't manage it alone.

I slipped outside. I walked to the end of Dad's driveway, and I placed the call.

"Get here as soon as you can."

BILLINGS | SEPTEMBER 22, 2007

I LAY IN BED because there was nothing else to do. Sleep wouldn't come. My emotions were tapped, but still the thoughts ping-ponged in my cranium.

I had carried Jerry with me every day since the news came to our door in 1983. I proudly shared his name; it was his legacy that weighed on me. I lost him when I was fifteen, and I labored under his shadow. By being buried a hero, he became a better athlete, a better student, and a better human being in death than he had ever been in life. It's not that I didn't love Jerry and miss him desperately. It's that I longed for someone to speak of him as I knew him—hardheaded, mischievous, arrogant, and yes, good-hearted—instead of presenting him as some sort of ideal I couldn't match for no other reason than, one, I was alive and, two, I wasn't him.

I flipped over and pounded my pillow. I chafed at the memory and at my stale grievances. I had to learn to let go of some of these things.

And, as I reminded myself, *it's not as if Mom and I weren't guilty of the same reverence to the dead.*

We suffocated in our house on the upper eastside of Olympia after he was gone. It had been our home since the early seventies, and his absence tore a hole in it that we couldn't fill with memories or regrets. Mom found us a townhouse nearer the bay, and we moved. I stayed until my high school graduation and my departure for California and college at Berkeley. She stayed until she died. Another loss.

I turned again on the bed and replayed Dad's revelation about why Mom had left him. It rocked me to my core. I closed my eyes and conjured her, and I remembered how I sometimes wondered why she never again let a man into our lives. My mother was not a cloistered woman, but at the end of the day, the men in her life were Jerry and me, and then, finally, me alone. For thirteen years after I moved away to college and then to my own life, she stuck to the routines and friendships she had in Olympia. If she ever regretted her decisions, she took that sorrow with her.

The torrent of memory carried me back to that November day in 1999 when I found out she was gone. It was only by inertia that I held it together on the flight from San Jose to Seattle, on the ride down Interstate 5 to the hospital in Olympia. I made the dutiful calls to the mortuary and to Cindy, summoning her to help me say good-bye.

The grief got the better of me only after I found the ground beef thawing on the countertop, put there by my mother on her final morning, before her final car drive, before her final breath. She had planned tacos for dinner. The soft-shell tortillas, the tomatoes, the cheese, the avocados were in the refrigerator, waiting.

I sat at the dinner table and I wept. Then I cooked the tacos, though I had no appetite. She would have hated to see it wasted.

In Mom's closet, I found photo albums that stretched to her early days in Montana with Dad. Flipping through them was like making bygone years flicker to life, if only for a moment. As the pages rolled past, so too did the arc of our family. First, it was just Mom and Dad, fresh-faced and young, all the possibilities and promises of youth in front of them. Later, baby Jerry appeared. I saw images of trips I had heard stories about—Mom, Dad, and Jerry, perhaps four years old, at the Grand Canyon. Then I showed up, bouncing on my grandfather's leg, riding in my father's arms. More pages went sliding by. Dad fell away, and the landscape changed. Jerry, in his early teens, frowning into the camera while Mom and I smiled in Pioneer Square. Jerry graduating from high school. Jerry, square-jawed, in his Marine uniform. Then it was just Mom and me. I grew up. She clipped out newspaper stories about my football games at Olympia High. The honor roll. My senior prom date. And then, as I finished high school and headed to Berkeley, the pictures ended.

I found something that made me angry all over again at Marie. Written during that summer in Milford, the letter from my mother asked Dad if he had given thought to private school for me. Across the top, Marie scrawled, "Leave Jim alone. Mitch doesn't want to go there."

I cried myself to sleep.

I remembered Mom's going-away day, and I wondered when it would come for Dad. In the darkness, I whispered a prayer and asked God to let me be here for Dad when it was time for him to leave. Though I could well recall every slight, I also remembered that when it was down to him and me, he had come through.

The day we buried Mom, I left her house and made my way through the early morning traffic in Olympia to the mortuary. I rapped on the door and told the man that I wanted a few minutes. He took me to her and graciously cleared out.

I went to unload thoughts I didn't want to clutch too tightly in that morning's service, to say the words I wouldn't want anyone else to hear. Whether Mom was in that room with me that morning is beyond my grasp; I don't know if it was her or just her temporal vessel, now empty of whatever it was inside that made her vivacious and funny and kind, always in the light and never in the shadows. The intervening years haven't granted clarity on that question. I just don't know, and I distrust those who claim to have the answers.

The face I saw looked like Mom, and that was good enough. I stroked her hair, and I started with a thank you.

After the service, Cindy and I lingered at the grave. Mom would be set to rest next to Jerry. It didn't make much difference to me—I would be on this side of the dirt, missing both of them—but I hoped it would make a difference to them, wherever they were. If they were.

I took Cindy's hand and we walked to the car. About halfway up the path, Dad stepped out from behind a massive fir. He wore a blue suit whose heyday was two decades earlier, and his thinning, gone-gray hair was slicked back.

His tie, grappled into a haphazard Windsor knot, hung askew. He fidgeted and looked anxious.

I hadn't seen him in twenty years. Cindy smiled and thanked him for coming, and I knew then that she had placed the call. There was much that it occurred to me to say, and I dismissed it out of hand.

He had come to my side.

The three of us walked away together.

MILFORD | JULY 7–10, 1979

AT THE GAS STATION in Bozeman, Brad stood waiting for us.

"I'll be damned," Dad said. He had spent the previous couple of hours doubting that the "hippie guy" would show up. That he had showed up was our first surprise.

The second came the next day, when the work began. Dad started Brad in the number-two spot, formerly held by Toby and me. He proved a quick study, and by the end of the second day, he was doing exactly what needed to be done without Dad prompting him. That brought a promotion, and Toby ended up at his old post, lugging explosives and shoveling out the pit and wondering what the hell had happened. Toby was none too happy with the way the work dynamic had changed, but I found that I had little room to care. The motorcycle had made the trip south with us, and I whiled away the hours rocketing across the sand and the sage.

At the end of another workday, we pulled into town, and Dad dropped Brad and Toby off. When we'd hit Milford a few days earlier, Dad had steered the pickup to the front door and rapped at it until Toby roused from a nap on the couch and answered. With no preamble, Dad had said, "Meet your new bunkmate," introduced them, slipped Brad a C-note to tide him over until payday, and that had been that. Social engineering, Jim Quillen style. In just a few days, Brad had invaded where Toby lived and where he worked.

We were climbing out of the pickup when the campground manager scurried up.

"This came for you today," he told me. I looked at the postmark on the envelope: San Diego.

"What is it?" Dad asked.

"It's from Jerry."

"Ah, yeah. Well, I'm going in."

"Don't you want to hear what he wrote?"

"Go ahead and read it," Dad said. "Fill me in later."

July 6, 1979
Hey, little bro—

I guess by now you know where I am.

Things are picking up around here. Still a lot of weeks to go before I find out where I'm headed and what I'm going to be doing.

I talked to Mom the other day. She says she didn't hear much out of you while you were in Montana. By my figures, you ought to be heading back to Milford in the next day or two. Make sure you give her a call. I wish I'd done better at it than I have.

If you see Denise, tell her I said hello. But just leave it at that, OK?

I hope you're doing good and enjoying your summer with Dad. If he asks, tell him I'm not mad anymore. If he doesn't ask, don't bother.

Your brother,

Jerry

Dad didn't ask. I didn't warrant much of his attention. He and Brad scarcely touched their food as they pored over charts and maps, plotting out the next day. Technically, Dad's helpers were on their own from the time we got into town each day until the next morning at five. Brad had eaten with us every night, and Dad had been all too happy to have him there so they could talk shop.

I guess I saw things Toby's way. Dad had moved fast to elevate Brad to the pipe duty, and he hadn't delivered the news kindly to Toby. Still, I knew that the results bore out Dad's decision. I would be on my motorbike, cutting doughnuts into the brittle earth, and I would look up and see that the rig had moved on. Brad was just damned efficient. He anticipated, he hauled ass, and he didn't make mistakes. He was better at the job than Jerry was, and that's saying something.

With nothing to do and no one to talk to, I ate ravenously.

"Dad," I said, plugging the last of my fries into my mouth. "Is it all right if I go up to the park?"

"Yeah," he said, not looking up. "Just be back before it gets dark."

I scooted for the door before he changed his mind.

I cut through the park and up the hill to Jennifer's house. It felt odd that I had missed a girl, but I really did want to see her again.

Denise answered the door. I gave her a big grin and a wave. She looked blankly at me.

"Jerry says hi," I said.

"When did he say that?"

"I got a letter from him today."

"Can I see it?"

"I don't have it on me," I lied.

"I've heard from him too."

"When?"

"A couple of days ago."

"What did he say?"

"He told me to stay here."

"Huh?"

"I said I would go out there and be with him. He said to stay here."

"Oh, I don't know anything about that."

"Anyway, what do you want?"

"Is Jennifer here?"

"Wait a sec." Denise closed the door on me.

Jennifer came outside. She wore a T-shirt, purple shorts, tennis shoes, and socks. She looked…well, she looked, beautiful.

"Hi, Mitch."

"Hi."

"I'm glad you're back."

"Me too. Can you come out for a while?"

"Yeah, I think so. What do you want to do?"

"I don't know."

"We could go to the school and shoot baskets," she said.

"Great."

She went back into the house to retrieve the basketball, and then off we went, dribbling it down the street.

"Did you have fun in Montana?" Jennifer asked.

"It was all right, I guess."

"Good."

I stopped.

"No. It was terrible."

"Why?"

I told her, all of it, as we walked the final couple of blocks to the school. She kept saying "Wow," which really didn't help, but I was glad to have a listener, anyway. Since we had been back in Milford, Dad had fallen into tunnel vision about work, and now he had a new buddy in Brad. Being with Jennifer made me forget that for a while.

We started by playing H-O-R-S-E, and Jennifer embarrassed me by winning easily. She had a gorgeous shot—squared up, elbow tucked, perfect follow-through. Mine was a bit erratic; I could shoot from farther away than she could, which was great if I made the shot, but she could hit baskets with more consistency. In the end, it was H-O-R-S-E for me to H-O for her.

"Let's try P-I-G," I said.

This time, I made her shoot with her off-hand, and I worked in a few trick shots that she wasn't as good at—reverse layups and such—and I beat her handily.

She fixed me with an evil grin.

"Around the World to settle it," she said. I never had a chance. She sank every shot around the key on her first attempt, finishing me off with a flourish.

"I know," I said. "Let's just shoot." Jennifer started laughing.

"How did you get so good?" I asked.

"My dad. He's been bringing me out to shoot baskets since I was a little girl."

"You *are* a little girl."

"Yeah, but I'm big enough to beat you."

She won again.

We filled a half hour shooting the ball and shooting the bull. We noted how the summer was quickly draining away. Time is a strange thing when you're a kid. The school year drags by in slow motion, with each Monday launching an inexorable wait for Friday. In September, six-week grading periods—six of them—seem like all the time in the universe. But eventually the breaks come. Two weeks at Christmas that are over in a flash, and then that last school day in June, a vantage point from which you can see three glorious months of freedom set out in front of you. Those twelve weeks go by so quickly, school starts anew, and time slows down again.

It's only after your twenties go by in a day and when things you think happened last year really lie five years back that you realize that time doesn't slow at all. Indeed, it only gains speed. And then you curse yourself for ever wishing it away.

I spotted Brad walking along the sidewalk.

"Hey, Brad." I waved to him.

"Who's that?" Jennifer whispered.

"He's working for my Dad."

Brad came in through the gate and joined us.

"Basketball, huh?" he said.

"Yeah. Do you want to play?"

"Sure, I'll give it a whirl."

We played H-O-R-S-E. I went first, followed by Brad and then Jennifer.

I couldn't do anything, and Jennifer met her match in Brad, who put five quick letters on her. Then he finished me off, laying the R-S-E on me to complete what Jennifer had started.

"Losers!" he said, pointing at us and laughing.

Jennifer looked upward. Ribbons of light streaked against the darkening sky.

"I have to go home," she said.

"Loser is going to take her ball and go home," Brad taunted.

"Hey," I said.

"Nah, man, I'm kidding," he said. "We'll walk you."

"Never mind," Jennifer said, and she walked off.

I squeaked out a "Bye, Jennifer," which got a curt wave in return. What an asshole Brad was for saying that to her. I hoped she wouldn't be too mad at me.

"I guess I better go too," I said.

"Want me to walk down there with you?"

I shrugged. "It's a free country."

"You don't like me much, do you?" Brad said.

My ears burned. "You're OK," I said.

I picked up the pace, and Brad easily matched me.

"Nah, look, Mitch, your dad and me, we're hitting it off, and that bugs you, doesn't it?"

I shrugged. "Maybe."

"I get it, man. I understand. Listen, don't worry about me. I'm not muscling in on you. I'm just trying to do some good work. This is my chance to learn a trade and make something of myself, you know?"

The edge of my animosity toward Brad softened. The very doubts he described had started to creep in, and I knew I couldn't compete with him in terms of work, which was really the only way get to Dad's good side. It made me feel better to think that Brad recognized this.

"Listen, man, I've picked up from Jim what's going on these days, and I know it's rough," he said. "Hell, my family situation is a mess. Don't know my dad. My mom's a fucking drunk. I know how it is, truly. But you're a good guy, Mitch, and you're gonna be just fine. You need anything, you need to hang out, you just come see me, all right?"

"Yeah, OK."

"Cool."

We walked on.

"How long have you lived in Bozeman?" I asked.

"I don't. Some of my friends do. I was lucky to catch on with you guys in West Yellowstone, because I wasn't sure where to go. My mom lives up in Kalispell, and I guess if I hadn't had anywhere else to go, I would have gone there. When Jim offered me the job, that was it. I crashed at a buddy's house for a week, then waited for you guys to arrive. Some things just work out, I guess."

"Yeah."

We reached the park. I saw the trailer down below in the twilight.

"You got it from here, man?" Brad asked.

"Yeah."

"All right, bud. I'll see you in the morning."

I returned to an empty trailer. The lights burned, and the TV was on, but Dad was gone. His truck sat out front, so I did what I could do: I dropped anchor and I waited. Soon, I seethed.

We were in Milford not even a week, and Dad's particular brand of bullshit was on display again. I bristled at the nerve of his telling me to be in by dark when he wouldn't even be here.

I could have stayed out with Brad, or gone back to Jennifer's house. Hadn't her father told me to come by any time? They wanted me around.

I stood and paced from the couch to the bedroom and back, and then I made up my mind. I'd go find him and shame him into coming back.

I hit the jackpot at the first place I looked, the bar around the corner from the Hotel Milford. The door to the street stood open, and I saw Dad and Toby standing at the bar. Toby jabbed his finger at Dad, who responded by slapping his hand onto the bar.

This went on a few seconds more, with Toby's arms flailing and Dad shaking his head. Finally, Toby clearly said, "Fuck you," and Dad dropped him to his knees with a quick, chopping punch to the solar plexus. I stumbled backward at seeing it.

The others in the bar, who had watched the scene unfold with growing interest, moved in to separate Dad and Toby. Dad was shown the door, his welcome worn out.

"Don't you puss out on me, Swint," Dad yelled. "Your ass better be there in the morning."

Dad didn't see me. He shouted some more, until the bartender stepped to the door and told Dad to get going or get arrested. Dad trudged toward the trailer park, and I galloped to catch up.

"Dad, what's going on?"

"What the hell are you doing here?"

I ignored the question.

"What happened back there?"

"Nothing. Another fucking hand with an opinion."

"Why'd you hit him?"

"Shut up, Mitch."

He walked on. I lumbered a step behind, quiet, as ordered.

BILLINGS | SEPTEMBER 23, 2007

Awake in the darkness, I envied the old man's ease at falling asleep, even as he knew that each breath led him closer to his end. I stared at the plaster ceiling of his double-wide, and I listened to the silence. Late evening had yielded to midnight, which had ceded to the early morning hours, and sleep still kept its distance. I waded knee-deep into the universe, pondering things that didn't seem to trouble Dad. What would I do if I knew my time was desperately short? Could I look down the barrel of my final days and be proud of my life? Could I say that I had done the things I needed to do and wanted to do?

I knew the answer was no, across the board. It disappointed me, but I clung to the idea that I had time, a luxury that no longer rested with Dad.

And then I stopped short. Time, as I knew all too well, has its own ideas.

I let my recollection carry me where it would, and it dove into corners that I hadn't visited in years. I conjured a memory of Dad from the summer of '77, in Sidney. On a day we broke early from work, Dad and some of the other drillers barbecued burgers in the park across the street from the motel where we stayed. The revelry went on for hours, and I loved seeing my father loosened from the grip of work. For most of that day and evening, he was everyone's best friend, quick with a joke and a smile.

Then a helper for one of the other drillers brought out boxing gloves and suggested some friendly bouts, and another good time crumbled.

A boxer from his Navy days, Dad turned frolic into intense competition, chopping down each opponent, one by one, until the only willing foe was the hand who had brought the gloves out. He was long and lean, his abdomen ripped with muscle, and he was more than a match for Dad—and probably half Dad's age.

When the fight began, the young hand bounced side to side on the periphery of Dad's range. Dad stalked his quarry. He loaded up a right hand and sent it screaming toward the kid's jaw. The young man slipped the punch, shuffled left, and plowed three quick jabs into Dad's face.

Dad came at him again, still cocking the right hand. When he let it go, the punch just missed, crashing loudly against the hand's sternum. The young man's eyes grew wide; he knew that a couple of inches higher would have laid him out. He slid to his right, out of Dad's reach, and offered recompense with two jabs to the face and a right cross that sent sweat flying off Dad's head.

Dad bore in hard and paid for the strategy. Lefts and rights hit Dad, splitting his lip and leaving a welt under his left eye. Dad swung wildly, and missed even more wildly. Each misstep carried a heavy toll of leather.

Dad cast off his gloves.

"Enough of this shit," he said. "I'm too damned old."

His opponent smiled and removed his gloves. He offered a handshake to Dad, who accepted it.

The guy never saw it coming. Dad gripped with one hand and crashed a fist into the guy's mouth with the other, toppling him. He got in two kicks to the guy's ribs—punctuated by "Now who's the tough guy, motherfucker?"—before Dad's buddies pulled him off.

I saw it all from my perch atop an old steam engine, just yards away. I watched as one of Dad's friends walked him out of the park and back to the motel. I watched as the young man rose slowly to his feet and spit up blood.

I quaked with fear as I returned to the room, scared of who I'd find on the other side of the door. Dad said nothing when I came in. He stared at the TV set. I quietly undressed and climbed into the bed opposite his.

My father's indestructibility left me awestruck. His ability to turn vicious draped me in fear.

Thirty years later, lying there in a bedroom adjacent to his, I found it difficult to comprehend that he no longer possessed much of either quality. The clock always winds down, whether we think of it or not.

I thought, too, of Cindy's admonition when I had called her hours earlier. "Just let it come."

We both sobbed over Dad's news, and we laughed wistfully at how it all made perfect sense, once the facts had come in. A week earlier, his aimless calls to our house in San Jose had been a nuisance. That interpretation was informed by the Jim Quillen we knew, an irascible old man who sometimes seemed to delight in manipulation. Now we knew that our clumsy caller was someone else. He was a scared father who needed desperately to talk to his distant son and yet didn't know how. Cindy had recognized it as a plea for help, although it was beyond her, or any other mortal, to divine what exactly the problem was. She had sent me on that errand.

The awful news delivered, I had turned manic on the phone. I had held the man at a distance for years, just as he had done to me. Now, I had to race death to get close to him.

"Just let it come," she said. "You have the time to say what needs to be said. Take your time, do it right."

Morning greeted me with a shove.

I opened my eyes and found Dad grinning at me.

"What?"

"Sport, you wrecked my shed," he said. "I figure the least you can do is help me fix it."

Fuzziness flooded my head when I sat up. Too quick, too early. I cupped my head in my hands and sat perched on the side of the bed.

"Not feeling so hot?" Dad said.

I waved him off.

"Just give me a minute. I'll get dressed and be right out."

When I emerged, Dad handed me a cup of coffee, one he had doctored to my specifications.

"You did a number on that shed," he said.

"Wouldn't have if you'd left the old lock on it."

He smiled and shook his head.

"Are you pissed off at me?" I asked.

"Nah, not really. I'm trying to understand you."

"Well, don't strain yourself," I teased.

"No, what I mean is, I understand why you did what you did."

"You do?"

"Sure. I gave you something to knock down, and you did."

"Jesus, Pop, did you get up early and take a philosophy class?"

"Screw you," he said, grinning.

We worked into the early afternoon, taking down the busted doors, pulling the twisted hinges, building a new jamb, cutting new doors from leftover plywood inside the shed, fastening them into place, installing the closing mechanism, and painting our handiwork.

Before we closed up the shed, Dad pulled down the box that had inspired my violent crashing of the place and handed it to me.

"It's yours," he said. "You earned it. Take it home."

"You kicking me out?"

He laughed.

"No. But I imagine your family misses you."

Dad was on the toilet when the knock came.

"Who's that?" he bellowed.

"I don't know."

I opened the door and greeted Kelly Hewins. Tears spilled down her cheeks, and she cupped my whiskered face in her hands. They were warm and soft and strong.

"Mitch?" she said.

"Yes."

"I can see him in your eyes."

I heard footsteps behind me. "Mitch, who is it?"

I stepped out of the space between brother and sister.

Dad's eyes flickered with recognition. "Jimmy," she said, and she stepped toward him. He took a half step back, and then he rushed forward to meet her.

I slid through the door and closed it. A piece of the reunion was mine to share, but it would come later. Besides, I had my own long-overdue reconciliation to get to.

I walked to the end of the driveway, a place where I had stood almost every night for a week, and I dialed. Cindy picked up on the first ring.

"Hi, babe. I'm coming home."

MILFORD | JULY 11, 1979

TOBY AND BRAD waited in the booth at the diner. Toby had taken Dad's shot and come back. My respect for him rose, as did a fear of what he might have unleashed.

"Morning," Dad said. The hands mumbled in kind.

The waitress we saw most mornings sidled up to the table, looked us over, and said, "The usual?" We all nodded our heads, and she left straightaway to get to it. Coffee, black, for Dad and Brad, orange juice for Toby and me.

Slowly, the torpor lifted, and the men chatted about the coming day. I watched and listened, and I tuned in particularly to the words between Dad and Toby. When Toby spoke, which was rare, Dad wore a measured gaze. I knew the look. Dad was watching for clues about where Toby's sensibilities lay. Whatever trouble existed between them, Dad wouldn't soon forget. I imagined that Toby wouldn't either. Having struck out with Dad, I resolved to ask Toby what had happened in the bar.

Dad caught me watching.

"Eat up," he said. He waved at my plate. "It's going to be a long day."

Our bellies full, we milled around the counter while Dad settled the food bill.

The manager ambled up to Dad. "Can I talk to you for a sec?"

"Get on out there," Dad said, shooing us toward the truck. "I'll be out in a minute."

Outside the door, Brad jabbed Toby in the ribs. "I'll bet he's telling Jim to have you shit somewhere other than his bathroom."

"Screw you," Toby said.

We sat in the truck a good while. I saw through the glass door that Dad had turned animated. The restaurant manager shook his head slowly and pointed repeatedly at something at the cash register.

Dad reached into his back pocket for his wallet and fished out cash. He walked out the door, his right hand aloft, as the manager talked to the back of his head. A few jabbing steps brought Dad to the pickup.

"That fucking bitch," he said.

"What?" I said.

"Marie. She drained the credit card. I'm down to what's in my pocket."

"How much?" I asked.

"Never mind. Enough to get us through the day. I'll figure something out."

I thought about the money folded into my wallet. I had done as Jerry instructed. Dad didn't know about it, and I hadn't spent it. It seemed to me that the right thing to do was to hand the cash to Dad and improve our lot, even slightly. But I knew that doing so would bring a lot of unpleasant questions my way, and I didn't want that. Further, Jerry had given me the money as a contingency, and as far as I could tell, that possibility remained in play. If Marie were up to no good, Dad could soon be in orbit. I might need the money yet.

I kept quiet and listened instead to Dad's profane composition as we rolled toward the work site.

Marie threw us all off-kilter. Dad, chewing on concerns that stretched beyond the patch of ground we stood on, wanted things done faster than usual, and even Brad couldn't keep up with his demands. The morning devolved into a series of half-comical errors. Toby tripped and fell while rushing with a bag of powdered mud, tearing it and sending a cloud of dust billowing across our faces. Brad missed a pipe as it slid down the chute toward him, and it came within inches of clipping my head as it sailed past. Toby dropped the hooked poles, and they scattered. With each misstep, Dad's burn gathered speed.

Much as I wanted to, I couldn't escape. With Toby and Brad screwing up, Dad said, "Stay off that motorcycle, Mitch. We need your help today." I was back on shovel duty.

And then, in a single moment, the day ended. As Dad pulled the pipe from the third hole of the morning, Toby yelled at him. "Hold up there, Jim."

Dad eased down from his perch and peered underneath the rig. The drill bit had thrown a cutter, probably while Dad coaxed it through a layer of rock deep below the surface.

"Son of a bitch," Dad said.

"Can you fix it?" Brad asked.

"Hell no. Don't have the money for it, either. We're done, boys."

Dad kicked at the ground and spat out Marie's name.

Nobody spoke on the ride back to town. Dad was a phantom driver, his head lost in the problem of what to do about his dire straits. He intermittently mumbled to himself, and I began stitching together his plan. When we dropped off Toby and Brad, he filled us all in.

"I've got to go to Cedar City and see if I can get this bit fixed and do something about the money," Dad told us. "Can Mitch stay here with you guys?"

"We done for the day?" Toby asked.

"At least."

"I'm going to head over to Beaver."

Dad looked blankly at Toby, and then he shifted his gaze to Brad, who hung on the doorframe, peeking into the cab.

"Yeah, sure," Brad said. "We'll hang out."

"Appreciate it," Dad said. "I'll bring him by in a bit. I should only be a few hours."

"It's no problem," Brad said.

Dad didn't even change clothes; when we got back to the trailer, he made us bologna sandwiches and poured Cokes.

"What are you going to do?" I asked.

"One of the bosses on this job is there," he said. "I figure I can get an advance from Stanton to tide us over. I've got to get to the bank and shut her down. If I'm lucky, I can pick up a fresh bit while I'm at it."

"What if you're not lucky?"

"Don't want to think about that," he said.

I had nearly screwed up the courage to ask if I could tag along when he said, "Look, sport, I know you want to come. I have to see a lot of people, and you'd get bored. You'll have more fun here."

Brad and I went over to the burger joint near his and Toby's place and had soft-serve ice cream. He showed me some cool tricks at pinball, like catching the ball with a single flipper, then letting it roll to the sweet spot for another shot up the gut. He hung out with me and talked to me like I was a grown-up, like him, and not just a dumb kid.

"That's crazy, what happened with your mom," he said.

"Marie's not my mom."

"Your stepmom. Do you think she took all that money?"

"Yeah, probably. She can be pretty mean."

"How so?"

I told Brad about the night at the Livery when she ignored me and instead hugged Jeff, and then ignited a barroom brawl with her catting around.

"Wow, that's crazy," he said.

We left the burger stand and went downtown. Brad wanted to check out eight-tracks at the convenience store.

"What do you listen to, Mitch?"

"I really like the Bee Gees."

Brad clutched at his chest and staggered around the store, a blond, blue-eyed Fred Sanford.

"No, no! Not them."

"They're good," I protested.

"They're not good, bud. They're popular." He pulled a tape off the shelf and handed it to me. "Here's what you need."

"Molly Hatchet. Who's she?"

Brad busted out laughing and took the tape from me and put it back on the shelf.

Swear to God, it was five more years before I figured out what was so funny. By then, nobody liked the Bee Gees anymore.

We walked back into the sun. It was damned hot, the temperature stretching toward three figures, and the ever-present wind propelled the oven waves fast across the landscape.

"Too hot," I said.

"Yeah. Want to go sit under the air conditioning? Maybe we can find something decent on TV."

"Yeah, let's go."

On the way up the hill, I told Brad about my nightly stalks in Split Rail, exploring the old hotel, slinking through backyards, and especially, about my first beer.

"Did you like it?" he asked.

"I guess."

"Warm beer," he said. "That's pretty gross."

"I guess. It's the only beer I've had."

Brad unlatched the door and ushered me in.

"Want another?" he asked.

"A beer?"

"Yeah. I think that dipshit Toby has some here."

"Sure, I guess."

I sat on the couch while Brad went into the kitchen. I heard the clank of bottles and then the caps hitting the countertop.

He came back into the living room and handed me a bottle. He kept one for himself and plopped down on the couch next to me and fired up the TV.

I drank in gulps, the cold beer sliding through my throat and into my chest, infusing my midsection with a shot of refrigeration. Brad nursed his beer as we watched cartoons broadcast from a station in Salt Lake.

"Don't drink it too fast, man," Brad warned. "It only seems like it's quenching your thirst. Beer's a diuretic."

"What's that?"

"It wrings water out of your body."

I drained the bottle. I could feel the rush in my head.

"Jesus, Mitch."

We gazed at the cartoons for another ten minutes or so while Brad took slow draws on his own beer. Finally, he knocked back the last of it.

"You got it out of your system now?" Brad asked. "You want to try another one and take it a little slower this time?"

The beer, so quick to go down, hit me with urgent force. Still, I didn't want to appear weak.

"What if my dad finds out?"

Brad stood up.

"He won't know if neither of us says anything. I'm not."

"Me either."

"Piggy promise?"

We locked fingers and gave them a twist.

"Another beer, coming up," Brad said.

A grin flopped across my face. I was glad I hadn't gone to Cedar City. Milford, to my delight and surprise, was just perfect.

BILLINGS | SEPTEMBER 24, 2007

DAD STOOD WITH ME in the ticket area of the Billings airport. I thought of when I was a boy and how he would walk me all the way to the gate and sit with me while I waited to board. But I wasn't a boy anymore, and 9/11 took care of something as innocuous as waiting at the gate to see a loved one leave. The security line had mostly cleared out, and the TSA guy looked expectantly at me while I tried to make my legs move.

"I'll be back in a few weeks," I said. "This isn't good-bye."

"I know."

"We're bringing the kids. They need to know their Grandpa Jim."

"I know."

Emotion had been battering me for two days, knocking me back each time. It happened again, right there.

"Don't you die on me," I said, my voice cracking.

"Mitch?"

"Yeah?"

"Get on the fucking plane." Dad grinned at me.

I half stepped toward the X-ray machines, and then I came back.

This time, Dad wrapped me in the hug.

On the flight, my heart kept leaping into my throat, goosed by anticipation. I had been gone less than a week, and yet the tingle in my body reminded me of my first trip to Europe and the sense of wonder that poured over me as I saw, with my eyes and through the eyes of my bride, sights that had existed only in imagination and on post-cards. A week in Billings—or, to be fair, the decades Dad and I crossed during a week in Billings—had turned San Jose into terra nova, my promised land. New beginnings awaited me, in my work and in my home. I made a prom-ise and crossed my heart. More than eleven years into our marriage, Cindy and I would start anew. All I needed was to see her sweet face.

When the jet banked left over the Santa Cruz Moun-tains and made the turn, my heart thumped hard against my breastbone. Below, I could see our neighborhood. Ten-nis courts and swimming pools and the sports arena passed beneath me, and as the jet glided ever lower, I looked right and saw the skyline of San Jose, so close that I could almost reach out and touch it. I was nearly home.

I came off the Jetway at the tail end of the terminal, as far from the baggage area as I could be. Two other flights unloaded with mine, and I fell into a sea of humanity swim-ming up the concourse. When we hit the confluence, our mass broke down. Some of us continued straight to another gate, some of us peeled off for coffee, and my group headed for the exit. I looked down the row at the expectant faces that awaited friends and loved ones and business associates. I didn't see her. I scanned left and then right, searching every face.

And then she stepped out, her hands attached to the smaller hands of our twins.

"There's your daddy," I saw her say, and my freckle-faced progeny barreled toward me in an arm-flailing run. I scooped Avery and Adia up and kissed them until they begged me to stop.

"Hi, stranger," Cindy said, sidling up to me.

I set my children down, cupped my wife's cheeks in my hands, and I kissed her like there was no tomorrow.

While we waited for my luggage to come off the carousel, I pulled the notebooks—five of them, filled front and back with my scrawl—from my carry-on bag and handed them to Cindy.

"These are yours," I said.

"Do you mean…"

"Yes. It's all there."

She opened the first one. I had left the opening page blank until the very end, for the words I saved until I was on the plane home.

My darling Cindy,

You were right. You always were. I've worked it through, and I'm done with it now. No more secrets.

I love you,

Mitch

MILFORD | JULY 11–12, 1979

THE ROLLING THUNDER and a flash of lightning stirred me. The gauze pulled back from the corners of my eyes, revealing a world cloaked in nighttime gray. The hallway light strained against the dark but gained little purchase. I lay on the couch and swam through the fog in my brain, trying to find my bearings.

When I sat up, the blood rushed to my head. I had to brace myself against the table to keep from passing out.

When I finally dared to look up, I saw her staring at me. Toby's girlfriend.

"What are you doing here?" I asked.

"Your dad asked me to look after you for a while."

"Why?"

"He didn't say."

My breathing leveled out and the fuzziness in my cranium receded. I lifted my head slowly and tried to make sense of where I was. I peered into the half light and tried to bring the clock on the stove into focus. 11:12. Where had the hours gone? And what was I doing back here?

"Are you OK?" my watcher asked.

"No."

She said nothing else. The rain pelted the trailer.

"What's your name?" I asked her.

"Teresa," she said.

"What are you doing here?"

"I told you."

She hadn't answered me, though. I ignored that and moved on to the most pregnant question, one I had asked too many times.

"Where is my dad?"

"I'm not sure. Out."

"Where are Toby and Brad?"

She looked away.

"They're with him."

I screwed up the gumption to stand. My head throbbed at the scant exertion it took, and my legs turned rubbery. I paced in the trailer's living space and tried to clear my head.

"How long was I asleep?"

"A long time," Teresa said.

I tried to reconstruct the day. I was missing a hell of a gap. Brad and I returned to the house in the afternoon. I remembered drinking one beer, then another. Things got hazy fast after that.

Remembering the beer frightened me. I wondered if I should ask Teresa what Dad knew. I wondered what she knew. If my illicit drinking were common knowledge, it would be to my advantage to be aware of that. If I was telling on myself, it could be quite bad for me.

"Does Dad know I was drinking?"

She looked away from the floor and back at me.

"I think so."

"Is he mad?"

The pause between question and response seemed interminable.

"Mitch, I don't really know."

I ran to the bathroom and heaved my guts into the toilet. On wavy legs, I returned to the couch, and sleep overtook me again.

My eyes flickered open. Dad's face greeted mine. He sat in a chair and hovered over me from the edge of the couch. He studied my face. The stench of dirt, sweat, and booze peeled off him.

"What time is it?" I asked.

His eyes didn't leave mine, and he didn't answer.

"Where have you been?"

"Out," he said.

"Where?"

"Places."

Each word sent alcohol-laden breath crashing into my face.

"Why did you leave me here with that girl?"

"You were asleep."

"So what?"

"You were asleep," he said again.

"I'm sick of this," I said.

"What?"

"Everything. Sick of you. Why do you always leave me?"

Dad kept a steady gaze on me. Finally, he spoke.

"Mitch, I think it's time for you to go back to Washington."

My heart cleaved into two imperfect pieces. I tried to shove the hurt back down into my gut, where he couldn't see it.

"Why?"

"It's time. You're better off at home."

"Is this because I drank beer?" My voice had gone shrill.

"No."

"Why then?"

"It's time."

"What does that mean?"

He didn't answer. Tears made tracks down my face.

"Take a shower and change clothes," he said softly. "I'll pack up your gear. We'll go to Salt Lake tonight and get you on the first flight out."

I didn't move.

"Don't make me go, Dad. I'll be good. I'll never drink another beer, ever again. Please let me stay."

Dad looked back at me with red eyes.

"It's better that you go."

"Can't I stay just a few more days? I want to say good-bye to my friends. Jennifer, Brad, Toby. Please?"

Dad stood up and reached for me. "Come on, Mitch. I'll tell those guys good-bye for you. Hop in the shower."

I slapped at his hand.

"I hate you," I said. "I did one thing wrong, and you're sending me away. What about all the things you did?"

He pursed his lips. I shoved him as I made my way to the bathroom, and there I hid my tears in the spray of the showerhead.

When I came back into the main trailer, I bore in on Dad again and begged him to reconsider. The grim look never left his face, and he never wavered.

"I hate you," I said.

"I know."

I loaded up my right hand and I punched him in the gut. Dad winced. I punched him again and again, and he took every shot. When he stepped closer to me and said, "Mitch," I belted him in the mouth, and my hand felt as though it shattered.

Dad punched me in the breastbone. I slumped to the trailer floor.

"Goddammit, Mitch. Grab your stuff. We're going."

I slept most of the way to Salt Lake, and in my moments of consciousness, I turned to the window of the pickup and faked it. I didn't want any more words. They hurt too much.

Dad kept a firm grip on the wheel and his eyes forward.

In Salt Lake, I stood apart from him at a pay phone while he called and woke up Mom and told her I would soon be on the way. Ever the skillful liar, he spun a good cover story. He told Mom that things had blown up with Marie and that he was going to have to shut down for a while to deal with it—all of which might well have been true, but it also skirted the fundamental truth that his decisions had brought us to this point. Jerry was gone, Marie was gone, and I was on my way, a month ahead of schedule. A summer that had started with such promise had gone to shit.

"Your mom wants to talk to you," he said, handing me the phone.

I said my hello. She asked if I was all right, and I said I was. She said she would see me soon. I told her I loved her, and I handed the phone back to Dad.

"I don't want you sitting next to me," I told Dad. We were at the gate, waiting for the boarding call.

He stood up and moved a couple of chairs down.

"Why are you doing this?" I asked him.

"It's for the best."

"Best for you. Not for me."

The quiet settled back into the space between us.

"Mitch, maybe someday you'll understand this."

I had grown weary of the it's-for-your-own-good bullshit. He wanted me gone. I wished he would just say so. Just acknowledge that I was in the way. Just be honest.

"I'll never understand."

He looked at me and smiled. It turned my stomach.

"In time, you will."

"Dad," I said. "I'm never coming back."

"Don't say that."

"You don't want me. I don't want you, either."

The airline agent called for my row number.

"That's you," Dad said, standing up. I rose.

Dad tried to hug me. I offered a handshake.

Then I pulled out my wallet and removed Jerry's sixty dollars. I handed the money to Dad. I didn't need it anymore.

BILLINGS | FEBRUARY 1–8, 2008

I HELD VIGIL AT DAD'S BEDSIDE for three days after Kelly called and summoned me to Montana. My newfound aunt and I alternated shifts of sleeping and sitting. I read a lot of books. I watched a lot of TV. I played the satellite radio I had bought for Dad and ensured that he was as comfortable as he could be.

I grew to love Kelly in those days spent with her, to love her as if she had always been in my life. Her own life, full and robust, was on hold while she tended to Dad in his last days. She called it a gift. I saw it that way too.

Dad's lucid moments were few, but each time he opened his eyes, he looked into a face of love. There was little we could give him, but we could do that.

In the quietest moments, late at night, I watched the snow fall outside his bedroom window. I held fast to the fresh memories we had made. I remembered Avery and Adia, initially so distrusting of him when we came to Billings a few weeks earlier, finally warming up to this plodding grandpa who played hide-and-seek and showed them how to do magic tricks. On our last night in Billings, they sat on his lap and snuggled into his chest as he read them a bedtime story. They would never forget him, I was sure. I needed it to be true. They had a chance to know only the good.

In my darker moments, usually in the wee hours as I silently fought my stubbornly open eyes, I wondered if I might someday be able to be so fortunate. My gratitude for these last days with Dad knew no bounds, but even so, I could still feel my heart's hard soil passing through my fingers.

On Sunday afternoon, while Kelly slept, I sat next to Dad's bed, reading a Louis L'Amour Western from his bookshelf. I lost myself in the pages, which amazed me. I had held L'Amour in such disdain without ever having read him. Pity my closed mind.

"Mitch."

Startled, I dropped the book. Dad looked up at me, his blue eyes clear as a July day.

"Do you need anything, Dad?"

His voice was weak, but his words were sure-footed. "Mitch, we need to talk."

"OK."

"I want you to take me to three places."

Before the cancer had started its final march, we had talked about cremation. I was ready.

"OK."

"Havre, where I was made."

"OK."

"Split Rail, at the ranch."

"Whatever you want, Dad."

"And Milford."

The hairs on the back of my neck stood rapt.

"Milford?"

Dad smiled.

"That's where it went on sideways on us, wasn't it?"

"Yes," I said. I felt as though I were choking.

"You find Toby Swint. He'll show you."

"Toby? What?"

"I did the best I could, Mitch," Dad whispered.

Sleep overtook him again, and I listened to his deep, labored breathing as I tried to pick up the pieces of what he had dropped on me.

Milford?

Toby Swint?

Just after five that afternoon, Dad's breathing became shallow and then, finally, stopped. I stroked his forehead.

"You old goat." Tears spilled from my eyes.

On Dad's face, a smile turned up at the corners of his mouth.

We cremated Dad, and I invited his buddies to come over to lift toasts. Charley Rayburn, Pete Rafferty, Ben Yoder, and maybe a dozen other coots I didn't know showed up and told stories about him into the wee hours. Kelly and I laughed along, and we shed tears for the side of the man that we had rarely seen. There is no universal standard for judging a man; it's all a matter of degrees and a question of where you stand. In that room, I saw Dad from vantage points I had never considered, or never even thought to consider. He was surprising me yet. Later, LaVerne Simms showed up, and I must have stared at her for an uncomfortably long time after giving her a hug.

"Mitch?" she said.

"God, LaVerne, I'd have known you anywhere."

Slowly, over several hours, our visitors left. Charley Rayburn was the last to go.

"He was lucky to have you as a friend," I said.

Charley grasped my shoulder with his meaty hand.

"You've been a good boy," he said. "He was proud of you."

I bit my lip.

"You know, I didn't feel it until these last few months."

Charley smiled at me. "It's never too late, kid. You've got to remember that."

In those last few days with Dad, Kelly and I had time to sort and divide his belongings. She got her letters back, and we split family pictures and other keepsakes, which were few. We agreed that his clothing and household goods would do others some good. The Montana Rescue Mission happily took them off our hands. I put the trailer up for sale and left it to a Billings agent to take care of the details.

I kept Dad's pickup. To do what he asked of me, I would need it.

On Friday, we convoyed the eighty miles to Split Rail. I led Kelly up through the buttes and down into town, and we followed the gravel road that ended at the gate to Dad's old ranch. Its current occupant was working a section of barbed-wire fence when we rolled up, and he walked down the line through the snow to see what our business was.

"Do you remember me?" I asked.

The rancher peered from under a cowboy hat.

"You look familiar."

"You turned a shotgun on me and my father a few months back."

"I remember."

"Dad used to own this place. He said he would like to have his ashes spread here. I was wondering if that would be all right."

The rancher didn't answer. He considered me. He looked at Kelly and tipped his hat. "Ma'am."

He studied me some more and said, finally, "Sorry to hear about your dad. Come on in." He fished out his keys, unlocked the gate, and pushed it open.

A vicious wind berated us as we walked up the road a piece. After about twenty-five yards, I stopped and said, "This will do fine."

My hands trembled. I pulled the canister from my coat pocket. I struggled to get a grip on the lid. Finally, I gave it a hard turn.

Kelly put her hands on the canister too. The rancher stepped back in deference.

"Well, Dad," I said. "Go where you will."

We lurched the canister skyward just as the wind shifted, and it carried Dad up the road to the place he once called home.

Kelly and I parted in Split Rail. She carried some of Dad, to fulfill the Havre part of his request. I carried the last of him. I had one more chore.

"Thank you for bringing him back to me, Mitch," she said. She wrapped me in a hug.

"Thank you for being there."

We didn't linger. There was little else to say.

That night, from a room in Salt Lake, I dialed the number of a T. Swint in Milford. My heart raced.

A girl picked up.

"Hello?"

"Is Toby Swint there?"

"Can I say who's calling?"

"An old friend."

I heard the phone set down, and her little-lady voice boomed, "Grandpa! Phone!"

"Hello?"

"Toby?"

"Yes."

"This is Mitch Quillen."

I waited. Toby didn't speak.

"Do you remember me?"

"I do. It's been a long time. How's your dad?"

"He just passed away."

"Oh, Mitch, I'm sorry."

"He wants to me to spread his ashes there in Milford, and he said I should see you."

"Oh?"

"I'll be there tomorrow morning. Can I see you?"

"I think so. When?"

"Say around ten?"

"That'll work. Do you remember the old diner? You think you can find it?"

"I think so."

"Town hasn't changed much. You'll be fine."

"So I'll see you then?"

"Sure," he said.

I heard Toby's voice as I started to hang up.

"What did Jim say?"

"He said you'd show me."

"Oh. OK. I'll see you tomorrow, Mitch."

I hung up the phone. Milford lay a few hours in front of me. My thoughts went decades in the other direction.

MILFORD | FEBRUARY 9, 2008

TOBY SWINT RAISED HIS HAND and flagged me down. I was glad he did, because I wouldn't have spotted him otherwise. As I moved in and he came into better view, I picked out pieces of my memories inside the jowly, corpulent face that looked back at me. I recalled the angled nose that dove hard toward the floor. The dimples. The lopsided, goofy half grin. The rest of the Toby I remembered had been buried deep in his hair gone gray and in the canyons of his face and in the soft angles of his body, ravaged by time and gravity.

I shook his hand and sat down opposite him. "Thanks for signaling me," I said. "I guess I'm an obvious stranger here."

He chuckled.

"You are, at that. You sure have changed, Mitch."

"I was thinking the same thing about you."

When the waitress swung by, I asked for an iced tea. I wasn't thirsty, but I could feel the cottonmouth coming on, just as it had the night before, when Toby was on the other end of my phone call from the motel in Salt Lake and I was scarcely sure where to begin.

There in the restaurant fourteen hours later, I was no more certain of my footing. But when the tea was set in front of me and the chitchat was done, I told Toby what had been told to me a few days earlier.

I watched the hulking man in front of me as I spoke, and he looked as though he might shrink into nothingness as I skirted the edges of a story too long to tell properly over a restaurant table. It had started in Milford, and I had returned for the ending. I just didn't know where or how to find it, exactly. So I showed my cards and hoped that Toby would show his.

After I came up for air, he fiddled with a straw before speaking.

"I was surprised to hear from you, Mitch," he said. "But as soon as you said your name on the phone last night, I knew. It couldn't be anything else."

I smiled but said nothing. Toby rolled his ham-hock shoulders and squirmed in his chair.

"I'm relieved. Jesus. I really am."

I pursed my lips. The poor bastard seemed to think that he and I had reached an end, but it was only a beginning. I had come back to this place that had cast shadows over most of my life—to get answers, to reclaim something that had been taken, and to honor a wish. It looked like I'd have to do some prodding to get what I was after.

"So," I said, "what am I supposed to do?"

Toby played with his straw a while longer.

"I'll show you," he said. "We'll have to make a little drive."

He pushed up from the table, and I followed.

From the passenger seat, Toby guided me out of town by a familiar route. A few minutes later, we were shooting east on the Ely Highway, that road of a long-ago summer. The winds barreled down off the foothills and whipsawed the Ranger, and I dug in, fighting against the tension from the moment and the strain of keeping the truck on the road.

"I hated this road," I said.

"Yeah, so did I," Toby said. "Still do."

We filled the miles with chitchat about families and jobs and the trivial frustrations of men pushing into middle age. We made a halfhearted effort to cover the years since we had last seen each other, but it was no use. Then, we had passed through each other's lives in the way that so many people do, taking up space when we were there but not leaving much of a hole once we were gone.

And yet…

There Toby and I were, riding into the country in my father's pickup, both of us holding tight to something.

"Turn left here," Toby said, pointing to a dirt road intersecting the highway. I eased the truck across the eastbound lane and onto the gravel.

"Didn't we dig around here?" I asked.

"Yep, up and down here."

"How far do I go?"

"It's up there a piece."

The route battered the Ranger's shocks, bouncing us around the cab despite my effort to poke along. Toby's voice, a presence most of the way, fell idle, and he took to staring out the window at the country.

It was as if I were standing outside myself, looking through my past while seeing my body propel through the present. A dull pain clawed at my gut. I wondered where we were headed. The highway fell away in the rearview mirror, and I recognized the ache in my stomach for what it was: fear.

"This is good right here," Toby said.

We'd come down off a hill into a grassy draw. I pulled over. Toby stepped out of the pickup, and I did the same.

We trudged maybe a quarter mile off the road. The shifting wind fought us, and sand slapped our faces. I hadn't dressed for the conditions, and I jammed my numbing hands in my pockets. I was just about to suggest that we turn around and hoof it back to the truck when Toby stopped and pointed at a wash that crossed the sandy floor of the broad valley.

"There," he said.

I looked around. I couldn't see the truck.

"What's so special about this place?" I asked.

"I wouldn't call it special."

"So why here?"

"Jim didn't tell you?"

"Tell me what?"

"Oh Christ," Toby said.

"What?"

He wailed. "Oh Jesus Christ. Oh shit."

It took a long time to settle Toby down, to get him talking in a straight line.

"Let's just go back," he said. "Let's just go."

That wasn't going to happen. Slowly, delicately, and finally, angrily, I implored him to talk. I needed this. I'd come too far.

"You don't need to know this, Mitch. Just walk away from it now. I would."

"Jesus, man, are you serious?" I said.

Toby stared at the dirt. He swallowed hard. He didn't speak.

"Tell me," I said. "Tell me now."

MILFORD | FEBRUARY 9, 2008

Toby stood in the sand, the wind blowing through him, and he cried.

With each whimper, my anger grew.

"Goddammit, Toby, talk to me. You have no clue what I've gone through to get here."

The pathetic bastard tried to pull himself together. He wiped his hand against his running nose, peeling off the snot. He dabbed at his eyes and tried to find his voice.

"OK," he said. His eyes were red and glassy.

"I don't even know where to begin," he said. "Jim and me, we buried that guy Brad up on the high side of that wash."

I slumped to my knees as if my legs had been taken out by a baseball bat.

"What? When?"

"You remember that day that Jim shut us down and went to Cedar City?"

Brad's face flashed in my head, over and over.

"Yeah."

"We buried him that night."

"Jesus, Toby. Why?"

"You don't want to know."

"You're wrong. I have to."

He couldn't look at me when the words came.

"Jim killed him."

I couldn't speak.

I sat on the ground, struck dumb by the revelation as Toby filled in the gaps in my last hours in Milford, the moments that my addled mind had tried to reconcile on that July day in 1979, and on so many days since.

"Teresa and I had to come back from Beaver," Toby said. "I went to pay for dinner, and I realized I'd left my wallet behind. So we came back. But the thing was, I couldn't find it in my room, so I opened Brad's door. Look, I didn't trust the guy. I thought maybe he took it."

Toby looked skyward. He sniffled.

"Mitch, you were on the bed. Brad had your pants off you, and he was—"

Everything in my stomach revolted and charged back up my gullet.

"Shit, Mitch," Toby said, stepping toward me. I held up my hand to keep him back, and Toby returned to where he had been standing. He watched and waited for me to control the spasms. I rode out the vomiting and the dry heaves that followed.

"Did he...was I..."

"No," Toby said. "I don't think so. It looked..." He rubbed his eyes.

"It looked like he was just getting started."

A chill braced my spine. I grabbed at my scattered thoughts and forced myself not to walk away.

"OK. Then what?"

"You sure you want to know about this, man?" Toby asked.

I set my jaw.

"Then what?"

"I tackled Brad and started whaling on him. He was stronger than me. He threw me off him and choked me. I felt like I was going to black out."

"Jesus."

"Yeah. Teresa heard what was happening. She came in and cracked him over the head with a beer bottle, and that stopped him. He'd have killed me, I think."

"Jesus." It was the only word I could find.

"I lost it, Mitch. I absolutely lost it. I couldn't move. Teresa took control. She made me help her tie Brad up. She dressed you, and we carried you out to my truck. He drugged you, I'm pretty sure. You were gone. We couldn't wake you up. I told her to find Jim and send him up to the house."

"What did Dad say?"

"I don't think he believed her, but he showed up. He didn't believe me, either. I'd been bitching to him about Brad for a few days. Hell, I got into it with him at the bar one night and—"

"And Dad punched you."

"Yeah, right. How'd you know?"

"I saw it."

Toby shook his head.

"Mitch, I just didn't like the guy. I had no idea he was like that. I'm telling you, man, if I'd even thought he was, I never would have let you be alone with him. I'm sorry. I'm really fucking sorry, man."

I waved him off.

"Just tell me what happened with Dad."

"Jim came into the bedroom and saw Brad there, tied up. I'd shoved a bandanna into his mouth to keep him quiet. Jim squatted down in front of him. Brad's eyes were bugging out. He was scared, man. Jim told him not to yell, and he took the bandanna out of his mouth."

"And?"

"Brad was scared, man. He told Jim that whatever he'd been told, it was a lie. He said he never touched you. That was fucking dumb, because then Jim knew what had gone down."

Another chill ran through me.

"What did he do?"

Toby looked to the sky, and he pawed at his face, stained with the tears that flowed in the retelling.

"He put the bandanna back into Brad's mouth," he said. Toby's voice wavered. "Then he reached over and covered Brad's nose with his hand. Brad thrashed, and Jim got thrown off. Jim pushed him down and straddled him. He placed his hand back over Brad's nose. It didn't take long."

I sat there next to my own sick. Toby knelt beside me.

"It's been a lot of years, but I always see that face, Mitch. I close my eyes sometimes, and I see Brad's eyes. He knew what was going to happen to him."

My jaw was slack.

"I'd never seen a man die before," Toby said.

I found my feet, and Toby kept talking while I stared at the wash that crossed the valley and our lives.

"Jim and I undressed Brad and put all of his clothes and stuff into a trash bag. It was eerie. It was like Jim knew exactly what to do. He told me we'd sit there with Brad and wait for night to come."

I shuddered.

"Your dad, he wouldn't let me move. 'Sit still,' he said, and I did. He kept asking me if Teresa was going to talk, and I kept saying, 'No, she won't talk.' But shit, I didn't know. I couldn't think straight."

"Did she ever talk?"

"No."

"What if she does someday?"

"I married her, Mitch. I think we've got this one locked away pretty tight."

"When night came, we loaded Brad into the pickup and we drove out here. Parked about where you and I parked today. We carried Brad and a shovel. The rain was coming down fierce. God, it was hard. We were stepping through this hard country, carrying a full-grown man, the thunder and the lightning all around us, and we couldn't see shit. It took us a long time to find the spot. Your dad didn't want to bury him in the valley floor, so we went up on that wash, where the wind and the water wouldn't get at him.

"When we started digging, the whole thing hit me, and I got sick. But your dad just kept going. It was like he was possessed or something. He dug the hole mostly by himself. He packed Brad into it. And he covered the guy up and tried to make it look like we hadn't been there. I was useless. I sat there in the mud.

"When he finished, we walked back to the truck. Jim, he had a fifth of whiskey. We drained it. It didn't help."

"What about Brad's clothes and wallet and stuff like that?" I asked.

"It all went down one of the wells a couple of days later. Your dad's idea. He had it all figured out."

I pulled the canister of Dad's ashes from my jacket pocket. I finally felt steady enough for what I had come to do.

"I wonder why he picked this spot," Toby said.

I knew that answer. Dad spent the last days of his life making peace with his past. I had brought him the final miles.

I shook the canister, and a fair wind took him away.

Dad's Ranger bounced along the two-track road as we headed back to town. My head swirled. My heart ached, for Dad and for this old friend beside me in the cab. They had carried a terrible secret. Now I was under it too.

"I'm not proud of this thing, but I'm not ashamed of it," Toby said. "Your call, Mitch. If you think we should say something to the cops and let the chips fall wherever, I'll do that. Either way."

I had been pondering that question for miles. And no matter how many times I looked at it or from how many angles, I returned to one conclusion. Sunshine disinfects, but so does darkness. Toby and Dad had put themselves on the line for me. For three decades, they had carried a burden so I wouldn't have to. It was time for me to take some of the weight on my own shoulders.

"You've got kids and grandkids. I'm not interested in wrecking your life," I said. "Nobody else needs to know about this."

"You sure, man?"

"Yeah, I am."

A few wordless miles fell behind us.

"Thank you," Toby said softly.

"Didn't you worry that somebody would come looking for him?" I asked.

"Every day," Toby said. "But nobody ever did. It got easier as the years piled up. There are nights, you know, where I lie in bed and I think about it. Brad was a bad guy, and he tried to do a bad thing. But death…it's final, man. That's it."

A shudder ran through me.

"How are you holding up, man?" Toby asked.

I couldn't lie. "Shaky."

"I'd tell you it gets better, but…"

"Yeah."

"I tell myself that Brad made his choices," Toby said. "The kind of things he did, you don't always get to call the shots on what comes next, you know what I mean?"

I nodded.

"How did Dad explain his absence?"

"He didn't. Guys on drilling crews, they come and go. Nobody ever asked. We worked alone for a couple of days, making sure we got rid of everything connected to Brad. Then Jim went his way, and I stayed here."

I drove on.

"Dad came back that night and sent me away, you know."

"He had to," Toby said. "He kept taking swigs of whiskey and talking about it. There was no other way. You can see that, can't you?"

I could. Seeing it, though, blew three decades of grudges all to hell. I was struggling with the letting go.

"I hated him, Toby. It was bigger than just that night. He sent me away, and I never forgave him for it."

"Well," Toby said, "maybe you can now."

We weaved through Milford back to the diner, where Toby had left his car.

"Do you remember that girl Jerry dated? Denise?" I asked.

"Yeah, sure."

"Is that family still around?"

"The old man died a while back. Denise married a guy from Salt Lake and lives there. Her sister's still around, though. Works at the Chevron. You looking to see somebody? I don't want to be an asshole, Mitch, but maybe it's best that you get on out of town. You know what I mean?"

"Yeah. I'm just curious. I'll go quietly."

I pulled into a parking spot at the diner.

"I want to thank you, Toby," I said. "It's weird to say that, I guess, but...well, thank you."

Toby shook hands with me.

"Mitch, keep in touch."

I started to leave, and he tapped on the glass. I rolled down the window.

"On second thought," he said, "enjoy the rest of your life."

I looked at my watch. Nearly two p.m. I had plenty of time to make Vegas. Then, the next day, I would be home to stay.

The gas tank full, I walked toward the store. Though vivid thoughts of an awful night still assaulted my head, the nausea was easing, and I knew that hunger would eventually come for me. I picked out a bag of chips and a big bottle of water.

The woman working the cash register scanned my items. She was about my age, a little heavy, with long brown hair and a freckled nose. I looked at the tag on her blouse and saw the name I knew. A little girl who looked like an old friend peered at me from the picture on a large button that read "World's Greatest Mom."

"Anything else?" she asked.

I smiled at her.

"No, I'm good."

I left Milford the way I had come in with Marie all those years earlier. I drove south to Cedar City, and then I veered into new territory on the way to St. George, where I straightened out for the shot into Vegas. The yellow line led home, where I needed to be. I thought of lessons and losses, and of the burden I had taken on. I decided I would carry this alone. I hoped that my shoulders were strong enough to hold the load.

My thoughts drifted to my little boy and little girl, and I willed the highway to slide past faster. I thought of the world they knew now, and the one they would come to know. My heart brimmed as I anticipated being able to hold them again. Every opportunity they could imagine stretched in front of them, waiting to be discovered. Maybe I knew enough to help them find the path that would bring their dreams within reach.

Maybe.

And still I wondered: if my children someday learn my secrets, what will they think of me?

THE END

ABOUT THE AUTHOR

Photograph by Larry Mayer, 2009

Craig Lancaster, a journalist and novelist, is the author of *600 Hours of Edward*, named a 2009 Montana Honor Book and the 2010 High Plains Book Award winner for best first book. He lives in Billings, Montana.